IMPETUS

By

SCOTT M SULLIVAN

DIGITAL INK
PUBLISHING

ISBN-13: 978-0-9904823-1-4
ISBN-10: 0990482316

Also by
Scott M Sullivan
THE TRINITY SIGNS
IMPERFECT INSIDE

im·pe·tus (*noun*)
a driving force

CHAPTER 1

"I think this about sums it up," Phillip said. He centered the single sheet of paper in front of him on the small mahogany table, then glanced toward the three members of his executive science team. "Thoughts?"

Sid, who had not agreed with the plan since its inception, looked up with a familiar scowl. "I'm sorry, Phillip. But this still seems unethical to me. If we could—"

"Here we go again," Rebekah interrupted. "I thought we had worked through this, Sid?"

"Well apparently we haven't," Sid said, frustrated.

The room was well lit. Not by the kind of government-issued overhead fluorescents that would seem fitting for The Facility, but rather by several decorative sconces scattered around the posh space.

Rebekah sighed loudly. "We've been over all of this ad nauseam, including your well-documented objections. We're past the point where ethics has a place in the conversation." She turned to Phillip. "I realize I've said this before, but if the committee had simply listened to me in the beginning, we may not be in this predicament. They said a triple-pump air filtration system was a waste of taxpayers' dollars." She gestured to the lavishly appointed room, shaking her head in disgust. "Classic government ignorance. At least we don't have to deal with them anymore."

"Yes, Rebekah," Phillip agreed hoarsely. He poured himself a glass of water from a blue pitcher and quickly took a sip to clear the tickle in his throat. "But pointing fingers at dead people does little to help us now."

Rebekah leaned back in her chair. "You're right, Phillip. I'm sorry. My point is that we simply don't have the luxury of morals at this time. We need to find that immunity strand. And we need to find it now. Talking about it over and over isn't getting us any closer to what we need."

"I understand that, Rebekah. Remember this?" Sid asked, pointing to the logo on his sterile white jumpsuit: a dark-green circle adorned with a light-blue double helix. "When The Initiative was formed, it came with a promise to rebuild once the meteorites did their damage. We were to help the people that survived, not hurt them further. And we've fulfilled little of our promise so far. So morality should be a certainty, not a luxury."

Rebekah looked over at the last of the group, who happened to be the youngest and most even-keeled. "Your friend is at it again, Alex."

"Sid is entitled to his opinions just like the rest of us," Alex said calmly. "It wasn't so long ago that you disagreed—pretty loudly, I may add—with our plan to increase the water flow in the filtration plant. Sid listened to you then."

Rebekah backed off a bit. "I guess."

"Think about who we are affecting here," Sid said. "We are intervening in lives that have already endured more than most. We are lying to them. What gives us that right?"

"It is not a right, Sid," Phillip said. "It is an imperative at this juncture. Time is something that we simply do not have enough of."

Sid looked around the small table. All eyes were on him. "How did I become the bad guy in all of this? I want what you all want. I want to live. But I don't want to do so if it means hurting even one more person."

"What would you have us do, Sid?" Phillip asked somberly. "Tell these people the truth? Do you really think anyone will believe us?"

"Probably not," Sid said. "But what do you think will happen once people find out what we have here? What we have been hiding all these years? Once we let our secret out, it's out. And there are bound to be some pretty pissed-off people."

"If we don't find the immunity soon, then it won't matter who knows what," Rebekah pointed out. "There will be nobody left to be pissed off."

"Enough," Phillip interjected. "The childish bickering is getting us nowhere. This test is our best shot at success." It was time to get the discussion back on track. His track. "We have to do this. If what we have done over the past ten years is to mean anything, we must follow through."

Sid stood and ran his hands through his already messy hair. He paced to the back of the room, careful of the Persian rug's upturned corner. "I'm sorry, Phillip," he said, instinctively fixing the rug with his foot before turning back. "Deterring the process has never been my intent. I hope you all know that. Not a day goes by that I don't see Dr. Shaker's image in my head. I'll never forget what the virus did to him."

"Use that as your motivation, Sid," Phillip said, his voice taking on an air of authority. "Because we will all share a similar fate if we don't act now."

Sid clenched his jaw and nodded reluctantly. There was nothing he could do or say at that moment that would make a difference.

"Very well then," Phillip said. "This is settled. We will print this bulletin and have the security team distribute copies along with the test kits under the cover of night. I pray, for the world's sake, that the match even exists."

CHAPTER 2

Mick sat on the peak of a barren hill and stared out at the desolate remains of the once-thriving city of Boston. His home for as long as he could remember, the city was now a fading imprint of his long-ago life. The crumbling buildings, empty streets, and ominously dark corners held nothing worth looking for. But hidden in the shadows were plenty of things to run from.

He slouched in his dilapidated lime-green beach chair. The chair was a broken remnant of better times, and it meant more to him than it should have. But it was the little things that mattered nowadays. He was able to look past the chair's missing right arm, torn from its thin white frame at some point before he found it. It still had one good arm, after all. And that was better than none.

Like the tip of a dagger, a rough piece of metal jutted out from the back of the chair where the violent amputation appeared to have taken place. The poorly healed scar on Mick's elbow, the aftereffect of carelessly leaning into the point and then three stitches with an improvised needle, was a constant reminder to never get too comfortable with the way things were. Something was always looking to bite you in the ass in the new world.

Mick tried to appreciate the chair for what it was *now* and not for what it used to be. His pre-Impact mentality had been forever altered by post-Impact reality. And no matter how diligent he was in his drive to stay positive, to focus on the tiny bits of good and ignore the vast swaths of bad, it seemed like an impossible task most days. The devastation left by the meteorites was absolute. Even the most optimistic of minds, of which Mick was not, could not look past it.

He didn't climb the hill to lament, as may seem to be the case, but to clear his head when he could. Mick tried, usually in vain, to remember what they all had lost ten years ago. And something on that hill helped him do just that.

Flowing green hills and spacious center-hall colonial houses were plastered across what was left of the ravaged frame of a billboard that leaned from the earth some fifty yards from where Mick sat. The stubborn structure's torn and bubbling paper was somehow still imbued with colorful, yet deeply faded, hues that no longer existed in any other place he could find. Grays and browns, devoid of any sort of vibrancy—that was the world Mick now slogged through.

Two quick gunshots snapped him from his thoughts.

He casually glanced to the left of the billboard and toward the city. It was difficult to really see the finer details. Thick and permanent haze smudged most things in the distance into blurry silhouettes at best. But the shots sounded far enough away. And it certainly was not the first time he had heard them from up there. Gunshots and a varying amount of other abrasive sounds had long replaced anything worth listening to.

At times, when he was transfixed by the colors of the billboard and lost in yesterday's thoughts, Mick tried to remember the better sounds, ones he so often took for granted when they were plentiful. Chirping birds frequently came to mind. Those that darted in and out of the lush green trees. He missed the birds' spectrum of colors and the variety of playful songs they provided free of charge. Their high-pitched tweets and synchronous conversations had awoken him entirely too early on many a summer morning. Now he would give almost anything to hear them just one more time.

He shielded his eyes from a sudden whip of wind.

The billboard tilted more to the side as each year passed, a reluctant victim of the eroding soil beneath it and the high winds that sometimes tore past. Mick knew it was a miracle that the billboard had even remained standing for this long. Eventually it would lean too far to the right, break free of its aged mooring in the loose soil, and rumble to its final resting place someplace at the base of the hill.

Mick dreaded that day. The rusted relic helped him to remember the way things used to be when his mind failed to — something that seemed to be happening more frequently. His memories didn't snap to attention the instant they were summoned. Not like they had when he was younger. It was as if something in the air, invisible and silent, slowly stole who he once was, sneaking into his head on the few nights he could actually fall asleep and erasing his memories one by one. The good memories, anyway. It felt as though he was being replaced by the person he'd been forced to become rather than the person he wanted to remember.

He rubbed his eyes and looked to the bleak sky. The grim brown of the air was an uninspiring reminder of what had taken place all those years back. The subtle shift in light told him all he needed to know. It was almost time to head back for the day. He figured a few more minutes wouldn't hurt. It was not like he truly had anywhere to be.

"Come to Shady Springs!" was the message plastered across the top of the billboard in a bold red font, cursive and twisty, which had faded to more of a pink over the years. Time and the constantly blowing dust had stolen the letter *i* in the word *springs*. And the word *shady* had been reduced to no more than *ha*. That seemed sadly fitting to Mick. As if this billboard somehow realized just how comically sad everything had become.

Those who were not wiped out by the main meteorite's blast, Colossus as it came to be known, or the thousands of subsequent smaller impacts like the ones that had destroyed Boston, now dotted the Earth like newly fallen leaves on the first days of fall. They stuck out on the soon-to-be-dormant grass, longing to be where they had been only days prior: thriving in life and not teetering on the edge of irrelevancy. And while the meteorites could not possibly have been selective in their destruction, Mick felt like not enough good remained behind to overpower all the bad. It was as if a speck of evil had been hidden deep in man's DNA. Someplace the conscience could never find it. But someplace readily available to grow given the right circumstances. The meteorites provided those circumstances. And grow the evil seed did.

A year or so following the impacts, after the new reality began to take shape, Mick had tried to rally those around him to rebuild what they could. Rather than working together to drive a stake into the ground for mankind's new start, man had turned on his fellow man as he had been subconsciously trained to do throughout years of ignorant intolerance and a lack of understanding of the differences that made everything possible in the first place. Pleasantries and civility went the way of electricity and clean running water. Mick had given up hope of ever rebuilding what was lost. The effort had been wasted and never repeated.

Another series of gunshots rang out into the gusty wind. More of them this time, followed by a scream for help. A man's unnerving scream. Mick shielded his eyes from the whipping dust and kept staring ahead. The shots did not sound any closer than the previous ones had. No need to worry. Not yet. What happened down in the city rarely made its way to the hill.

Someone without an understanding of how things now worked may think Mick was uncaring, a coldhearted observer who didn't embrace the plight of his fellow humans. How could he not rush to help when someone else was in distress? Where was his sense of compassion? But that was not how people went about their business anymore. Rules, even those of the conscience, no longer applied in the post-Impact world. People were better off once they learned to ignore their morals and trust their more primal instincts. Those were what would get them by in times of need.

A couple more minutes on the hill. Then he would really have to leave.

His absolute favorite part of the billboard was what remained of the sun in the top right corner. Most of the paper had torn away over the years, sticking only where the glue had been applied the thickest. The paper sun's fading yellow rays provided about the same amount of heat that the real sun did after impact, maybe a bit less. Mick longed to feel the real sun again. To close his eyes and bask beneath the warmth of the giant star just one more time. To feel its invigorating radiation reach deep inside, touch his bones, and warm him from the marrow on out like a warm bowl of soup on a cold winter day.

Mick looked to the sky one last time. Time to go.

He begrudgingly pushed himself up from the creaky beach chair. He arched his back and tried to expel the age that had slithered its way into his body; more so, it seemed, over the past couple of years. He then reached up and adjusted his dark-blue baseball cap, pushing his shaggy head of hair more neatly beneath it. The embroidered red *B* of *Boston Red Sox* had darkened to more of a dingy gray thanks in large part to the amount of grime that seemed to be everywhere. Mick didn't care what the cap looked like. Vanity no longer held a place in his world. Unlike his chair, however, his cap was not about utility. It was simply his favorite, one that had carried him through some very tough times. It was also the final gift he would ever receive from his wife. He clung to his Sox cap as if it were her.

He shouldered his rifle for the short walk back down the hill.

Mick followed the same path that he did every day: down the backside of the dusty brown hill, careful of the loose rocks that ran the path's length. He could ill afford to be immobile because of another twisted ankle. The path wound through a toothpick-like grove of trees that stood haunting in their stillness. Though to still call them trees seemed a misnomer now. With little sunlight penetrating the thick atmosphere and rain, when it happened, more like a shower of mud, most of the planet's vegetation had died long ago, taking with it anything that could be considered natural beauty. Now the trees before him were nothing more than grayish dead sticks in the ground, wooden warriors silently killed by the invisible and unrelenting enemy known as time—an enemy that was certain to get them all eventually.

The trek down the hill was quick and lonely. The wind bared its proverbial teeth at times, whipping through the honeycomb of steel buildings left vacant both inside and outside the city's limits and shifting the dust in never-ending cycles. It was something Mick had become all too accustomed to, much like the gunshots. The omnipresent dust seemed like a mindless organism sickly bent on the destruction of those who remained. Inside every crevice. Floating in every stream. Coating the entirety of the planet's surface. It was the dust that he feared the most.

Mick reached down, lifted the bandanna that hung around his neck, and cupped it over his mouth. The bandanna, a rag whose faded silver fleur-de-lis pattern was still somewhat noticeable against the thin blue cloth, did not stop all the dust from getting in his mouth. But it stopped enough to matter. In this new world sometimes a little bit meant a lot.

The remains of the old MIT building came into view as Mick exited the grove of splinter trees. Situated at a relatively safe distance outside the city's limits, the structure resided at the base of the far side of the hill that Mick had sat atop only moments before. It was hidden from view within a natural horseshoe of rocks. An idyllic setting when it had been built. This was his home now. It held what was absolutely most precious to him.

The building's rows of pane glass had long been broken. Some by the global rioting that had spread like wildfire after Colossus, when society unknowingly stood on the precipice of its own demise and the thieves' feeble minds still believed what they stole would somehow hold value in a world where no value remained. The rest of the glass had shattered when the enormous natural gas tank on the side of Interstate 93 exploded and sent a rippling shock wave for miles.

"All clear, Mick?" sounded the deep baritone voice from three stories above as he neared to within thirty feet of the building.

Mick looked up from beneath the curved brim of his cap and toward the roof. He realized a small headache had snuck into his head. He'd kill for a couple aspirin. "All clear," he said, nodding to Greg. It was the same as yesterday and the countless days before that. That was a good thing in its own mundane way.

Greg gave him a thumbs-up and leaned back on his chair.

Mick had found Greg wandering the streets of Boston still dressed in his police department blues two months after Impact. Seeing as Greg was an officer of the law, or had been back when laws were still a thing, Mick had figured he would be best suited to watch over "the herd": the name he had subconsciously given to the seven other people he'd shared the building with. Greg's sworn duty before Impact was to protect and serve, something he still admirably embraced.

Mick walked up the cracked concrete walkway and over the broken glass that seemed to always be underfoot. He passed the charred remains of an old MIT shuttle bus and through what remained of the building's front entrance. Inside was no different than outside: dusty and barren, a shell of what it had once been. However, this part of the building was unimportant. The structure below was what had kept them alive all these years.

The building had been in the process of being repurposed as a bleeding-edge medical wing of MIT, or so Mick surmised from the paperwork left behind by the workers. When he'd first entered the building after Impact, he had come upon a room stuffed with ten large cages of somehow still shiny steel. Within those cages rotted the carcasses of ten decomposing monkeys. The rankness that hung in the air was like nothing he had ever had the displeasure of smelling before or since. And that was saying a lot. The monkeys must have died of starvation after their captors had fled, which, all things considered, was not the worst way to go. He had seen worse ways. Much worse.

Mick was midway into the building when he noticed it: a red box lying on the ground, one with the word *open* written across the top. He smiled. *What a nice surprise.* He must have missed it on the way out of the shelter that morning, when the dim light had been even dimmer. The kids hadn't left him a treasure box in quite some time, years probably. This one was larger than the others they used to leave for him. He'd figured the children had outgrown such things. They were, after all, teenagers now.

He turned the box around in his hand, looking at the vibrant red paint that coated the exterior and feeling something shift against the sides. The paint job was thorough, much more so than the scribbles of crayon they'd used to decorate their other treasure boxes. He thought about opening it. His curiosity had been sparked. In the past, the kids typically left him items they found lying around: bottle caps, sticks, glass. Anything they deemed to have some kind of worth. But he figured it was best he checked in first. He had been gone longer than usual. No need to worry anyone.

He opened the brown leather satchel he had hanging over his shoulder and put the box inside.

He followed the worn path through the rest of the cluttered room and approached a door beneath a dangling Exit sign. A single red and partially frayed wire held the sign aloft, refusing to let it fall for reasons apparent to only it. Mick pounded twice on the door with his left fist and waited. A minute later the locks clicked open from behind the door, three in all.

"Welcome back," Sarah said as the door opened. Her skin was grimy and worn from the present-day trials they all went through, but her beauty refused to be masked beneath it. She had pulled her long brown hair into a loose ponytail that hung freely over her right shoulder, exposing her high cheekbones and sculpted face.

"Thanks," Mick said. "How's everything here?"

"Same as always," she answered, turning to walk back down the flight of stairs. "I don't know if that's a good thing or a bad thing."

Sarah had worked for the local news as a field reporter before Colossus. A shooting here or a multicar crash there were what she'd mainly dabbled in. Not out of desire, as she would later tell Mick, but from a need to climb the proverbial ladder to a better job. Mick used to watch her on the six o'clock news on the nights he didn't have to work late. He'd always appreciated her zeal for reporting. She just had a knack for it, as if she was born to do it. She had found out only days before Impact that her request for the open investigative journalist spot at Channel Seven News was approved and she was about to move up in the ranks. Sarah would finally be doing what she'd always dreamed, what she had worked so hard for.

Then the rocks fell, and everything changed.

Sarah and Mick turned left through another metal door at the base of the stairs.

"Hey, Sarah," Mick said as he felt his way

forward. It seemed awfully dark. More so than usual. The cheap aluminum furniture usually reflected enough light to navigate.

The single kerosene lamp that had been noticeably absent flickered on in the center of the room and revealed three more of his seven roommates huddled around it.

"Happy birthday!"

Mick couldn't help but smile. He was surprised by both the gesture and the fact that the group had pulled something off without his knowledge.

"I forgot it was my birthday," he lied.

Rather, he'd chosen to forget. Turning fifty had seemed a harrowing event back when the world was somewhat normal. Now it just meant he had spent another year surviving, not living. Mick peered to his left in the dull glow the lamp provided. At least another year older had brought with it another year with them.

"Happy birthday, Dad," Nate said, reaching out and hugging Mick loosely, closer to a pat than a hug. Even with the breakdown in society, his son still had the right of every young man to distance himself emotionally from his father. Mick did not take offense. He was happy that some things did not change.

"Happy birthday, Daddy," Kathryn said, shuffling past her twin brother and pushing aside a beautiful shock of bright-red curly hair; tendrils darted away in every direction like bottle rockets frozen in time. She kissed Mick on his cheek and hugged him tight.

Her hug was different than Nate's. It was solid and heartfelt, filled with a love that was exuded through her embrace. Mick felt her heart beat in rhythm with his and her breath on his neck. Not to say that Nate didn't feel the same way. Mick knew he did. But Kathryn was not ashamed to wear her feelings for everyone to see. Mick's simple hope was that she would stay that way forever. Though he doubted that very much. Like her brother, she, too, would soon become captive to the chemical changes that puberty brought. Because even in such a depressing world they still found ways to be angst-ridden teenagers, forgetful of all but their own issues. Mick certainly did not blame them for it. In fact, he was glad to know some form of normality still existed.

"Thanks, you two," Mick said, smiling.

They were his everything, two colorful flowers blooming against the odds in a place that had become so adverse to growth. There were times when he almost wished the twins had not been born. Not for any other reason than to spare them the hardship of life in the new world. But the selfish side of him could not even entertain the idea of an existence without their bright lives in it. His life would have ended many years ago had they not been there to drive him past the doubt.

Forced to raise them by himself since Impact, Mick was proud of who they had become. He frequently thought of the stories his father would share with him whenever he complained as a child; the stories of how his father walked to school ten miles each way, sometimes in a blizzard, sometimes barefoot, sometimes both. Or how "in his day" kids did what they were told without question. But his father's day, as well as Mick's own, had been easier times to go through childhood. Mick could not imagine growing up in the world that his children would inherit, if they inherited anything at all.

Life was tough enough for him to deal with, and he was a grown man with knowledge of things well beyond his children's years. It was difficult for him to intuit what went through his kids' minds at times, what they thought and felt knowing that hope had left them to salvage their own futures so many years back. His children had been robbed of their chance to enjoy growing up. To hang with friends, go to parties, do well in school so they could do well in life. Their lives were spent wondering if they had enough clean water to drink or diesel fuel to last through the ever-growing winter season. It didn't seem fair. None of it did. But despite it all, Mick was determined to give them the best future that this horrid world could provide. He would find hope, wherever it had disappeared to, and wrangle it back by its neck if it was the last thing he did.

Laurel shifted from out of the darkness like a shadow. The speck of a woman squeezed Mick tightly. "Happy birthday, old man," she said as a smile spread across her face. "It's about time you got back. We've been waiting."

Mick looked down to his left at Laurel. "This is your doing, I take it?" She was an old soul with knowledge and understanding beyond what any thirty-five-year-old should know. She had also been a registered nurse before Colossus, which made her a god among men.

Laurel grimaced slightly, more of a knowing grimace. "Actually, Mick, it was your children's idea. I told them you wouldn't want a celebration. But you know how they are." She nodded toward the kids, who smiled back.

He knew quite well how his children were. And he was sure this was not their doing. He loved the twins, and they loved him. But he was sure Laurel was simply trying to make the teens look good and him feel better, both of which he appreciated immensely.

When times got tough, which they so often did, and everything seemed beyond repair, Mick simply closed his eyes and thought of Nate and Kathryn. They reminded him that life was what you made of it. There would always be peaks and valleys. Though the peaks seemed rare nowadays and the valleys stretched for miles and miles.

Mick looked around the room and thanked those there with a warm smile. He had seen Greg on the way in, but that left two of their group unaccounted for.

"Sandeep and Chester are in the back taking inventory," Sarah said as if reading his mind. "They're missing a can of beans." She rolled her eyes. "Chester thinks they miscounted. Sandeep thinks something nefarious is going on. You know how those two can be."

"Like an old married couple," Mick said, followed by the tiniest of chuckles.

He'd brought his children to the shelter shortly after the world began to crumble from within. This was his extended family now. They had their quarrels like any family would, but they also watched out for the other, cared for the other's well-being.

"Did you see anyone out there today, Daddy?" Kathryn asked. "People, animals, anything?"

Mick could see in her eyes that she wanted him to say yes, wanted him to tell her that the sky had cleared and people had begun their migration back to rebuild what had been lost.

"Not today, sweetie." He smiled halfheartedly as he removed the rifle from his shoulder and leaned it against an old metal desk near the door.

Unless it was good news, which it rarely was, Mick kept the finer details of his outings to himself. They lived in an adult world full of adult things. There was no hiding that. There was no time for a kid to be a kid. But he refused to subjugate his children to undue stress until it was absolutely necessary. They did not need to know about the gunshots and how they seemed to get closer each day. Nor did they need to know about the howling he'd heard last week a few blocks from the shelter. Or the myriad other things that were better left untold. When and if an emergency arose, and he was sure it eventually would, he would deal with it then. Until that time, Mick resolved to paint as bright a picture that he could on the sullied canvas they had been forced to create a life on.

Mick leaned against a support pillar. "Are you both finished with your studies for today?"

Kathryn and Nate nodded at the same time and in the same manner as only twins could.

"What subject did Sandeep teach you today?"

"History," Nate said dejectedly.

Math was Nate's strength. He seemed to truly enjoy it, often making a game out of solving for x and y. It was just how his mind worked: computer-like and step-oriented. But Nate detested history, which, ironically, happened to be Mick's favorite subject in school. He still loved it. History held better times in its grasp.

Mick turned to Nate.

"I keep telling you—"

"I know. I know," Nate said, cutting him off. He then furrowed his brow, what Mick could see of it beneath his hair, and said in his best impersonation of his father, "You can't move forward without knowing where you've been." His voice traveled the road of puberty, crackling as it went.

"It's true," Mick said, smiling at his son's

25

impression. He was getting better at it. "Besides, you need to be well-rounded."

Nate scoffed. "I still don't get it, Dad. Why, exactly, do I need to be well-rounded? It's not like I'll be applying for jobs anytime soon. I should be out there with you. Not stuck around here all day."

Nate was right. What better way to teach him than for Mick to show him firsthand? But in Mick's mind, Nate would never be prepared to venture out with him. It was safer around their building. He could get hurt out there, or worse. It was a state of mind that Mick knew he would eventually need to change. It did neither of them any good to use yesterday's standards as a crutch. For now, though, he was perfectly content with Nate learning about better times and broadening his horizons. He would protect his children from certain aspects of reality for as long as possible. That was his right as a father.

Kathryn, who casually leaned on the table, piped up. "You think you know so much, Nate. The world can change. Sandeep is always teaching us how society will find a way to rebuild from its ashes. It's happened before. It's bound to happen again."

"Keep dreaming," Nate said.

To which Kathryn resolutely replied, "I will, thank you."

Mick could not help but to smile. Kathryn exuded an admirable eternal optimism, just like her mother. Mick loved that about her. Even though it was naive to think the world would truly ever improve. The devastation was too vast to ever go back to how it had been. Nothing could change that now. But her attitude was a bright spot among all the gloom. And to squelch that seemed like a disservice to them all.

"Well," Sarah said, sliding up next to Kathryn at the table.

"Well what?"

She looked over to Mick's right and down at the table. "Aren't you going to blow out your candle?"

Candle?

Mick followed Sarah's gaze to the center of the industrial metal table. And there it was, just like Sarah said. A real wax candle. He hadn't noticed its flame hidden by the dim glow of the lamp. The flame's flicker quickly mesmerized him. The blue candle had a white swirling curve that ran from its bottom to its top, around its circumference, to where the dancing flame turned it to liquid wax, lessening it drip by drip. But what really caught him off guard was what the candle rose from. It looked like a cake, at least from where he was standing. A rectangular and strange-looking cake at that. It had to be an illusion.

Mick bent down to get a closer look. "Is this what I think it is?"

Laurel nodded, smiled.

He furrowed his brow, perplexed. "A real cake?"

"Well, sort of," Laurel said. "Remember a few months back when Greg went to gather supplies? You had that nasty flu or something?" She reached to her right and gathered a stack of time-stained plates while she spoke.

Mick remembered it well. Greg had been gone for nearly three days. It was much longer than Greg had initially intended to be gone, and far longer than Mick was comfortable with. It had turned out to be one of the most worthwhile trips any of them had ever taken. He had returned with two blister packs of antibiotics. If that had been pre-Colossus, it would have been like Greg walking in with an armful of gold.

"Well," Laurel continued, "Greg found something when he was out there. And he purposely didn't tell you about it." She placed the stack of plates next to the cake. "You're always the one to take care of us, Mick. So we figured we'd stash what he found and save it." She scrunched her nose in a cute way. "Heck, it lasted through a global apocalypse. What was another few months?"

With his face still close to the cake, Mick said, "You know, it's funny. This thing looks a lot like—"

"A big Twinkie?" Laurel laughed. "That's because it is. We mushed them all together."

"That's great," Mick said, delighted.

"Well, we'll see about that," Sarah said. "It was

the best we could do. The bakery was out of their fresh stuff."

Laurel went to the far side of the room and banged on the exposed heating conduit that led to the roof. "Greg," she shouted into the vent. "Cake." She then turned toward the rest of the group. "Or whatever we're calling it."

"I'll get the guys," Kathryn said, vanishing from the room to gather Sandeep and Chester from their task of inventorying.

Being the center of attention had never been Mick's thing. He preferred to lie low and let others rush around him. To silently observe whenever possible. However, it seemed as though this celebration was going to happen with or without his consent. Whether he liked it or not.

As the rest of the group prepared what would prove to be an awful-tasting "cake" experience, Mick reached into the inner pocket of his tattered blue peacoat and removed a faded and slightly burned photograph. With his back to the group, he gently caressed the picture of his wife with his thumb. The room was dim, but he did not need much light to see every contour of her face. He stared at it for hours at a time, memorizing what he could to replace what he had forgotten. At times he became so caught up in the moment that he could swear the picture smiled. The world would have been infinitely better if Sue was still in it.

The group then sang a rousing verse of "Happy Birthday," followed immediately by "How

Old Are You Now," at which point Mick cut them off. His body reminded him each day how old he was. He certainly did not need a verbal reminder.

CHAPTER 3

"You awake, boy?"

Solomon did not move. He continued to stare at the chipped concrete wall in front of him, a few inches from his nose. The one time it had rained over the past few years had left a dark water spot on the wall. He concentrated on that. It reminded him of a mouse; the thinner channels of water mimicked the mouse's whiskers, and the larger, more rounded stain formed its body.

"You hear me, boy?"

He wished he could run away from his life. Run back into the past. At least then he would be protected beneath Ms. Stella's umbrella of love and selflessness. The present stripped away his desire to live. His twenty-three-year existence had been filled with people calling him a retard or slow or different. The words hurt. He pretended as if they didn't, but they did. Rarely did anyone look deeper than his appearance or mannerisms to see who he truly was, to see the soul inside the skin. He wasn't any of those nasty things people called him. He was smart in his own way—a way that had carried him through times that no human should have to endure. What most people failed to understand was that just because he spoke slowly and stuttered when he was nervous didn't mean his mind worked that way. Very few cared to take the time to understand that.

The clinking on the metal bars told Solomon all he needed to know. He did not look over to where the sound came from. He knew who it was and what it meant.

He kept staring at the water-stain mouse. It had faded greatly over the years. But Solomon had memorized its shape having spent so much time looking at it. The closer to the wall he was, the less likely he would inadvertently look back at the old jail cell bars. And, more importantly, through the bars. Solomon refused to give him that satisfaction. Not today. Not ever.

More clinking. Loud, obnoxious clinking. A sound he reviled so intensely that it made his stomach knot and his lips purse. He wanted to explode in rage, bend the lifeless metal bars that held him captive during the nights. Reach through and crush the throats of his captors, specifically the one that was there now. It was nothing more than a perverse fantasy. He could never do that. They would kill him if he did. And his life was not his own to give. He lived it for another.

Solomon kept staring. And just like each morning before it, Solomon's refusal to look back brought Clyde into the cell. But Solomon knew he was coming in either way. Nothing he said or did would stop that. It never did.

Clyde fumbled with the keys with his nine pudgy fingers—the tenth had been lost before

Solomon had had the misfortune of meeting him during their early teenage years. He stared down at the ring of keys that hung from a chain on his neck through his hazy sports goggles; his glasses had broken some time ago. Solomon remembered hearing King ask Clyde once why he wore those "ridiculous things." "You look like something out of a science fiction movie," King had said. Clyde had told him it was part of his character and who he was in the world after Impact. He remembered King then laughing and telling Clyde that he looked like a fool and that one needed to have character before becoming a character. Or something like that.

It was one of the few things King ever said that Solomon agreed with. He tried to ignore whatever those around him said whenever possible. They spit poison from their mouths, hateful and cruel things. Ms. Stella had impressed upon him to keep away from people like that. That he was better than them in every way imaginable. He had little choice in the matter, however. There was no way to avoid these people. Prisoners lacked the luxury of choosing their captors.

Clyde finally unlocked the rusty cell door and swung it open. Its long moaning creak was a warning of sorts, as if the cold metal surrounding Solomon felt his despair and the pain soon to come.

Clyde waddled clumsily into the cell in his holey black boots. Solomon felt each step vibrate the floor in a way only someone used to being there for as long as he had could. He'd become so accustomed to this ritual that he'd found out firsthand that fat, of which Clyde had copious amounts, could actually make a rubbing sound if one listened closely enough; skin moved against skin in the most grotesque of ways. Solomon used that sound to gauge how long until the next part in their sadistic play began. The part he was resolute to win every time no matter the cost.

Thump, thump, went Clyde's stubby feet. Solomon counted. It typically took Clyde twelve steps to reach him, except on the days when he stumbled.

Ten, eleven ...

There was a short pause. The footsteps stopped. Solomon clenched his body tight.

Clyde reared back one of his thick legs and kicked Solomon square in the back with the toe of his boot, causing Solomon to inadvertently contort away from the kick and toward the water-stain mouse.

"Didn't you hear me, boy?"

Clyde then squealed in delight like the fat little piggy he was. This was what Clyde lived for: to torment Solomon in private, away from any form of remaining civility that might stop his barbaric actions.

He kicked again, this time with more power, aiming for the small of Solomon's back.

Solomon closed his eyes. He clenched his jaw. Like every morning, he tried to think of better thoughts. Ms. Stella had taught him to meditate to calm his mind. He tried, usually in vain, to drift to a better place. His back had become calloused over the years from enduring such torment. The bruises were harder to form as if his body stopped caring some time ago. But the pain was always present; he used it to drive himself. It was a pain he would never forget. If Solomon died one morning from this, and he felt as if he may at times, then he would die knowing that Clyde did not win. While his body was captive, his mind was not. Solomon's will was his alone to control. And this fat little man he'd once considered a friend would never take that from him.

"Ready to get up yet, boy?"

Solomon was a man. He detested the word *boy*. King, the man who had created this bubble of miscreants, called him that. And Clyde figured he could, too, seeing as he was King's lapdog. But as much as he wanted to, Solomon would not put up a fight. They would hurt *her* if he did. And they had already hurt her enough. So he would endure the pain for both of them.

Solomon opened his eyes and pushed himself up with his right arm, his back aching as he did. He got to his knees and then rose to his feet. He stood maybe an inch taller than Clyde. He knew he was stronger than him—much stronger. When they would play wrestle at the orphanage, Solomon would always come out the victor. Never once did Clyde win.

Since that time, their relationship had changed about as drastically as one could. Clyde's jealousy and weak mind had a lot to do with it; his inner turmoil took care of the rest. Now Solomon would rather spit on Clyde's grave than remember who he used to be. The anger that brewed inside Solomon was fierce, a captive much like himself.

He feared the day he knew was coming. When he would lose his control and do what needed to be done, what was begging so badly to come to fruition. But for such a "stupid" person, Solomon understood what the ramifications of that would be. So he continued to bite his tongue and take his unjustified daily punishment, mindful of the greater picture, hoping for change.

Clyde smiled, revealing his stained and rotting teeth. A black gaping hole stretched across his gums where his front two teeth had been. Solomon remembered when King had knocked one of them out. Solomon went to bed with a smile on his face that night. He didn't know or care where the other one went; hopefully into Clyde's belly where it may do some damage, rip his intestines open and slowly poison him. He wished he could knock the rest out, one by one. Clyde deserved that and so much more. Maybe one day Solomon would be given that chance. If he lived that long.

Solomon held his arms out. The handcuffs were old, but they still did their job.

"I went and saw your little friend downstairs already," Clyde said. He unlocked Solomon's cuffs and put them in his back pocket. "One day I'll have my way with her. And there is nothing you can do to stop it." He snickered.

Without so much as a word, Solomon turned his back to Clyde and walked from the cell. Clyde did his best to rile him up, make him do something he would instantly regret. But just like his refusal to turn around when Clyde came calling, he would not give in to his little game of words. He was better than that. He was better than Clyde.

Solomon knew where to go. This was the routine. He headed left out of his cell and down a short dark hallway. He then veered right when the hall ended and down the longer hallway that led to the large room where King presided over his kingdom.

The dark hallway gave way to a well-lit room, or, rather, well lit for the times and conditions. Anything more than nothing could be considered so. Two long rectangular tables flanked either side of the room, where the other hungry savages ate their filthy meals. Chomps and gargles filled the room as if the feeding trough had opened in the hogs' pen. Not a single person looked up when Solomon entered. No one but King.

"About time you got up, boy," Matthew King O'Conner said as he picked something from his teeth with his long pinkie fingernail. He'd long ago pompously shortened his name to simply King, as he'd felt it was more fitting for a man in his position. He sat on a large leather recliner atop a smallish wooden platform. A faux throne for a faux king. He wore a long black trench coat that had the appearance of a cape as it melted into the black of the chair. His cleanly shaved head seemed out of place among all the filth that surrounded them. But when you were King, you had certain privileges that others did not. A razor being one of them. Hygiene being another.

Solomon said nothing. He did not look at King out of fear that his true feelings would be conveyed in an instant. And while he could take a beating, as evidenced by Clyde's morning wake-up call, he was not about to volunteer for one in any possible way. So he simply skulked off like he did every morning, into a dark corner of the room, and watched as the subhumans fed their faces with whatever scraps they were able to find.

Solomon ate what he could when the others were done. Scraps of scraps were what he had. He thought about eating nothing and letting himself slide off into death from starvation, but he did not want to give them that satisfaction. And then *she* would be all alone. They all thought he was too slow to comprehend anything. And he used that to his advantage. He found ways to sneak out of the old police station when nobody was looking. That was when he found his food in whatever form it took that day. He would wait.

King wiped his mouth with his sleeve and then waved Clyde in closer. He whispered something to him.

Clyde promptly turned around and addressed those in attendance. "Shut up and stop feeding your traps," he said. "King's got something to say."

Most of them stopped what they were doing. Solomon stared out at the group of forty or so people. Most of them men. All of them despicable. King knew how to fill the place with weak-minded people that would gladly do his bidding rather than face his wrath.

King rose from his recliner throne. He rubbed his bald head slowly with his right hand and then smoothed his perfectly trimmed goatee. He took a great deal of pleasure in being in charge. This was his sad kingdom. And his alone.

"My people," he addressed the room. "It has come to my attention that rations have been found near the harbor. I will lead our army to gather them. Do I have any volunteers?"

The room sat quiet. Dirty faces looked from one to another. Not a sound from anyone. They were as lazy as they were predictable. Solomon knew it was not a request despite its phrasing.

Clyde stepped forward and pulled a Magnum revolver from his pants. He pointed it at the crowd, waving it from side to side. Slowly hands began to rise. Voices that had been muted moments ago came to life. The room of dolts had figured it out.

"I'll go," said one man reluctantly, looking around at his fellow heathens.

"Me, too?" said another, phrased in as close to a question as possible.

One by one the room began to stand, until there was only one left sitting: Solomon. Nobody noticed or cared that he did not stand. For even if he had the desire to go with them, which he never would, they would not want him there to slow them down. His job was anything deemed lower than menial. It was one of the few things that worked out in his favor.

"All right then," King said. "Let's go. We have some ground to cover."

And with that, the group spilled from the room and up another hallway toward the building's exit. The few in the back, those out of King's earshot, complained to each other. Solomon knew their words were wasted just like their lives. They were expendable. They simply had not figured that out yet.

Clyde turned to Solomon before leaving. He reached down and flipped a few of the plates onto the floor, spilling whatever slop was on them. "Clean this up," he said, waving his hand around the room. "Or your body and my boot are going to have another meeting when I get back." He snickered and then walked away, calling over his shoulder, "Or maybe I'll pay your friend downstairs another visit."

Solomon stared back. Hatred boiled inside him. Hatred not only for Clyde but for himself, because he would clean this mess up as much as he detested the fact. He hated them all for a multitude of reasons. But as much as he hated Clyde, he hated

King the most. He was the one that pushed Clyde over the edge of sanity. He was the one that nudged him toward the blackness that was inside him all along.

CHAPTER 4

Mick woke after another restless night spent worrying about things he had no control over. He drearily rubbed his heavy eyes and allowed them to adjust to the faintest of glows produced by the lamp from out in the main room. Each morning came like the one before it: melting into the previous night, not nearly as delineated as he remembered it once being. Very little light shone through the particulate-laced atmosphere to begin with. And while he could still differentiate between day and night on the outside, it became a much more difficult task while inside the subterranean world in which they dwelled. But the human body had the most amazing alarm clock built into it; one that woke him around the same time each morning.

He reached to his left to nudge his kids awake.

Nate grumbled, his eyes still firmly shut, and rolled over in his sleeping bag. "Five more minutes," he said, haphazardly waving his arm to leave him alone.

Nate would get up soon enough. He always did. And it would do Mick no good to pester him. While his fatherly instinct was to make sure Nate stuck to a schedule and did not "waste his day away," as his father would put it, it was his hope that Nate would fall back asleep and into a dream that carried him to a better place, if only for a few more minutes. To rob him of that opportunity didn't seem fair.

Kathryn rubbed her eyes and yawned. "Morning."

"Morning, sweetie."

It was at these times, when the dim light played tricks on his eyes, that he could not help but stare at Kathryn and see his sweet little four-year-old baby instead of the fourteen-year-old young woman she was. He liked to hold on to the trick of the dim light, hold on to his little girl. In the brighter light, he could see that over the past year her face had begun to morph into that of her mother. And each day she matured on both the inside and out, making him prouder than he'd ever imagined he could be. At times, he could swear it was Sue, his sorely missed wife, looking back at him, telling him that everything was going to be all right and that he was doing a fine job of raising the twins.

Mick swung his feet over the edge of the cot and scratched his scraggly head of hair, which had recently begun to bald in the back center. Ironic, considering his graying beard seemed to get thicker with time. But few things made sense anymore. With his head bowed in tiredness, or maybe just simple reluctance to rinse and repeat the day before, Mick forced himself off the rigid cot. It was a more difficult task than he ever would have foreseen. With very little to look forward to motivation became elusive, especially first thing in the morning.

Chester, typically the first one up in the morning, was in charge of the food store and its upkeep. He was not fat. He was husky, or so he told Mick on more than one occasion. And Mick believed him considering they all ate the same meager meals, yet Chester stayed the same round shape. Rarely did the food store grow. But Chester helped to keep it from diminishing before its time. It was an important job that he took a great amount of pride in.

"Morning, Chester," Mick said, exiting the sleeping quarters and stepping into the glow of the single kerosene lamp.

"And a good morning to you, my friend," Chester said. "Hungry?"

Mick took a seat at the table. He was starving, actually. "What's on the menu today? Poached eggs? Pancakes?" he said, yawning. Then something so cruelly delicious popped into his head. "Bacon?" Why did he even think that? What a tease. But he could have sworn the unmistakable taste of pork had hit his tongue with its salty deliciousness. His mind suddenly salivated for it. He would have traded his rifle at that moment for a seat at a greasy spoon.

"No," Chester said. "None of those things. I have something much better." He smiled.

And Mick knew all too well what that something was.

Chester reached down and laid Mick's plate in front of him. One slice of canned meat, thinly cut as usual, still with a bit of the yellowish gelatin preservative on it. He also placed a cup to the right of his plate half filled with water from the storage tank. Each morning was the same, rarely a deviation and never anything worth waking up for.

The building they called home had been sanctioned by the city as a fallout shelter twenty years back, ten years before Colossus. Mick had been hired to help wire the building's telecommunications during its remodel. There was enough food, water, and fuel for up to one thousand people to survive for three months; plenty of time for the nearby residents to ride out almost anything imaginable. Turns out they did not imagine the right things. And, luckily for Mick and crew, the city had not officially opened the facility as a shelter before Impact. So few people knew of its existence. And those who did know apparently did not survive long enough to reap the benefits. The large conference hall that would have been used as the living quarters for the one thousand people had collapsed before Mick had brought his kids there, and the remaining sections of the shelter held the eight of them comfortably. Most importantly, though, was the fact that the food had been untouched when they'd arrived. It was like winning the post-apocalypse lottery, if there ever was such a morbid thing.

Mick picked up his fork from the table, which

Chester had laid out in a neater manner than the times demanded, and flipped it over as he always did, checking for his name written in permanent black marker. Dishes were not washed. Clean water was only for drinking. So utensils and plates were all permanently assigned to each person. Germs were less likely to be passed that way. At least that is what they told themselves.

It became more of a habit than anything: checking for his name. Mick knew full well that germs were going to spread regardless of proper utensil hygiene. The eight of them could be locked in a box for only so long before becoming one giant organism, living and dying by each other's woes. But he still practiced the ritual. As far as he was concerned, there was nothing wrong with being a stickler for routine.

With a certain level of care it did not deserve, Mick used the fork to push the remaining gelatin off to the side of the slice of canned meat like a plow clearing a wintery street. Except this street had been covered in slimy yellow goop. The overly processed meat concoction had an infinite shelf life as long as the temperature was right. The taste, if it even had one to begin with, had deteriorated over the years to the point where it and cardboard were indistinguishable from one another. But it was the protein that mattered, not the taste.

Mick folded his slice of canned meat in half, now clean of all gelatin preservative, and shoved it in his mouth whole. All he needed was the bit of nutrition it provided. And the quicker he got it down his throat the better, as he gagged almost every meal. Something about the texture and the way it slid around inside his mouth did not agree with him.

Sandeep was next out of the sleeping quarters. "Morning to you both," he said, rubbing the sleep from his eyes. He pulled out a chair opposite Mick at the cold metal table and plopped his lanky frame down. He then scratched his patchy beard down to its brittle roots.

"You're just in time, Deep," Mick said, yawning again. "Chester's serving up bacon this morning."

Mick called him Deep for two reasons: the first being that he tended to shorten people's names without knowing it, a bad habit from growing up in a neighborhood where everyone had three- or four-syllable names. There was no time for full names back then. They had games to play and places to run to during their busy childhood; a time when life was simpler and still relatively normal. Sandeep was also quite intelligent, having been a teacher before Impact. He waxed philosophical on more than one occasion. His thoughts were as deep as his soul was good. Deep would constantly tell Mick how thankful he was that he took him in after Impact. In reality it was Mick who was thankful for Deep.

Sandeep looked over his shoulder as Chester put his plate down, identical to Mick's. "Truly amazing things they can do with bacon these days."

Chester smiled. "Bon appétit," he said, removing his hand from the plate and vanishing into the dark food pantry behind them.

Sandeep, like Mick, pushed the thin patches of gelatin off the canned meat. He then cut the mushy slice of canned meat with the side of his fork into six equal pieces like he did at every meal. He put the first piece in his mouth, always the top left corner. He chewed slowly, hunched over his plate as if contemplating just how gross the canned meat had become, and stared down at the five remaining identical pieces. He then looked up from his breakfast and across the table at Mick, gave him a quick smile, and forked bite number two into his mouth. The second piece was always the top right corner. That was followed by the bottom left corner, the bottom right corner, then the two center pieces at once—never a deviation. Mick had come to find out that he was not the only creature of habit remaining in this broken world.

Chester reappeared from the panty. "Will you be joining us for prayer this morning, Mick?"

Mick looked up and slowed his chewing. He peered at Chester through the corner of his eye. He then swallowed his breakfast and washed it down with a bit of water. "The answer never changes, Chester," Mick said with a quickly vanishing half-smile. "Your perseverance is admirable, though."

Chester nodded as he always did before

turning to prepare the others' breakfasts.

Before Impact, Chester had worked as a minster at a local Unitarian Universalist church. He still practiced his beliefs daily. Each morning after breakfast, Chester would sit and read scripture. Some of the others came and went from these sessions. Greg, an Irish Catholic who was raised in South Boston, made a habit more than most to attend before going up to the roof for lookout duty.

Mick made a point to tell his kids that it was up to them to decide what they believed in; it was a choice they would need to make for themselves when and if they were ready. When it came to his own beliefs, Mick was resolute that there could be no possibility of God—not in this life or the next. If there was a God, then his wife would still be here with him. A true and good God, the one preached about across the globe, would never take such an important soul away before her time. And truly, if a divine being did exist, then the meteorites never should have hit in the first place, leaving a people supposedly created in God's image to wither and die. No. Mick simply believed in what he could put his own two hands on. Practicality was his religion, and it had served him well up until that point.

He downed what remained of his water, which over the past year or so had taken on the taste of its large plastic holding tank. Sandeep assured him that the water was still perfectly fine, just a bit different-tasting. Sandeep said the storage tank had held their water for longer than they had been there, and that the water was bound to take in some of the tank's essence, as he put it.

Mick said his good-byes and kissed his kids; Kathryn on her cheek and Nate on his forehead. He then donned his dusty blue peacoat, shouldered his rifle, and made his way back up the stairs he seemed to have just come down only minutes ago. Chester followed him up and locked the door behind him.

"Safe journey, Mick," Chester said.

"Be back soon."

As the door swung shut, Mick took a deep breath to gather his senses. He itched for a break in the monotony. This was a new day. And while the day felt no different from the last, or the hundreds of days before it, he could change that. No. He *would* change that. *Today's going to be different*, he told himself. He was not sure if he believed it. But he found that sometimes words could motivate actions. Maybe today was one of those days.

CHAPTER 5

Solomon reluctantly cleared the mess the heathens had made when slopping their various scraps down their worthless throats. He tried not to think while doing it, as the anger brewed the more thought he put into it. He cleared his mind and thought of Ms. Stella. She'd taught him to control his anger, that it would only end up hurting him in the long run. People were going to act the way they wanted to. Solomon had no control over that. Ms. Stella had reinforced in him to do the best he could and ignore whatever he was able to. He used that knowledge each day. He let the others around him stew in anger and hatred because of what had happened to them, to the planet, to those they loved. He had resolved to dwell in a better world inside his mind where he had complete control. For it was truly the only place he felt safe.

Solomon's mother, a heroin addict who had later died of her addiction, had blamed Solomon for pushing his father away. He, too, had been an addict and destined to leave regardless of Solomon. His mother had later insisted that he'd abandoned them because Solomon was "different." That it was his fault they had no money. That her life would have been better if he had not come into it. In her drug-clouded mind, it was newly born Solomon that had ruined her life and not her true master, the one she injected into her veins whenever she was able to steal enough to reunite with the darkness. It was a miracle he had been able to survive as long as he had given the mental anguish he had endured. Aside from the care of Ms. Stella, Solomon had never felt wanted.

After his mother passed, Solomon found himself alone in a society that did not want him. With a mere seven years of age under his overburdened belt—seven years that had matured him before his time—Solomon was forced to fend for himself, to learn things on his own that should have been taught to him. He learned to eke out a life on the streets. And he did so until the ripe old age of twelve. It was then that he met Ms. Stella. Very few things made Solomon smile. The world gave him no reason to. Yet the memory of her, especially the first time they had met, still forced a grin to break the gruff exterior he was forced to adopt.

Solomon remembered the day vividly. Probably because he tried to forget so many painful things, the truly wonderful memories did not have to fight for space.

It was dusk, and the pre-Impact city of Boston bustled with those leaving work for the weekend. The streets were cluttered with honking horns and slowly moving traffic. Nothing abnormal, aside from where Solomon was looking for food. He did not go around that particular neighborhood often.

Too many of the residents tended to come outside and sit on their stoops. Too many eyes watched what everyone was doing. It was bad enough that he had not eaten in days. The last thing he needed were the judging tones and shooings away that tended to happen when he intruded on a close-knit community. It had happened before. Many times at that. And it wasn't like Solomon really cared what others thought of him. He was nobody to them—just another dirty beggar on the street, even though he had not begged a day in his life.

"You shouldn't be in there," he remembered Ms. Stella saying to him. Her first words in what would become a life-altering relationship.

He was Dumpster diving. In the alley a few streets from her house. Solomon was halfway into the Dumpster, his legs dangling over the outside, when Ms. Stella found him. He stopped sifting through the trash.

He heard her shoes click and clack down the alley. Ms. Stella then lightly tapped his leg. "Are you all right in there?" she said.

Her voice was soft but firm. It was the first time that Solomon had not been afraid to listen to what someone had to say. It was as if the bond they would ultimately share reached out and invited him in instantly. A strange sense of worth that he had never felt in his life up until that point washed over him. Solomon pushed himself out of the Dumpster and came face-to-face with Ms. Stella.

She was nicely put together in a long

burgundy dress with a sweater over the top. But what he remembered most was her smile. For whatever reason, Ms. Stella seemed genuinely happy to interact with Solomon. He was not accustomed to that. In fact, he could not remember a time when that happened. Most people refused to make eye contact with him. He had been the bastard child of the world for so long that he did not know how to react. His instincts, wrong at the time, told him to run; he shouldn't trust anyone. He would only get hurt.

As he started to flee, Ms. Stella again did something he was not accustomed to. "Young man," she said. "Why don't you come with me? You look like you could use a nice hot meal. Would you like that?" She walked closer to him and gently brushed a tuft of hair from his eyes. "I don't think a shower would hurt, either."

Solomon said nothing. He rarely spoke. Typically because he had no one to speak with, but also because he had been so jaded over the years from being called stupid and the harshness society surrounded him with was less so when his mouth was shut. He wanted to speak, though. He knew in his soul that Ms. Stella was not one of those practitioners of pain. The tiniest bit of hope grew inside him as he stood in front of her. But he still did not speak. He simply nodded. Old habits were hard to break.

Remembering the times he had with Ms. Stella somehow lessened, to a minor degree, the pain he lived in now.

Solomon finished clearing the room the best he could. Not that it made much difference. The entire abandoned police station that they lived in was rife with filth. But it was enough of a change so he would not have to listen to that idiot Clyde.

CHAPTER 6

Phillip sat in his office and stared at the abstract oil painting on his wall. Contorted shapes and exaggerated swishes fought each other for space on the small canvas. He loved abstract art. Abstract allowed him to view the work in the way he wanted. Other types of art seemed more rigid in their meaning. And he did not like to be told what to think or do. This particular painting happened to be his favorite. As with most things Phillip admired, this was done by his own hands.

He leaned back in his chair with his hands behind his head and his feet up on his desk, and he admired his work. He vividly remembered the day he'd created this masterpiece. It was two years before Colossus. He was working tirelessly for the Department of Defense on a new strand of airborne bacteria that would render whoever breathed it unconscious for anywhere from eight to twelve hours. It worked instantly, was odorless, and only known by a select few because of its top secret designation.

A colleague of his at the University of Massachusetts who was constantly pestering him to get out of the lab and "back into society" invited him to a party. Phillip initially dismissed the idea. He did not have the luxury of personal time. There were far too many important things to do. And he valued his work over anything those of lesser intelligence could offer. That was until he discovered that Lucy would be going. The party then became of interest. He figured it couldn't hurt to take an hour or two out of his busy schedule to socialize.

Lucy and Phillip started as colleagues, but became something more. The flirting ramped-up the night of the party, especially after Phillip had a few vodka and tonics. They talked about many things, but mostly about work. Phillip was attracted to intelligence above all else; it was his weak spot. And Lucy had copious amounts of it to go with her curvaceous body. It did not take long after that for the two to become one. Their relationship was a sweet crush that quickly soured, lasting for less than six months. It was all Phillip's fault. They both knew that. He chose his work time and again over her. Having never been in a relationship for longer than a minute, and usually with a snooze-worthy medical book, he'd doomed their relationship from the start.

He painted this picture during one of his dates with Lucy. *Date with Paint* was the name of the place. He had never been much of a painter, aside from the careless smudges he made as a child. But there he was, a celebrated pathologist with a PhD in microbiology, dressed in a goofy art apron two sizes too large, swooning over a woman he knew in his heart he had no way of keeping.

The painting reminded him of her, of that night. Most of all, his picture reminded him that his work should never come second to anyone or anything. Since then, it never had.

There was a knock on the glass door to his office. Phillip looked over and waved him in.

"Dr. Jones," said the man who entered. He was dressed in a dark-blue jumpsuit, tight around the waste, with a gold shield emblem on both shoulders and over the right breast. The words *Initiative Security* were emblazoned above the shields, with the word *Captain* below.

"How did it go, Jon?"

"Fine, sir. We distributed all twenty test kits without incident."

"Were you seen?"

"Yes. But we needn't worry about her." Captain Jon Teague moved closer to the desk.

"How so?"

"She was in the late stages of CV-1. Maybe a week or so left. Limb paralysis had already set in. And her corneas were blackening."

"What do you mean *was* in the late stages?"

"We did the humane thing. She was in pain. We ended that pain."

Phillip soaked in the information. "And you made sure the kits would be seen?"

The captain said, "Yes, sir. We painted the boxes bright red as requested. There is no way anyone is going to miss it out there. It might as well be a friggin' rainbow."

Phillip paused for a moment, caught in his thoughts. He then looked back to Captain Teague. "Well done, Captain. Let's hope this leads us to the answers we desperately need."

**

Sid sat on his bed and bounced a tennis ball off the far wall. With each bounce he thought of all the experiments he had run on the virus's makeup. He would throw and then catch, pausing in between the routine as he thought. The virus had been broken down, diluted, spliced, heated, frozen, and everything in between. It seemed impervious to anything they knew or had: a true enigma. All the tools and instruments that they had packed into The Facility before Impact made little difference. Hundreds of millions of dollars' worth of medical equipment: CT, genetic splicers, nanobots. They had it all and more, and none of it mattered. And that was what worried Sid the most. There may be no answer to the question the virus posed.

The fact that they had yet to put a dent in the virus kept him up at night. But it was what they were doing now, the testing outside the doors, that gave him nightmares. What they were doing went against his Hippocratic Oath. The respect for life seemed to be uncaringly brushed aside. Now he simply felt like a hypocrite. On more than one occasion, he brought those feelings up. His peers quickly reminded him that the oath they all swore was to a world that no longer existed. The rules had changed, they said. But he did not see it that way. These were the same people he'd sworn to protect. The same lives he'd vowed to respect. It was nothing more than convenient to ignore all that under the premise of change. It served *their* purpose. It helped *them* sleep at night.

But he was not sleeping. All he could do was think of what they had just done.

The door to Sid's quarters slid open automatically as Alex entered from the hallway.

"Hey, bud," Alex said. "I hope you aren't mad about yesterday's meeting?"

Sid shook his head. "I'm not mad. I'm disgusted. What we're doing isn't right, Alex."

Alex sighed and then sat at the end of Sid's bed. He put his back to the wall and held out his hands, requesting the ball.

Sid tossed it to him and Alex began bouncing it on the opposite wall. "I hope you know that I'm not fully on board with what Phillip is doing, either."

Sid looked at him, raising his right eyebrow.

"Don't do that. You've known me a long time, Sid. I don't want to fool these people any more than you do. But what choice do we have? If we don't do this, then we all—"

"We may die regardless of what we've done," Sid said, sensing what Alex was about to say. They had been through this countless times. "I feel like we are getting off course. The Initiative was created to rebuild what the meteorites destroyed. It doesn't feel like we are rebuilding anything. It feels like we are helping to destroy more lives."

"I know," Alex said.

"Then why not say something, Alex? Why am I the one that always has to play devil's advocate? At this point I wouldn't be surprised to wake up outside the doors one morning. I think Phillip is getting fed up with my bleeding heart crap."

"Stop it."

"I'm serious, Alex. Phillip isn't going to put up with it much longer. Especially when everyone else simply agrees with his plans. I seem to be the only one who disagrees on a regular basis. Remember when Shaker started showing signs of infection?"

Alex nodded. It was hard for any of them to forget.

"His symptoms came out of nowhere. Much quicker than we had seen in the others. It was like he drank a gallon of liquid virus."

"Of course I remember, man. I liked Shaker as much as you did. It wasn't easy on any of us watching him die like that."

"It doesn't seem strange to you how quickly he came down with the virus?"

Alex shook his head slowly while thinking. "Not really. He dealt with the virus in its raw form. He was the one breaking it down every day. Out of all of us, he was the one with the most daily exposure to it. It was probably just a matter of time before he had an accident."

"What if it wasn't an accident?"

"Oh, come on, Sid. You don't really believe that someone here sabotaged his work, do you?"

Sid remained quiet. He didn't know what to believe anymore. But he'd known Dr. Shaker well, from his early days working for the CDC. Dr. Shaker was many things, but careless was not one of them.

"Sid, I don't necessarily agree with how Phillip is going about—"

"Then speak up," Sid interrupted. "How can you sit there while he puts this into motion? These people are all going to think once they inject themselves that they are safe. That the virus can't affect them any longer. But in reality all they are being is unknowingly tested without consent. What happens if one of those people has an adverse event to the serum? What if they die from it?"

"They are going to die regardless, Sid. We didn't cause the virus. Remember? We are simply trying to eradicate it."

"But at what cost, Alex?"

"What are our alternatives, Sid? Please. Let me know. Because I'm all ears. If you have something else, then let me know. I'll march down to Phillip's office with you right now."

Sid said nothing. He knew, despite his strong reservations, that there were no alternatives. He had worked tirelessly in the lab to find one. Night after night, and typically into the early morning hours. There had to be something else they could do. Some miniscule speck of hope that he had missed. Something so elusive that once found it would be a eureka moment for them all. That was what he searched for. If found, they could cure those inside The Facility without having to hurt those that had already been hurt so much. He had never felt easy about living at The Facility while so many others suffered. And he worked to make sure it was not in vain.

"You're a good man, Sid. Better than the rest of us. But you know this is the only way. We've both spent every waking hour in the lab trying to find something to beat this thing. You don't have to like it. Hell, I don't like it, either. But this is where we are."

"Who's to say this works? It's nothing more than a needle in the proverbial haystack. And we don't even know if the immunity exists."

Alex stopped throwing the ball against the wall. He eyed it a minute before tossing it back to Sid. "We have to believe it exists, Alex. If we don't, what else do we have?"

Sid stood from his bed. He walked over and placed the ball on one of the three shelves in the back of his room. He then picked up a picture of himself, one taken the day he'd graduated from medical school. A beaming smile cut his face from ear to ear. That was back when his purpose was defined, his future determined. Now it all seemed so worthless.

He turned to Alex. "I don't mean to lash out at

you. I hope you know that."

"I know," Alex said. "To tell you the truth, though, if you didn't get all heated over this, then I'd be worried. You have always been the voice of reason. You kept me grounded in medical school and pushed me through some long nights during our residency. I take what you say very seriously. Just try to remember that I'm on your side. Just because I don't go against Phillip doesn't mean I necessarily agree with his methods. Remember Professor McKay's first rule?"

Sid thought and then said, "Of course I do. It's not like he would let us forget it. 'Wasted energy is the direct result of disagreements without solutions.'"

"That's the one. Trust me—I'd love nothing more than to find a different solution to this thing. But this is all we have. You never seemed this concerned when we tested on the dogs in the lab."

"Those were dogs, Alex. These are humans. Different reactions. Different meaning."

"Same principle. Same morals. I know dogs are not humans, but if you had no compunctions then—"

"It's not the same and you know it, Alex. It's just eating me up."

Sid turned and put the picture back down on the shelf. If the virus did not get him, his own conscience would.

CHAPTER 7

"Please," the elderly woman begged from down on her knees. "We have nothing."

King stared past her, toward what remained of Boston Harbor. The water moved like the sands of a desert, covered in ash and dust, swaying in place just enough to reveal it was not solid land. He took a breath and looked down at the woman with disgust. To him these people were no different than cockroaches; pains in the ass that stole what was left of the world's supplies. *His* supplies. And from *his* land.

"And now you have even less," King said. He motioned to Clyde with nothing more than a quick glance of his eyes. It was a look he had given more times than he could remember. It always meant the same thing. Something he trained his son to do at his unspoken command.

The woman said nothing. Nor did her husband as he knelt beside her. They simply looked at one another in fearful confusion. It was only moments ago that they had been dragged from their own shelter: a small apartment atop the charred and empty remains of a once-thriving convenience store in what used to be one of the busiest sections of the city.

The couple's shared look was quickly

interrupted.

Clyde reached down without so much as a word, and, in one swift motion, he cut the old woman's throat from ear to ear with a dagger he had stealthily removed from his boot. The woman gasped, which quickly turned into a gurgle. She instinctively reached up to her throat, blood seeping between her fingers. She then fell face-first onto the pavement. A small clap of dust wafted around her as her body thumped down, dead.

Her husband's face turned white in horror. "No!" he screamed. Then his eyes burned red with anger. Instinct and rage took over. The old man sprang to his feet in a manner that seemed unfitting for such aged legs. He turned to Clyde. And that's when Clyde stuck him in the gut with the same blade that had seconds ago taken his wife's life.

"Till death do you part," Clyde said, smiling crookedly.

The man did not look away until the last breath escaped his now lifeless body. He fell beside his wife, his hand coming to rest atop hers.

King did not look. He kept his eyes on the harbor, never turning his attention to the vulgar matters that had transpired a mere three feet from him. Clyde was good at what he did. Like father, like son. He'd been trained by King himself. He lacked the finesse King had, of course. Clyde was brutish in his ways. Like a child first learning to color inside the lines: sloppy and rough. The end result was the same, though. And that was really all King cared about. His will would be done.

Boston Harbor was where King had moored his yacht, back when people strived to have such things. He went looking for his once-prized possession a year after Impact. *In the Shadows* was the name he'd chosen for her. The yacht was the only "female" he ever treated with an ounce of respect; in his darkly twisted mind, she was the only one that deserved it. His own father had taught him early on that women were to be subservient. If they did not obey, then they were to be punished.

Toward the end of things, his work had run him ragged. Long flights coupled with longer nights had worn him down. His work situation had neared a tipping point a few months before Colossus, and King had strongly considered leaving it all behind. He had enough money to last the rest of his life. And to him money was nothing more than a pleasurable by-product of a job he loved. Those were the days. Patiently waiting for his mark. Methodically planning his kill down to the last detail. And when the time came, he was always precise. He considered himself the brain surgeon of killers. It was an art form to him. And that was why he could not be bothered with amateurish killings such as Clyde's.

"There ain't nothing in there," said one of King's men as he stumbled out of the broken glass and metal structure of the old convenience store. He looked down quickly at the two corpses at his feet. "Oh," he said.

King took a large breath and then exhaled a larger sigh. He turned to the ragged man, Richard, he thought. Though it did not really matter what his name was. Only that he was loyal like the rest of the dogs that obeyed him. Once the loyalty was gone, then so was the dog.

"You searched the entirety of the building?" King asked.

The man nodded unconvincingly. The longer he nodded, the less sure he appeared. "Let me take another look, King." And with that he turned and shuffled back into the dilapidated structure they had come to pillage.

Nowadays King did little killing. He had Clyde for that. And if not Clyde, then he was sure he would be able to find a suitable replacement. The meteorite seemed to have spared many terrible people's lives. Either that or the new world had created them. Either way, finding people lacking in morality was as easy as finding dust. Clyde was his son, but only because it was convenient for King at the time. Ever since he'd rescued him from that terrible life within the orphanage. Granted, he had been the one who'd abandoned Clyde at that orphanage in the first place. He felt like a good person for taking him back out after the Earth fell in upon itself. In his mind, King was nothing short of a saint.

His seat in life was that of a ruler. And before Impact that would have been an impossibility. He would never had been president. After all, "killer for hire" would have been frowned upon as his previous employment. But now that a government, or a president, or really anything that once was, no longer existed, he was free to make his own kingdom. And that is what he did. One built on fear and death, atop the bodies of many a man.

The same ragged man again appeared from within the dark store. "We searched again. There ain't nothing in there, King. The store ain't got nothing in it but dust and some rat skeletons."

King said, "And what of the upstairs?"

The man's eyes widened. It was readily apparent that he lacked the intelligence to realize there was an upper level. King did not fault him for that. He knew surrounding himself with neophytes had its disadvantages. They were grunts. He was the mind.

King walked past the man and inside the store. His men scurried around like ants, turning and tossing anything not nailed down, searching for anything useful. The floors were more clutter than anything. And the entirety of the inside reeked of decomposing organic material. The dead rats they had failed to find yet, he figured. Unsurprisingly, the rats had seemed to fare better after Impact than almost anything else. But he realized the stench may have been from his own men. He was not entirely sure if some of them showered even when it was available.

There was no basement that he could see, so he

pried open a metal door on the far side of the shop that had been haphazardly hidden behind an old wire rack. The handle was clean and dustless. It had been used recently. He figured by the two dead elderly people outside.

King climbed the short flight of stairs that had been hidden by the metal door. The old wood creaked and moaned with every step, announcing his approach. He exited the stairs and stepped directly ahead into a small bathroom. The room was empty. When he turned to leave, he was faced with his own reflection in a well-preserved mirror that hung over the bathroom's sink, or what remained of it. He wiped a bit of dust off his bald head and stroked his goatee. It was a rare occurrence to see an intact mirror. As fragile as it was, glass did not fare so well in the world's current state. His own appearance had not changed much. He always kept a cleanly shaved head. A throwback to his working days. It made disguising himself in wigs much easier. He figured a mirror would provide quite the sight for some that still imagined themselves as close to who they had been and not as who they had ultimately become—the dogs that served him, for instance.

Aside from the bathroom there appeared to be two small bedrooms, one in each direction. He went right out of the bathroom.

King had his minions as any reputable king would. But he also had a network of eyes and ears scattered throughout the city; those that were not privileged enough to live directly in his castle. They were probably more valuable to him than the dogs he surrounded himself with. Those on the outskirts were the ones that pinpointed his next conquest. They were the ones who kept a lookout for things he may need. People had become so desperate to survive in the post-Impact world that they aligned themselves with whoever helped them do just that. King spared most of them. He even protected a few. It was good to be in King's company, if for nothing else than to live one more day.

One of these people had told King about the food stash here. So far the information had proven fruitless. For the informant's sake, King better find fruit soon. He did not like to be jerked around.

The first bedroom was clearly not the one the couple used. The room was empty as empty could be. Nothing. Not even a closet to search. The walls and ceiling were preserved well and solid-looking.

He left and walked the short distance down the hall and into the second bedroom. Pushed into the far corner was a mattress. A holey green comforter neatly covered it. Aside from that the room was sparse. It did have a closet, however, and that was what interested King the most. People tended to hide things in closets. Closets held their secrets and skeletons until someone looked hard enough to find them.

King pulled the handle. Locked. The door looked weak. Not one of the solid doors, but one with a hollow center like himself.

He brought his knee up and then thrust his booted foot into the door, breaking it in on the first kick. King grabbed the splintered remains and pushed them aside. A small chest, a hope chest he figured, lay on the floor. It, too, was locked. The man or woman must have had the key for it. But that would take more effort than he wanted to waste. So he reached into his waistband and removed a 9 mm handgun. He fired a single round, shattering the lock to the chest.

"You all right, King?" said someone from downstairs.

"Of course I'm all right," he replied. The last thing he needed was his gang of goons thinking he needed protecting.

King holstered his gun and opened the chest. Mostly empty, it contained a few pictures of the couple throughout their lives. They must have been together for a long time judging by the assortment of years between them. There was no food, however. In fact, there was nothing but the pictures and a couple of trinkets. Nothing to make this trip worthwhile.

He slammed the lid of the chest down. When he looked up, he noticed a clean spot on the wall. He leaned in closer. An old knot in the wood was gone, leaving a smallish hole. After reaching in with his index finger, King pried away the loose board. He stared in. While he couldn't see what it was, he knew it was something. And that was better than the nothing he thought they had a moment ago. He pried another board off and then another. With each new board, the hidden contents came more into view.

Here was the food and supplies he had been told about. His minion on the outskirts had done right by him this time. He'd make sure he received a percentage of the loot. He was, after all, a civilized man.

CHAPTER 8

Rather than heading up the hill and through the gathering of dead trees as he usually did, back to his vantage point by the billboard, Mick detoured through a rusty old chain-link fence and down the hill toward what was left of the outskirts of Boston. The city was still plenty inhabited. People just tended to keep to themselves and out of sight the best they could. It was safer that way. And, like Mick's own group, folks tended to stay gathered in packs. There was safety in numbers. These packs rarely communicated with one another, typically out of fear of running into the wrong type of person. The groups of survivors were all just islands floating in a sea of uncertainty, consciously unaware of each other.

There were still good people in the world. There had to be. But Mick also knew for a fact that there were bad people remaining. Many of them. He had run into his fair share over the years. Societal rules were a thing of the past. Human decency was an afterthought. Not that he blamed anyone for becoming who they had. Colossus had left them all with little choice. But that did not mean he shouldn't avoid them whenever possible.

While Mick was determined to scout for new food, anything besides the canned meat, he was also a realist. He had been into the city many times before; a few months ago was the last time he'd ventured down. And he fully realized that this would not be a trip to the grocery store. If only it could be that easy. Anything and everything useful in any way had long since been scooped up. Shelves in stores had been bare so long that thick layers of dust could be used like the rings of a tree to date when they'd last held anything. Mick would have to think outside the box this time. Do something different. Do something he knew that he probably should not.

Mick paused near the base of the hill and crouched down, his knees cracking as he did. He surveyed the dusty gray city. Aside from the scattered howls of wind, all seemed quiet. He then closed his eyes and listened, really listened. The years had taught him that his senses could, and quite frequently did, lie. Quiet could mean a trap. Noise could mean a distraction. He had learned it was best to question his senses if given the opportunity to; simply allow the best possible outcome to rise to the top. If one should even exist.

Swirls of debris, captured by a sudden gust of wind, spun down the street in front of him, tempests without meaning or direction. He paused again, bringing his rifle to the front. While his caution was less, his preparedness could not be. He rarely encountered anyone or anything in his journeys down from the hill. But he would not be caught off guard. He could not afford to be. He owed it to his children to protect himself. He owed his group. And his survival depended on acting first and thinking later.

Normally, Mick went straight down Main Street where most of the shops had once thrived. But he had been down there too many times already. Einstein once said that insanity is doing the same thing over and over again and expecting different results. Deep had told him that after his last unsuccessful trek to find food. He may be insane—he certainly would not rule it out—but he was not stupid. He needed to go a different, and therefore less safe, route.

A burp of canned meat solidified that notion.

To his left, about a mile or so away, flowed the Charles River. What had once been a favorite spot for showing off one's kayaking prowess was now nothing more than a sewage spillway, clogged and contaminated like all the rest of the water around them. Mick had seen everything float down the Charles from half of a school bus—where the other half went was something he did not care to worry about—to bodies to picnic tables to dead trees to things he wished he had not seen and seemingly everything in between. He felt like there would be nothing of interest down that way, so he headed to his right and toward some of the old brownstones that once housed the wealthier Bostonians.

The sky above was just as dreary as always: gray and overcast with a constant tinge of brown from the dust. Before Impact, in the days when the seasons still came about, Mick had always found himself becoming grumpier as the weather turned colder, especially near the end of the year. The worst months were typically January and February in New England: cold, bitter, and gloomy. People were rude and tired of the season by then. That feeling now hung in perpetuity, thankfully minus the snow. Though the cold seemed to linger forever. Not the biting cold he was used to in the heart of winter. More of a steady cold that never left the air. He figured the sun was still up there somewhere. Else the Earth would have already turned into a giant ice cube.

Mick pulled his bandanna over his mouth and flipped the collar of his coat up close to his neck. He kept a steady pace for the better part of an hour, winding into the city proper, his gun at the ready. The old brownstone buildings that lined the street to his left began to melt into larger apartment complexes built into the city as the population expanded. Burned-out and crumbling storefronts littered the street to his right. His shuffling footsteps were the only true sound to be heard, echoing off the buildings between the spurts of gusty wind.

Another two hundred yards forward and he paused in the street. One storefront to his right grabbed his attention like a slap to the face, pushing long forgotten memories back to the present. Memories he tried to keep forgotten simply to avoid the pain of remembering them.

He figured it must have been a dress shop of some kind. Broken mannequin parts were scattered the floor inside and jutted out from beneath the dust on the sidewalk in front. What was left of the front display window contained remnants of a princess-like blue gown window graphic. It was the same vibrant color as the dress that Sue had worn when they'd attended the governor's ball a few years prior to Impact. It had happened to be their first true night out in the two years since the twins had been born. His mother had come over to watch the kids that night. Both Sue and Mick had been reluctant to leave the twins as most new parents would be. But his mother had pushed them out the door and sent them on their way to what would be a fun night.

Mick walked slowly over the store's remains, captured by his thoughts. He kicked away the debris at the base of the brick wall with his worn boot and slid down the wall and onto his butt. He removed the faded picture of Sue from his jacket pocket and stared at it, willing the picture to transcend reality and speak to him.

Let me hear your voice just one more time, my love.

Sue's voice, how he remembered it anyway, became softer and less recognizable as the years traveled forward, more difficult to grab from the other voices in his mind. He hated that. Her voice should never have to relent to any other. To be able hear it one more time would spark a newer, stronger memory. One he was sure to never forget.

But time was fickle, and his memories its slave. Mick did his best to hide his feelings in front of the kids. They were only four years old when Sue died. Their memories of her, the truly eventful ones, were unfortunately few as she'd traveled so much for her job. But Mick had many memories of her, and all but one was good.

On their wedding day, Mick's mother had given him one piece of advice. She'd said, "Never go to bed angry." He'd laughed when she said it, though not because it was funny. Rather simply because she was being a mom; she was always being a mom. And he had heard that saying before. It wasn't until Mick became a parent that he realized how wise she truly was. He had let his mother's simple words of advice slip to the back of his mind when they should have become a staple in their relationship.

The day Sue had left for Japan, three days prior to Impact, they'd had a blowout fight. The sad thing was he could not remember for the life of him what the fight had been about, only that he had regretted it ever since. They had no chance to make up, to profess their undying love for each other. Sue had left for the airport in a huff. She'd slammed their apartment door, catching part of her coat in it in her haste to leave. Mick's final vision of his wife was of the strap of her coat as it slipped through the crack of the door, like the grains of her life in the hourglass that was about to run dry.

Mick paused for a long moment, staring at the

picture, his mind adrift, before placing it back in his coat, standing back up, and continuing down the street. He had not come down there for that.

He watched the windows in the buildings to his left as he continued along the cluttered street. He would watch the windows to see if a curtain moved. Someone could be hiding behind it. He would study the rooftops. Someone could be watching. Greg had shown him what to look for; taught him what he'd learned in counterterrorist training at the Boston Police Department. If a place had been pillaged, which most were, the door would likely be busted open if even still on the hinge. Looters, like most of what remained of society, did not follow proper etiquette by shutting the door behind them. If the door was sealed tight, then odds were it was someone's home and most likely fiercely protected.

In the parts of town farthest from The Shelter, parts Mick had sworn he would never again travel to, the animals that had laid claim had gone so far as to crucify bodies in the streets, hanging them up on the streetlight poles, running as far as he could see. Whether those bodies were alive during the crucifixion or just cadavers used as props was not important. They were meant as signs to those that wandered too close; signs that crept closer to Mick's shelter as the years carried on. Anyone that would take the time out of his or her miserable existence to do that was not someone Mick chose to cross.

On a hunch, Mick turned left and down a dreary alleyway between two large brick apartment buildings. He had not been down this way in a very long time. His gut told him not to. To turn around. He ignored it. The lingering taste of canned meat pushed him forward. The alley was shadowed by ten-story buildings on either side that reached high above his head. While he fully understood that with newness came danger, it would take a more brazen approach to find anything worthwhile on this trip. And he was determined to find something.

Debris and several larger pieces of trash littered the alley, obstructing the path forward. An old busted tube television rested atop a pile of preserved black trash bags directly in his way. It seemed as if the bags had been put out recently; each still had a bit of man-made plastic shininess to it. His wife would harp on him to help save the world whenever he could. "Use less trash bags," she would say. "They don't decompose, Mick." She was such a good woman. Too good to be taken by that damn rock.

He put his foot down firmly in the pile, using the brick wall of the building to steady himself, and pushed himself over in one quick motion. His wife could take heart in knowing that mankind could not possibly do any more harm to the planet than what had been done already; what was left of their species was just slowly finishing the job the space rocks had failed to.

The alleyway spilled into a large street dotted with abandoned vehicles; some upright, some not. Most of them had shattered windows and deflated tires—a graveyard of all things metal and glass. Mick paused again and looked from left to right. It never hurt to be overly cautious. Another thing he had learned over the years. This street looked like the one before and surely the one after. They all looked the same. But therein lay the rub. The quietest places were sometimes the most dangerous.

Careful steps carried Mick out of the alley and to his left as a rumbling gust of wind whipped up the dusty street into a mini-sandstorm. He tilted his head down, using the brim of his cap for protection. It would be over soon enough. Tiny bits of loose debris banged and crashed into anything opposing its forward momentum. A large radio antenna, awkwardly perched atop the three-story building across the street, swayed and creaked as the wind failed to take it down. A personal grudge match between man and nature that he figured had been going on for years; it had the look of something that would soon end in the wind's favor. As expected, the wind subsided and Mick pushed on, sticking to the cover of the buildings to his left, ducking below dipping awnings and over more dust-covered debris.

A clinking sound startled him to a stop.

What the?

He bent down and listened. The sound came

from up ahead, to his left. At least that was where he thought it came from. It may simply have been his mind playing tricks on him. It certainly would not be the first time that had happened. The sound could have been an aftereffect of the most recent gust. But it had sounded distinctly like an empty tin can being kicked, maybe accidentally, maybe not. If it was a can, and it was kicked, then someone had to do the kicking. And that meant he was not as alone as he'd first suspected.

With the rifle butt tucked firmly up against his right arm, the barrel close to his body to limit its movement, Mick crept forward, listening, slowing his breaths that fought to come out faster. The silence was uncomfortable and heavy, almost palpable, to the point where he felt its weight pushing on his soul. The situation would be easier if the sound reared up again; if he could see what had made the noise, then maybe he could better track it down. But until that moment came, he would dwell in an infinite amount of what-if scenarios.

His thinking leaned toward everything bad. It flashed made-up images and terrible situations. It could be those damn cannibals that strung people up on the dark side of town for all he knew. What if it was some crazed group of disease-ridden lunatics that he did not have enough bullets to stop? The truly sad thing was that these were all distinctly real possibilities. Science fiction had become science fact since Impact. The human mind was powerful for sure, creating and destroying in less time than it took him to take his next breath, but it did not necessarily make those creations any less real.

His hands were steady, his breath controlled. He had been in situations like this before. His thoughts went to his kids, their beautiful faces and waning innocence. He valued his own life well below theirs, much like any loving parent would. *Maybe I should have stuck to the routine*, he thought, checking that the rifle's chamber was loaded and ready. *Always listen to your gut.* That was what his father had told him. Maybe he should have paid more attention to that.

He had been forced to fire his rifle twice in the past ten years. One bullet was a warning shot that had worked as intended. The second bullet was something he tried to forget every day. Even so, he was prepared to fire it a third time if left with no choice.

He hugged close to the wall, careful with his steps. He stayed on his toes to avoid the full weight of his feet and the added sound that would bring. *Control your breathing. Steady your mind.* Between each step Mick processed any and all sounds, of which there were few, and none sounded like what he had assumed to be a tin can before.

Closer he crept.

He looked in every direction, soaking in every piece of information that his brain deemed critical.

Ahead and to the left was another alley.

A shadow emerged from obscurity and vanished just as quickly.

Was that a shadow? He was not sure.

His heart beat faster.

He rubbed his dry eyes quickly and squinted back to the alley, staring at the brick wall, waiting for confirmation that he was not seeing things and that a shadow had indeed darted quickly out of his sight.

He paused at the alley's entry. He held his breath and listened. The rifle's barrel pointed upward in line with his body. He was a statue, stiff and unmoving. His heart pounded with the force of a runaway freight train that rumbled down the tracks.

Maybe I should just head back. Be smart, Mick.

Then another tiny piece of that morning's meat concoction dislodged from his back molar. It reminded him of why he was there in the first place. But at that point it almost did not seem worth the trouble.

In one swift and decisive motion, Mick leaned into the alley like a door on a hinge, prepared as best as he could be for what awaited. He swung the rifle ahead so it led the way. His senses were peaked, and his finger was on the trigger. The alley appeared to be empty, ending abruptly at a window-lined wall of brick that rose high above his head. A dead end. He remained still, watching, listening. If there was someone down there, then they were most likely watching him. He had the disadvantage in this sudden situation.

Still not too late to turn back.

The hair on his neck rose as another wind kicked up and whirled down the street behind him, but his eyes remained transfixed on the end of the alley. This was no time for lax concentration. He could have sworn he had seen something else. No shadows this time. No, this time he was sure someone or something was crouched near a large dented Dumpster whose green flaking paint had given way to large Rorschach-shaped patches of rust.

"Who's back there?" he shouted. He studied the alley for movement, but there was none to be found. He then shifted slightly left to gain a better view, while remaining at the mouth of the alley in case things turned sour. "I'm not looking for a fight." He went up on his tiptoes. The alley was too dark to make out what may be hiding there.

The way Mick saw it, he had two options: go back the way he came or give in to his curiosity. Having gone so long without seeing something new, the choice was clear to him, even though it was clearly not the safest one. He thirsted for an answer despite the danger he felt he put himself in.

"Listen," he said. "I'm coming down there. And I'm armed," he added, before realizing he should have just kept that to himself. But if someone was watching him, then the fact that he held a rifle was obvious. "I have no intentions on using it unless you give me a reason." And even then he was not sure if he could pull the trigger. Could he live with another death by his hand? He hoped he did not have to find out. The face of that deranged woman who'd left him no choice remained burned in his memory.

Mick stopped in his tracks about halfway down the alley.

The sound of metal on metal, while muted and hidden among the gusts of wind, was loud enough to convince him that he was not alone.

His heart pounded still faster. The blood flowed too quickly and freely to the wrong parts of his body as a sense of frightened light-headedness overwhelmed him.

"My name's Mick. Whoever you are," he said, thinking it could also be a whatever. "We can just go our separate ways. For my safety, though, I need some assurance that I won't need to keep looking over my shoulder." Nobody owed him assurance. Mick knew that. He simply hoped the rifle in his hands would afford him some.

He slowly made his way farther down the alley, cognizant of the open space behind him. Was this a trap? Could he be stupid enough to fall for something so easy?

The alley was short, but the journey to its end seemed exceptionally long. Like an actor onstage who forgot his lines, his mind went blank when he neared the alley's end.

At the front edge of the Dumpster, Mick used his height to peer over its lid. He inadvertently locked his jaw in a moment of nervous tension. Slowly the inky dark corner came into view. And then he breathed deeply, laughing to himself. *Stupid Irish bastard.* Much to his relief, the corner was empty—nothing more than a few scraps of paper and some loose bricks.

He closed the gap to the end of the alley with one giant purposeful stride and swung the rifle to his right and toward the corner just to make sure.

It was indeed empty.

He exhaled a large breath that he could not remember holding in the first place. His mind had gotten the better of him, coerced him into believing something that was not. Was he starting to lose his marbles?

He relaxed and shouldered his rifle. He then flexed his hands to pump more blood into his once-tight extremities. His eyes must have been playing tricks on him. The dim light that still reached through the atmosphere did that at times, made him see things that were not there. His arms ached from holding the gun prone. Thankfully, it appeared that his error in judgment would be forgiven this time. But what if it happened again? What if he was losing his edge? Was he becoming complacent with the way things were? If he was, then he knew it was the beginning of the end. Complacency led to death in the word after Colossus.

He exhaled another deep breath and calmed his shaky nerves.

He turned to leave the alley.

The Dumpster's lid pushed up from the inside, then closed in the same stolen moment.

"Who's there?" Mick shouted, pointing the rifle at the lid. He knew he saw something. This was no mind game. This was real. His heart again revved, and adrenaline coursed through his veins. The thoughts he'd just let die rose from their graves and crashed into the forefront of his mind. "I'm only going to ask one more time. Who's in there? Show yourself." Still no reply came. His mind told him to shoot now, put a bullet through the side of the rusty Dumpster, ask questions later when he would be afforded the opportunity to ask them. But he could not. The world was savage and inhumane, but that did not mean he needed to feed its hunger.

He inched closer to the corner so the Dumpster was in front of him, the lid only inches away from his fingers. Again he held his breath. He positioned the rifle in his right hand and freed his left.

One. He thought of his children. *Two.* And of the rest of the herd. *Three.*

He grabbed hold of the lid and flung it open. He pointed the rifle down into the darkness, half expecting some wayward jungle cat to pounce on him and delight in a fresh meal.

But it was a man that slowly rose from within the dark interior, his face filthy and ragged. Mick instinctively fell back against the alley wall behind him. He was startled but not fearful. Something in the man's eyes conveyed a sense of restless peace.

It only took a moment for Mick to realize that this hidden man was more scared than Mick was.

"Are you armed?" Mick asked. It was the most important question—a question that needed to be addressed right away for both of their sakes. The space between them was solidly occupied by Mick's rifle should he need it. The man looked to be in his mid-twenties, though it was difficult to tell with the amount of filth covering him. He said nothing, nor did he move. He simply stared at Mick with large saucer-shaped blue eyes that cut through the grime like a rainbow on a cloudy day. "Listen," Mick said. "I don't want to hurt you, but I need to know you feel the same about me. Okay?"

The man in the Dumpster remained still. Their eyes remained locked. Mick was unsure of what to do next, searching for options but finding none available. So he stared back, lost in the moment. The more he studied the man's eyes, the more comfortable he felt about not having to use his weapon. They said the eyes were the windows to the soul. Mick wholeheartedly agreed with that notion. More times than not the eyes told him more than words ever could. And he had already foolishly ignored his gut by coming down the alley in the first place. What was one more time?

He lowered his rifle while keeping his gaze locked on the man. It could be the last mistake he ever made. The man's hands were still out of sight. For all he knew, this guy had a pistol at the ready and was simply waiting for Mick's sense of humanity to kick in, a sense that was not as strong as it once was. But he could not stand there forever. The stalemate had to be broken.

"Listen," Mick said. "Why don't you come out of there?" He slowly walked past the Dumpster so that his back was now facing the way he had originally entered, toward the mouth of the alley. He would give the man some room to come out, put some distance between them. The alley was tight, so it was in his best interests to be able to retreat should he need to. "Come on," he said, waving the man out. "I promise I won't hurt you."

The man looked him over for another moment before timidly nodding his head. He then brought his right booted foot up to the lip of the Dumpster and pushed himself up and out. He landed clumsily on a rock and stumbled back into the wall, but his eyes never left Mick.

The man's hands were cut up and dirty. His fingernails were long and yellow, chipping at their tips like jagged teeth. He had no weapon that Mick could see. With the man's hands now visible, he felt easy enough to again shoulder his rifle.

"What's your name?" Mick tried to make the man feel at ease. He had a timid aura about him.

"S-S-Solomon," the man stuttered in a hushed tone. His mop of bouncy black hair flopped back and forth as he did. The longer hairs of his patchy black beard shifted ever so slightly in the captured alleyway breeze that left as quickly as it came.

"What were you doing back here, Solomon?"

Mick asked.

Solomon did not reply. Mick figured that maybe a different question would work.

"Do you live around here, Solomon?"

Solomon nodded again. This time it seemed to be a more accepting nod, friendly in a cautious way.

"I'm sorry if I scared you," Mick said. "Can never be too careful nowadays."

Solomon remained still and quiet. He looked toward the ground, away from Mick's friendly gaze.

Something about Solomon clung to Mick, like a precipitous fog he could feel but not see. And at the same time, something did not feel right about him.

Mick's compassion, something that had been buried for a while, found its way back out. "Are you all right, Solomon?" He sure did not look all right.

Solomon's chapped, cracking lips parted slightly, enough for the smallest of mutters. "Y-yes."

Mick figured he would ask again now that the proverbial ice had been broken. "Do you live around here?"

Solomon nodded once and looked over Mick's shoulder and toward the street.

Mick followed his gaze. Across the street was another longer alley that ended at an old movie theater that looked vaguely familiar.

"You live in the theater?"

"N-no," he said, hushed, almost in a whisper. "B-Behind. P-police S-s-station." It was at that moment that Mick put his finger on it. Solomon was special, challenged further than most folks should ever have to be.

"Have you lived there long?" Though Mick rarely came to these parts of town, he didn't remember seeing anyone around there before. He knew that other parts of town were more populated. This area bordered the savages' zone.

Solomon shook his head no, and then he gently pushed past Mick and back down the alley toward the street.

"Wait. Solomon." Mick hurried up behind him. He figured if Solomon lived around here, then maybe he knew where to find some food. It was a long shot, but what did he have to lose?

Solomon kept walking. His shoulders were tight and rigid and his steps were short and jerky, but he moved with a purposeful stride. When Mick caught up with him, he tapped his back to let him know he still wanted to talk. When he did, Solomon pushed out his chest and moved his back away from the tap, almost as if it was instinctive. Solomon then turned around toward Mick. His jaw locked and his face transformed from that of a timid man to that of one anguished by something that ran very deep into his soul.

"I'm sorry," Mick said. "I shouldn't have touched you. I just wanted to get your attention."

The look on Solomon's face softened a bit. He

turned and walked straight from the alley into the street.

"Solomon," Mick said louder than he would have liked. "Do you know where I can find any food or water?" Keeping up with Solomon was proving more difficult than he would have guessed it would be.

Solomon nodded and kept walking at his own quick pace.

A tiny pebble of happiness formed in Mick's belly, only to have common sense pulverize it back down to nothingness. Solomon seemed to do a lot of nodding. And who was to say that Mick could even trust him? After all, he had just met the guy not more than five minutes ago hiding in a Dumpster in a dark alley. Not exactly the best jumping-off point to a trustworthy relationship. Yet, for whatever reason, he felt as if he could trust him.

"Can you tell me where it is, Solomon? Can you show me?"

Now halfway down the alley, Solomon continued forward silently. No nod. No response.

"Please, Solomon. There are children …"

Solomon stopped. With his back to Mick, Solomon stared straight down at the ground for a long minute. He then gave three nods in quick succession, almost angrily it seemed, and crossed the next street and over to the cinema. Before Mick had a chance to follow him or try to stop him, Solomon disappeared into the darkness beside the theater.

I guess that's that.

As he stared at the theater, it hit Mick where he knew it from. He had been there once, before he met Sue, back when his only worries were how to pay for gas and where the next party was. He vaguely remembered the experience.

Much to Mick's surprise, Solomon suddenly lurched back out from the dark path to the left of the theater and across the street. He seemed to throw all caution to the wind as he walked, almost as if he was unaware of what the world had become. He reached Mick in a matter of seconds and stopped in front of him.

Solomon again stared down at the ground, averting his eyes. He then raised his right hand. In it he held what remained of a stuffed bunny rabbit, brown and what Mick assumed used to be white. Now it was closer to a filthy gray. The stuffed animal's left leg was gone and a bit of whitish stuffing protruded from the hole. One of its black button eyes dangled precipitously from a thick black thread that looked to be nearing the end of its time.

"Ch-children," Solomon spit out.

At fourteen, the kids were long past needing or wanting a stuffed animal. And while the gesture was most unexpected, it was surprisingly heartwarming. It was the first drop of civility, aside from his own group, that Mick had seen in quite some time. Maybe there was hope for the world yet.

Mick reached up and gently grabbed the stuffed animal. "Thank you, Solomon."

Solomon nodded, but he did not look at Mick. He then lifted his right hand again and pointed down the street. "Y-y-yellow house," he said. "Eight eight. P-please d-d-don't take m-much." He then quickly turned and again vanished into the darkness beside the theater. This time Mick had a hunch that he was not coming back.

CHAPTER 9

Solomon climbed the rusty fire escape in the dark alley adjacent to the old cinema. The third floor was his secret. He had discovered it the day after King decided to expand his kingdom further by moving a good chunk of his men into the police station. Their old place, a beat-up row house, was closer to Boston Harbor, where King would have preferred to stay. But every kingdom eventually outgrew its borders. King's faux kingdom was no different.

When they'd first moved here, King's men were so busy trying to appease him by searching the police station for anything useful that they did not mind Solomon's comings and goings. He had used that time to find a way out of the hell he lived in. He always came back. Not that he wanted to. Not in the least. But he had to. In his mind, there was no choice. His journeys to the outside had helped him stay alive this long. And he needed to stay alive for her sake. Without him, she would die. And if she died, he did not know what he would do.

After entering through the broken window of the third-floor fire escape, Solomon shuffled over the worn wooden floor and through a broken door frame at the back of the room. This room was small and dark. It was probably a closet at some point. But he did not need light to know where he was going. At the base of the wall was a hole. Exposed brick jutted out from beneath what little remained of the drywall.

Solomon went headfirst so he could push himself into the adjacent crawl space. There he headed to his left, sideways so he could maneuver the cramped space, and along the thick wall separating the cinema and the old police station. A few feet farther and another hole appeared. This one broke into the police station, and it took more skill to enter. He stole a quick glance through the hole to ensure he was alone. Thankfully the room was just as empty as it had been when he'd left.

From a standing position, Solomon made his way down to the narrow floor below him, lying on his side the best he could, his feet pointing toward the hole in the wall. He used one of the exposed studs in the wall to push his feet toward the hole and eventually through and into the police station's third floor.

A sense of relief washed over him once he was back inside. The third floor was off-limits to most. That was where King stored the food and supplies. Only King could enter this room. It was locked from the outside, or so King thought.

He next walked slowly through the room, keeping an eye on the only door. If he was caught in there, he was not sure what would happen, aside from it being very bad for him. He slowly shifted to his left and through the maze of varying supplies, which seemed to grow each time he left. The supplies consisted of cans of varying foods, cases of bottled water, and cartons of cigarettes to name a few. He did not dare take anything from this room as much as he wanted to. As primal and savage as King's group was, they still maintained a certain level of organization, much like a pack of wolves. They would surely know if anything suddenly went missing. And if they found out he was in this room, they would undoubtedly question him as to why, followed shortly thereafter by a beating. Of course, the beatings would come regardless. It's just that their severity would undoubtedly increase.

Like most of the police station, this room held its own secrets. At his feet and to his left, a grate rested loosely against the wall behind a broken crate. He carefully lifted the light crate an inch or so off the ground to avoid unneeded sound and pushed it to the side. He then shifted the grate and entered through another small hole where the air ducts used to be. Now it was just another hole that Solomon used to his advantage. And since only a handful of people were in the police station at that moment, he knew he could move more freely, while at the same staying alert for anything unexpected.

Most of the group had gone with King on the salvage mission. He feared for those that held the supplies. It rarely ended in their best interests. The few that remained behind would jump at the chance to rat Solomon out. They would do anything to please their faux king, move up in the ranks of a hierarchy that existed in the mind of one man.

There was only one person in this entire building that was on Solomon's side, and he was headed to her now.

Down the desolate stairway he went. From floor three to the basement, where few entered. This is where they kept what remained of her. Solomon could take the abuse that King and Clyde constantly dished out his way. He was still relatively young. His body still bounced back a bit. But she did not fare as well. Her frail body had become incapable of moving far, really at all. So King and his cronies did little to keep her there, aside from the bars they kept her behind. Solomon found a way to visit her every chance he could.

"M-M-Ms. S-S-tella," Solomon whispered as he approached her cage. He looked around to make sure they were alone.

If only she had not met him that day in the alley. Ultimately that day led her to this point, caged and withering.

On the day King came to gather Clyde from the orphanage, he'd decided on the spot to take all the children with him and his small band of misfits. After all, a kingdom needed future generations. Ms. Stella had vehemently opposed it. As the voices grew louder and the reasoning dwindled, Ms. Stella had ended up striking King across the face, her ring slashing the skin beneath his right eye. Since then, King made it a point to show Ms. Stella who was in charge.

Sadly, most of the children, their minds still malleable and easily influenced, had adapted to their new surroundings and become part of his kingdom, as King had wished. Some had not. Some had had courage beyond their years. They'd questioned the reasoning behind all of it. Why could they not stay where they'd built a life? Why must they leave Ms. Stella's side? They had pleaded for King to release them and Ms. Stella, return them to the life they loved despite the carnage that surrounded them. Solomon was the only one of those brave little men that was still alive. Though, at times, he wished that was different.

Ms. Stella sat slumped in the corner of the large cell, her back against the bars. Her knees were pulled up to her emaciated frame, and her head was slumped down on her knees. Her stringy white hair hung down and covered her face. This was how he usually found her. At times he was not sure if she would answer when he called. And at times he wished she would not. He wished she would escape her captivity in a way King could never prevent.

She raised her head slowly. The muscles in her neck, easily noticed as they pushed from beneath her thin skin, strained to keep her head upright.

Solomon went to his knees beside the bars. He

reached in and brushed the hair away from her wrinkled face. While Solomon was kept under lock and key at night, this was his true prison: seeing Ms. Stella in this condition and forgotten by all but him.

"Hello, my dear," Ms. Stella said, raspy and weak but somehow still full of joy to see her Solomon.

Solomon reached into his jacket. "I b-b-brought this for you," he said, removing a can of beans from his jacket. He had found it inside the Dumpster in the alley, right before he'd met that man with the gun. He'd also found a recently dead rat. He had picked pieces of that off for himself, having not eaten in days. Dead and uncooked rat was not something he'd ever thought he would have to eat. But he needed to keep some semblance of strength if he was to help Ms. Stella. His stomach still churned with the rotting flesh inside, reminding him that not all decisions were the correct ones.

Solomon went to the far side of the hallway that lined Ms. Stella's jail cell. At the end was a pile of brick from a destroyed interior wall. Solomon placed the can of beans on its side. He picked up the largest whole brick he could find and, with an uncanny precision for such a crude tool, he burst the can at its top seam, losing only a small bit of the grayish-red mass inside.

He hurried back to Ms. Stella. "P-p-please eat," he said, holding the can of beans through the bars.

Ms. Stella smiled as sweetly as her state of

being would allow. "Thank you, my dear." She took the can and quickly glanced at its contents before putting it beside her. "I'm afraid my stomach is not feeling well at the moment."

He looked at the can of beans by her side. He realized why she was not hungry. The beans had turned into a pungent goopy gray puddle inside the tin can. A far cry from what they used to be. What was left was most likely inedible and even made the raw rat meat inside his belly seem like a delicacy.

"I'm s-s-sorry, M-Ms. Stella." He shook his head, angry at himself for not providing something of sustenance for her. *Stupid. Stupid.*

She smiled. With her fragile left hand, Ms. Stella reached through the bars and caressed Solomon's cheek. Her skin had a gray tone to it and had become so thin that her veins were displayed prominently wherever her skin was exposed from beneath her ragged clothes. She wasted away more as each day passed. And as she did, so did Solomon's heart.

"Don't you ever be sorry, Solomon," she said, lifting his chin ever so delicately so he had to look into her eyes. "You are a good man. Far better than those around you." Solomon tried to look away at the ground like he did with others. But Ms. Stella would not have any of it. She nudged his chin up again. "I mean it, Solomon. You have never been able to accept how great of a person you are, even when you were a child."

As much love as he had for Ms. Stella, his mind had already begun to wander. He needed to get her food. Without it she would die soon. He did not want to imagine this horrid world without her in it. She was his hope. And he was hers. He knew what needed to be done. He would have to act fast, as he was not sure how much longer King would be gone.

CHAPTER 10

The theater grew distant, but Mick's thoughts of Solomon did not. These treks of his had been going on for years without running into another person for long enough to hold a conversation. Not that what he'd had with Solomon could ever be construed as such. Not by yesterday's standards, anyway.

Living with the same seven people for the past ten years, Mick had come to know their traits, how they acted and spoke, what made them happy and sad. He adapted and became comfortable with all of them. And life did not volunteer as many opportunities to meet new people as it once had. Not that he was complaining. But speaking with Solomon, for however brief a time it was, had sparked something inside him that seemed to punch a tiny hole in the darkness he had blanketed over his will to socialize. Given enough time, maybe that hole would grow.

Mick walked for two or three lonely miles, following the street as it twisted and turned, before he came upon a bend in the road.

That has to be the place, he thought, veering left at the bend.

The house a couple up on his right was the first hint of yellow he had seen. The shade reminded him of the paper sun on his billboard. And like his billboard, this house stuck out like a beacon against the grim backdrop the neighboring houses provided. The yellow house was well maintained, as if it had not been there during Impact, but rather gently placed there afterward from the sky above.

A large number eighty-eight had been painted in black paint with crude brushstrokes on the front of the bottom step of a short flight of concrete steps. The number was fading and dust covered but still noticeable. *That about settles it*, he thought, looking up from the steps and back to the house. This was definitely the place.

A second-story porch hung over the front entryway to the house. However, only a single screen remained in place above, and it was now more hole than screen. A few of the others were strewn across the tiny fenced-in front yard, bent and broken, one folded completely in half and off to the right.

A set of footsteps, barely noticeable under the newly blown dust, led up the steps and toward the front door. *I wonder who made those.* Did he want to find out? He should go back and get Greg. That's what he *should* do. But he was already there, and dragging Greg back for what could be an empty house did not seem like the most efficient use of time. Was the house empty? His thoughts came and went quickly, leaving him a bit frustrated. There was only one way to find out. And he had come this far. He would need to suck it up and see what the yellow house held within its walls. He owed it to the herd to check inside. He owed it to his children.

The first step he took was onto one of the previous footprints. His boot was much larger than whoever had come before him. That gave Mick a tiny bit of solace. At the very least he had the height advantage over some would-be attacker. Then again, it could just be a large man with small feet. It was not out of the question.

His buddy Jake was like that: very tall with disproportionately small feet. Jake stood close to six foot four, and he had size-ten feet. Mick would give him crap about that all the time. He could not for the life of him figure out how such a large man, both in height and ever-increasing circumference, could stay upright with such tiny feet.

Ah, Jake. He had not thought about him since the impacts. The thought brought a quick smile to his face. Mick missed his boisterous laughter and his spice for life. Jake also happened to be a drunk—a happy drunk, but a drunk nonetheless.

Seeing the bright-yellow house coupled with his thoughts of Jake reminded Mick of the time that Jake had dressed up as Santa for a Christmas party at a bright-yellow house like this one in the South Shore. Unfortunately for Jake, and really everyone else at the party, Jake had tied one on a bit too early in the unseasonably warm day. Somehow, in Jake's drunken stupor, he'd forgotten that Santa tended to wear pants with his big red suit. When he showed up and Mick pointed it out to him, amid cackles of delight from the other partygoers, Jake's response had been, "I thought this suit was a bit drafty." Mick laughed, remembering the funny times. The world could sorely use some of the laughter that his large friend used to bring.

Mick's next few steps brought him up onto the small wooden deck that spanned the short length of the front of the house. The deck had not fared as well as the rest of the exterior. Bulging and warped wooden boards ran the deck's length. Protruding nails forced their way free; a few had wiggled completely out and now rested beneath the blown dust like dried earthworms in a shallow grave. The two front windows to the right of the front door had their shades drawn. Mick wished they were not. If they were open, then at least he could sneak a quick look inside without offering his safety as collateral. Now he would be forced to enter blindly to satisfy his curiosity.

The footprints stopped at the closed front door. Against his better judgment, Mick shouldered his rifle and reached for the doorknob, pausing as he grabbed hold of its surprisingly chilly metal.

I could still head back to the shelter. It was not too late.

The voice inside his head begged him to listen. As much as he wanted what was in there, if there was anything to begin with, he hesitated to take the chance. Nobody from the shelter knew where he was. And even if Greg came to find him, it would be next to impossible. The city and its suburbs were vast. And, like all other footprints before his, the dust was sure to erase Mick's path before nightfall. He would be no more findable than an Internet connection.

Mick turned to leave.

When he did, he was face-to-face with Solomon, a mere two inches separating them.

"Whoa!" Mick said, stumbling back in surprise. He fell backward into the door, pushing it open and tripping over the threshold into the home's interior. "Solomon," he said angrily after he ended up on his back. It was the situation, not Solomon, that burned him. But he was caught up in the moment. His nerves were already on edge. Why hadn't he heard Solomon come up behind him? Over squeaky floorboards nonetheless. That bothered him. He was losing focus.

Solomon did not speak. He walked over and picked Mick up off the floor. For a man his size, Solomon was as strong as a bear. It was a deceiving trait considering he was much shorter than Mick and had no discernible muscle mass.

Mick rose to his feet without much of his own doing. Solomon then began to pat the dust off Mick's clothes.

"Thank you," Mick said, stopping Solomon. "But I can handle that."

Solomon backed away slowly but stayed on the front porch. He looked nervously down the street.

Mick finished the job that Solomon had started and patted the new layer of dust off his clothes. He did not know why he even bothered. His pants were sure to get dusty in another minute or two. Another habit formed in his youth, he figured; one that seemed impossible to break no matter how little it mattered.

Then, out of the blue, and again at the strangest of times, Mick thought of his father. It was of a saying his father loved to repeat, especially to someone from out of state. It worked best when they lived in a sunny state like California or Florida. He would say, "If you don't like the weather in New England, just wait a minute." It was never funny. And rarely did anyone laugh out of anything other than a sense of obligation. Of course, it may have been pity, too. But his father used it whenever he could. As unfunny as it was, his joke was borderline accurate. At least it used to be. Mick looked to the filthy sky. He would love to see the weather change to anything other than cold and colorless. Thankfully his father had died before the meteorites hit. He would have hated to have nobody to tell his awful jokes to.

Mick reached out for Solomon, to grab his arm in a humanistic way, to assure him that all was well. He regretted yelling when he had. The moment had gotten the better of him. And Mick tended to feel comfort when accompanied by touch. He had always been a tactile person. And he assumed, sometimes incorrectly, as in this case, that others felt the same way.

Solomon backed away a few steps.

Mick held up his hands. "Okay. Fair enough," he said. "Did you follow me here?"

Solomon nodded.

"Why?"

Solomon said nothing. He strode past Mick, gently brushing against him as he did in the alley, and straight through the open door of the house. Mick went to stop him, to warn him of the dangers this world posed, but he did not think Solomon needed him to explain that. Solomon had survived just like the rest of them up until that point. And for all Mick knew, he'd done so on his own.

"You sure you want to go in there?" Mick asked. But Solomon had already vanished into the darkness beyond the door's threshold.

I guess so.

Mick cautiously followed Solomon into the house. What else was he going to do at that point? He now felt a sense of obligation to protect Solomon if need be. To the best of Mick's knowledge, Solomon would not have even been there had Mick not asked about the rations. He felt as though he'd drawn him there. And Mick could not allow more misery to occur because of his poor decisions.

"Solomon?" he said in as close to a whisper as he could muster. The inside of the house was dark and musty. A very fine coating of dust had settled on everything that Mick could see. Despite the dust, the house looked maintained in a way. As if it had a post-Impact cleaning service.

"Solomon?" he said again, looking into the room to his right. *Where did he run off to?*

This room was relatively clean like the rest of the house. A large brown couch rested solidly against the wall to his left. A floral-patterned chair, with dull browns and blues, sat between the two front windows that had their blinds drawn. But it was the far wall that instantly caught his eye. Almost every inch of the wallpapered wall was plastered with pictures of varying sizes and shapes. Some of the pictures had fallen to the ground and left rectangular squares of clean, yet yellowing wallpaper behind them. All the pictures were of children, but they all had a constant variable to them: a short woman with the most genuine of smiles. In some of the pictures, she looked to be in the later parts of her life, well aged, the dark-brown hair turned white, but still with some lingering youth in her eyes. Mick figured she was the owner of the house—that, or someone had a strong affection for her.

After leaving the picture room, Mick passed through a narrow doorway into the kitchen.

"Solomon?" he said again.

The kitchen was tiny and run-down, much more disheveled than the other parts of the house he had seen. A few of the cheap white cabinet doors that lined the space above the countertop hung down by their hinges, broken and splintered, almost as if they had been torn down in a fit of rage. The shade over the tiny kitchen sink was drawn like all the others, but its cheap aluminum slats were bent and contorted in the center, allowing Mick to briefly view a messy back porch.

Mick walked through the rest of the kitchen, which took all of a few more steps, and into the small room adjacent to it. *There you are*, Mick thought as Solomon came into view. He stood still, swaying ever so slightly as gravity appeared to play with his balance.

"Is everything all right?" Mick asked.

Solomon nodded, keeping his eyes trained on the floor in front of him. He then reached down and tossed the oval red-and-black area rug off to the side. There, at their feet, was a trapdoor, like something out of an old pirate movie. A large black latch rested within the carved-out circle on its surface.

"How did you know about this, Solomon?"

Solomon paused, still staring down at the floor. He then looked to his right and put his feet in motion, disappearing out of sight down the hall. He quickly returned with one of the pictures from the many that hung on the wall. Solomon rubbed the dust that coated the glass cover of the frame off on his belly, then handed it to Mick. The photo had the same white-haired woman in it that all the others did. She looked to be maybe in her early fifties.

"Is this you, Solomon? In the picture with this woman?"

Solomon nodded.

The nose on the boy in the picture was unmistakably Solomon's: thin on the bridge with wide, flaring nostrils. Mick also noticed the distinct arch to his eyebrows on the boy, maybe in his early teens at that time. He was a handsome boy. Probably about the same age in this picture as Nate and Kathryn.

"Is this your house?" Mick asked, looking up.

"N-n-no," Solomon said.

"Is this her house?" Mick said, pointing to the woman.

Solomon nodded again.

"Does she still live here?"

Solomon clenched his jaw and then suddenly began to hit himself repeatedly in the head. Whack, whack, whack.

"Solomon," Mick said, reaching out to stop him. "You're going to hurt yourself." Stopping him was not easy. His strength was something to behold, firm and unwavering, the antithesis of his personality.

Solomon eventually did stop, but not before reddening the side of his head, almost to the point of breaking the skin.

Why the hell did he just do that? Mick worried that this was becoming too taxing for Solomon. He was about to back out of the situation, walk

Solomon out, and forget he even knew about this place, when Solomon reached down and picked up the picture that Mick had dropped in his haste. A small crack traced the front of the glass, running from the top to midway through the frame.

"I'm so sorry, Solomon." And he was. It didn't take a lot to understand that this picture meant something to him.

Solomon did not say anything. Instead, he walked back to the picture room, then quickly returned without the picture of himself as a child. He bent down without so much as a word and heaved the trapdoor in the floor open.

No sooner had the door locked in place when the shout came from outside.

"You in there, boy?"

Both Mick and Solomon turned their attention back down the hall and toward the front door.

Who the hell is that? He knew he should have left the yellow house when he had the chance. *Dammit, Mick!*

The voice from outside sounded harsh and agitated. Most of all, it sounded exactly like what Mick wanted to avoid.

A noticeable look of fear washed over Solomon's face. His eyes widened but remained locked down the hallway. Solomon quickly and quietly closed the trapdoor and replaced the area rug in exactly the same position it was in prior to them arriving, careful of even a centimeter of discrepancy. Solomon then walked past Mick and down the hall.

Mick turned and followed him back onto the warped wooden deck outside. He had a bad feeling about this. Solomon had already gone down the small flight of stairs and was now on the street. There was a group of three men in front of him. One in particular had both an air of authority and evil to him.

The man closest to Solomon smacked him in the back of his head. "Didn't I tell you, boy? Huh? Didn't I?" He again smacked the back of Solomon's head. "I told you what would happen if you did this again."

"Hey," Mick said. He knew he had to be careful with what he did now. The men were armed, and they certainly did not have the look of people that he wanted to mess with. "Listen," Mick said. "It was my fault. I asked—"

Solomon shook his head very softly but enough for Mick to notice. His stomach knotted at the thought of confrontation. This was not how he'd wanted the day to go. *Stupid canned meat.* He should have stayed on his hill and stared at the billboard.

The man next to Solomon, the one that had hit him and the one that Mick figured was in charge by the way the two others flanked him, trained his eyes on Mick.

"And who are you?" King said authoritatively. His voice was raspy, as if he had a slight case of laryngitis, but firm in its tone. A hint of a southern twang hung on his words.

"Mick." He could not find more words to offer. And it was probably better to leave it at that.

"Well, Mick," King said. "It looks like we have a problem here." He wore a long black leather trench coat over his dark-blue jeans. His hands were covered with black leather biker gloves, the type with the knuckles exposed. His head was clean shaven and razor smooth, which was not something Mick had seen in a long time. His head played the yin to the yang of his neatly trimmed goatee.

"There's no problem," Mick said.

"Well, now," King replied. "Unfortunately for you, I don't see it that way."

Mick's gut told him to run as fast and as far as he could. And that is exactly what he would have done if the circumstances were different. While Mick wasn't scared, the grounded adult inside him reminded him that he had priorities. The one thorn in this predicament was Solomon. If Mick ran, then he left Solomon to fend for himself. And while Mick felt that Solomon could handle himself, he could not bear to be the cause of problems for the young man. His conscience would never let him. The few hours of sleep that Mick managed a night would be filled with Solomon's image and lamenting his own lack of conviction.

Mick said, "I ran into Solomon outside the house. I followed him in because I thought he was in trouble."

He'd offered too much. That much he could tell by the look of pain that suddenly struck Solomon's face.

King laughed. His goons laughed with him. "Hear that, boys?" he said. "Our new friend—Mick was it?—followed the boy into my house because he thought he was in trouble." King stopped laughing, but the others continued. "You see, the problem with that is I don't much like people in my house. And we certainly don't like trespassers around these parts."

Mick held up his hand. "I didn't realize this was your place. I'm sorry about that." This guy seemed a little off. Actually, he seemed a lot off. Mick did not dispute his ownership claim even though he knew from speaking with Solomon that this was clearly not the bald man's house. Mick looked over the other two guys. And they kept their focus on him. One of them was tall with a wandering eye. Mick was unsure which one was looking at him, further cementing the uneasy feeling. The other was like something out of a comic book. He wore some type of goggles. He was short and stocky, and his fat jiggled each time he laughed.

The bald man paused and stared at Mick. He squinted, magnifying the wrinkles around his eyes. He looked to be Mick's senior by a decade or so. Despite his gruff persona, the man appeared to be well maintained—far better than most.

"All of these houses are mine, Mick." He let his

name roll off his tongue with a noticeable twinge of animosity, the hard *k* sound clicking pointedly. 'Everything you see is mine. And so is everything beyond that."

Mick looked around the street. "All of these are yours?" As soon as he said it, he wished that he could take it back. He did not want to engage in dialogue with this man any longer than he absolutely needed to. But to claim ownership over a city block was just plain mad. Then again, maybe that was exactly who he was dealing with: a madman.

"Don't question the Rubble King," said the goon to Mick's right, the plump nothing of a man with the goofy goggles.

Rubble King? Despite the gravity of the situation, Mick tried not to snicker. *What a stupid name.*

The man's goons made an aggressive move toward Mick, their pistols now in plain sight.

"You know what, Mick?" King said, stopping his men before the situation could escalate any further. "I'm in a forgiving mood right now."

The one with the lazy eye said, "You are?"

King looked at him quickly in disgust and then back to Mick. "So I'll tell you what. I'm going to let you walk away. This is a onetime deal. I don't want to see you in these parts again. If I do," King said, letting his words trail off and Mick's imagination brew. He then slapped Solomon again in the back of the head. "Say good-bye to your little protector, boy."

After eyeing Mick briefly, Solomon kept his head down. He then turned and walked away with the group of men.

Mick's mind, choosing a fine time to show up, kept him cemented in place and stopped him from making the wrong decision of chasing after them.

When they had traveled down the road far enough, Mick dropped his bravado and let the weight of what had just happened rush into his system. His hands twitched, and his pulse raced. He realized how close he'd been to getting into a gunfight. For a split second, not too much longer, Mick thought about aiming at the men as they walked away. Three quick shots would free Solomon. He was sure he could hit his marks. And he did not feel he would have much remorse over their loss. But Mick had no idea if they were the only ones around. For all he knew, there were others watching him, hidden from sight, strewn inside the surrounding buildings. It was a situation without any good choices. Because of that, Mick was not about to enter the yellow house again.

Not yet. Not alone.

CHAPTER 11

King pushed Solomon through the front door of the police station, causing him to stumble into an overturned and broken desk that lay on its side.

"I'm getting sick and tired of your actions, boy," King said, stopping next to Solomon. "What exactly do you think you were doing at that house? How many times have I told you not to leave this building?" He turned and walked away slowly, turning back when the nearest wall stopped his progress. "Clyde," he yelled.

Clyde slithered over in a way that only he could. He sneered at Solomon as he approached.

King said, "I need you to find out how the boy here keeps getting out."

"Show me how you leave," Clyde said to Solomon.

King smacked Clyde in the back of his head. "If that was all it required, don't you think I could have done that myself? Idiot. He's not going to willingly tell you. Find out how." Clyde waited. "Now!"

Clyde waddled away in a hopeless effort to locate Solomon's secret holes in the walls. Solomon knew he would never find them. Even if he somehow stumbled upon one of them, his rotund belly would never allow him further access.

When King spoke, Solomon rarely if ever looked him in the eye. He knew it irked him.

"I expect an answer when I ask you a question." King smacked Solomon across the face, sending him to his knees. "Don't you dare disrespect me."

Solomon stood and pushed King away from him. It was an instinct, one he instantly regretted. Not that his actions didn't reflect his feelings. In fact, he would do worse. Much worse. But as soon as he touched King, he knew it was the wrong move. There would undoubtedly be repercussions.

King stumbled back into a small group of his men and, like a rubber ball, bounced back toward Solomon, punching him square in the nose as he neared.

A bright light consumed Solomon's vision. Blood gushed down his face and over his lips, dripping onto the dusty floor. He blinked to regain his vision, while a sharp, shooting pain ran up his spine and into the base of his skull.

"How dare you," King said, getting right up into Solomon's bloodied face and grabbing him by his shirt. He stared at Solomon in disgust. King must have realized he was losing his cool in front of his men, as he quickly regained his composure and backed away a few steps. "See what you've done? Your insolence drives me to the brink of doing something that you'll regret." He stroked his bald head. "I've let you live all these years because it amuses me. As soon as that amusement dies, so do you. I will ask you again. Tell me what you were doing at that house."

Solomon said nothing even though he knew he should have. Out of everyone around him, King was the one not to be toyed with.

"Very well," King said. He grabbed Solomon by the shirt. "Come with me."

King pulled Solomon across the main room and down the stairs to the basement. He tossed him forward, over the last three or four stairs, and headfirst into the cold steel bars of Ms. Stella's cell. King wasted no time. He closed the space behind him, pushing Solomon's face hard into the bars, keeping the pressure on so he could not move.

"Now," King said. "Tell me what you were doing at that house. If you don't, I will show your little bitch friend how things get done in my kingdom." He then leaned in close to Solomon's ear and whispered, "And then she'll experience it firsthand. And it will all be because of you."

"I w-wasn't doing anything," Solomon said.

"Let him go," Ms. Stella said. "You are an evil man."

"Shut up, bitch. Don't open that mouth of yours unless I tell you to."

"I'll do whatever I like," Ms. Stella said.

King laughed. "As long as it's inside your cell." He then turned his attention back to Solomon. "Well, if you weren't doing anything, then why were you there? You think I'm a fool, boy? You were there for a reason."

"I w-w-was g-g-going for a w-w-walk."

"A walk?" King laughed again. "Out seeing the sights, were you? You hear that, bitch? Your little boy here was out on a walk. What have I told you about leaving the building, boy? Huh?"

Solomon said nothing. He looked through the bars at Ms. Stella.

King brought his arm back but stopped. "Last chance, boy."

Solomon gave in. It wasn't worth it to hold back. He decided to give in to King now. If he didn't, the only one who would lose would be him. Or worse, Ms. Stella.

"You t-told me not t-t-to leave."

King let his hand fall back to his side. "You hear that, bitch," King said. "He does understand." He snickered and leaned in closer to Solomon. "I expect you to listen this time, boy. The next time I will not be so easy on you." He then looked to Ms. Stella. "Or maybe the next time I'll go straight for her. We could have a little"—he paused—"talk."

Solomon tried to push his head off the bars. The anger inside him seemed all encompassing. He stopped as quickly as he started. It was useless. Even if he did overpower King, it would do him no good. Where was he going to go? What was he going to do? The King had claimed everywhere Solomon had ever known as home. To run would be stupid. King and his goons would find him eventually; King would never let Solomon go free without a fight. And Ms. Stella's health was a sneeze away from worsening. Solomon's life was an inescapable prison, both physically and psychologically.

"Now," King said. "This will be the final time I ask. What were you doing at that house?"

"I—I s-s-s-aw," Solomon said before stopping. He took a deep breath to try and calm his nerves. "The m-m-an went in. I w-w-as c-curious."

"And how did you stumble upon this man? Mick, I believe his name was."

Solomon tried to come up with an excuse, but he realized that the truth would do just as well. He knew nothing about Mick, so there was no way he could get him in trouble.

"H-he w-w-w-as on th-the street."

"Where?"

"Outside."

King smacked Solomon on the side of his head. "I get that part, dummy. Where outside?"

Solomon pointed toward the back of the station. "B-b-back there."

"I see," King said. "Well, I'll find out soon if you are telling the truth. I sent Robert to follow him to see where he goes."

Solomon had noticed Robert, the man with the lazy eye, disappear from the group as they'd headed back to the station. He hadn't given it any thought as King's henchmen came and went at King's bidding. But now he knew where he'd gone, and he realized that Mick's life was about to change for the worse.

CHAPTER 12

Mick struggled with the idea of telling the group right away about the encounter he'd had with Solomon and the self-proclaimed Rubble King. He went back and forth but ultimately decided against it, at least for the moment. The group deserved to know. Secrets did little but hurt in the post-Impact world. But Mick needed to figure out his own thoughts first, understand what exactly had happened back there. There was no use in getting even one of the herd excited about something that probably didn't even matter.

Mick waved to Greg as he neared the shelter.

"Anything new?" Greg said from up top.

Mick shook his head and smiled briefly to hide the story he was itching to tell.

Sarah was tending to her garden outside the shelter in a neat bed of dirt and dust. She called it a garden, so Mick did, too. However, it was nothing close to a garden by yesterday's standards. She pushed the dust away and cleared down to the cracked soil beneath it. Mick figured she did this each day as a way to bring a sense of normality into her life, like a runner going for a daily jog. He was not sure if she actually expected anything to grow or if she simply went through the motions. After all, the two most important things essential to plant growth were the two things most sorely missed: sunlight and water. But that did not stop her from trying. If anything were to grow there, it would have sprung from hope alone.

"Hey," Mick said with another smile.

Sarah looked up and wiped the slightest bit of sweat from her brow with her sleeve. "Hey yourself. How was your walk?"

He thought for second, probably less, before saying, "Dusty." That would suffice for now. And it was the truth no matter how obvious.

"No getting away from the stuff, unfortunately."

A quick breeze kicked up as if listening to their conversation and blew some of the newly cleared dust back into Sarah's garden.

She looked down. "See what I mean." She pushed the dust back off to the side with her hands, a chore she undoubtedly had done hundreds of times before. Smears of dirt marked her forehead and right cheek. Her hair, as usual, had been tightly pulled back and knotted in a bun.

"You're really determined to get something to grow?" Mick said.

She smiled. "Determined, yes. Naive enough to believe it will work, no. But I'll keep trying. Remember what they used to say about the lottery?"

Mick thought for a moment before shaking his head. He was never much of a gambler.

"You can't win if you don't play," Sarah said.

"It went something like that. The person with the winning ticket never thought in a million years that they would be the one to win. But someone eventually does. Or did, anyway. So I'm going to keep digging in this stupid dirt and clearing this annoying dust on the off chance that I'm holding the winning ticket."

"That's a good way of looking at things."

She stood from the ground, brushed the dirt from her knees, and gently touched his arm. "Unfortunately, Mick, It's the only way of looking at things that doesn't make me want to curl up in a ball and rock back and forth like a crazy person in a padded room."

"Would that be so bad?" Mick said with a wink. "At least you'd sleep comfortably."

She laughed. "True. Okay, I take it back. I'd prefer the padded room, please. Think you can make that happen?"

He said, "Sure," and pretended to pick up the phone. "Hello, Doctor? Yes, I'll need your nicest padded room please for my friend Sarah."

Sarah closed her eyes. "Imagine that, Mick. I bet they'd have a hot shower there. How good would that feel?"

Mick hadn't thought about a hot shower in a very long time. It was one of those things that he put out of his mind as it was certainly never going to happen—not today or in the future. He likened it to the sun. It did nothing but remind him of how many other comforts they all now missed. But watching Sarah soak in the hot shower in her mind forced him to do the same. And when he did, he soon longed for it more than anything in the world. To feel the thousands of warm drops wash over his body would be as close to orgasmic as things got for Mick nowadays.

"Can you feel it, Mick? The warm water rushing over your body. The smell of lathered body wash and coconut shampoo." She sighed happily. "I'd stand there for hours under the water. I'd get all wrinkled and prune-like, and I'd love it. Every single second of it. Hmmm." Sarah melted into the moment in her mind.

"Well," Mick said, cruelly shaking her back to reality, "maybe that can be your next project after your beanstalk grows."

"Beanstalk?" she said. "I wish. We could climb out of this crap if that was the case. No, I'll settle for a carrot." Sarah walked a few steps to the side of the building and picked up an old tin can. She had poked holes in the bottom of it and used a plastic cover to hold back the dirty undrinkable water until she was ready to use the improvised watering can. "Here's to hope." She removed the plastic lid and let the water trickle out and onto the patch of soil.

"You never know, Sarah."

"That's what I keep telling myself. Lottery, Mick. Lottery." The rest of the water emptied from the can. They both watched the drops vanish quickly into the dry earth. "You know, they say there is a secret bunker down by the harbor. I bet they have carrots growing down there."

He laughed. "And all the Twinkies we can eat."

Sarah held up her hand and suddenly appeared sick. "No, thanks. I'm not sure your cake was all that fresh. It didn't sit right with me."

"Same here. But it's the thought that counts. Plus, it was cool to see a Twinkie again. It brought back some good memories."

He had heard something a few years back about the bunker Sarah mentioned. He never put any stock into the story, though. That wasn't the only secret place he had heard about. Greg had told him about another one rumored to be located in Cape Cod, down by Woods Hole, where a group of scientists were feverishly trying to figure out a way to get the dust cleared from the atmosphere. There were even crazier stories about cities in the sky and some at the bottom of the ocean. As far as he was concerned, they were nothing more than fairy tales.

"Do you really think places like that exist?" Mick said.

"What? A secret base?"

Mick nodded.

"I doubt it," Sarah said. "At least not one so close to us. You'd think we would have seen someone or something during the past ten years, right? I mean, the harbor isn't that far away. There *was* a government submarine base being built there. That much I know for a fact. One that nobody talked about. It was going to be my first big story for Channel Seven. One night, I ended up hanging at a bar on Newbury Street with a naval contractor that was working at the base. He was all drunk and hitting on me. And you know what they say about loose lips."

"How do you know about his lips, young lady?" Mick teased.

Sarah shoved him. "Shut up, Mick. It wasn't like that."

"That's what they all say."

"Whatever," she said, smiling and blushing at the same time. "Anyway, this guy worked there. He told me all about this base in Boston Harbor that nobody knew about. He said they were working on a new kind of nuclear power." She stopped and thought. "No, actually, it wasn't nuclear. It was a fusion reactor or something. Whatever comes after nuclear. That's what they were working on. This guy said it was like the Area 51 of the East Coast."

"Well," he said, "I'll have to keep an eye out for it should I ever happen by the harbor." Which he knew he probably would not. To get to the harbor, he would have to pass through the crucifixion zone. And after his run-in with the Rubble King, that scenario was even less likely.

Sarah said, "Tell them I said hi. Ooh, and bring me back a carrot. I'll put it in my garden and tell Sandeep it grew there. That would sure freak him out."

He touched her arm and said, "Well, I'm going to head down. You coming?"

"In a minute." She looked down at her garden. "I'm going to brush the dust off one more time. Don't ask me why. It's just going to get covered again. I'm a glutton for punishment, I guess."

"Okay," Mick said. "I'll see you down there."

**

Mick rested on his cot, awake, and listened to the group as they slept. Inhales mixed with exhales and the occasional snore, a symphony of essential human functions, off-key but still soothing in a way. He wished he could join them in their rendition of sleep rather than observe, but his encounter earlier that day kept him awake as he'd known it would.

As his mind played back what happened, Mick found himself clenching his fists and tightening his arms, as if he were about to fight. Second-guessing himself was a bad habit he could not seem to break over the years—another habit that came from youth, a time when he made a lot of bad decisions and learned from too few of them. A person could only screw up so many times before the doubt set in. And when it set in with Mick, it became a permanent member of his psyche, presiding over his every decision, casting every light in a bit of a shadow.

He rose from his cot and shuffled silently to the main room. He could navigate their entire dwelling in the dark. Though he would not need to that night.

Chester, the eternal night owl, sat against the far wall. Being a night owl was rather unfortunate in the post-Impact world, considering there was not much to keep him occupied but the darkness and his own thoughts. Mick figured that Chester somehow managed to fill his head with better thoughts than he was able to, an envious position for sure. Chester tended to see the glass as half-full, while Mick failed to see the glass at all. The kerosene lamp burned dimly as he read from a book on his lap.

"You mind some company?" Mick asked.

Chester looked up in surprise. "Of course not, Mick. Please, sit."

Mick walked over and slid down the wall on the opposite side of the lamp. He crossed his legs and leaned his head back, letting out a small sigh as he did.

"Is everything all right?" Chester asked.

"As good as it can be, I guess."

Chester closed the book on his lap, which Mick could see in the faint glow of the lamp was the Bible. While Chester tried in vain to get Mick to join his scripture readings, he was good about not pushing his views. He realized that Mick did not believe what he believed, and he usually left it at that. It was probably one of the many reasons they got along so well.

"You don't sound so sure about that, Mick. You sure you're okay?"

"Ah, Chester," he said, exhaling regret. "To tell you the truth, I'm not sure."

"Care to tell me about it?"

At first Mick did not want to say anything more. It would open a can of worms that he was not sure he wanted open at all. But it was eating away at him from the inside. He needed an outlet. If for no other reason than to be reassured that he'd made the right decision. But if that wasn't the case? What if he made the wrong one? Did he truly want to know? If left alone, this nugget of his day, just one of thousands gathered over the years, would ultimately ruin him, cast all his decisions further into doubt. He suddenly realized that he was not protecting the group; he was protecting himself from knowing whether he'd made a bad decision or not.

He rolled the back of his head against the wall so he was facing Chester.

"For now, please keep what I'm going to tell you between us?" Before Chester could reply, Mick added, "It's not like it's a secret. I just don't know how I feel about the whole thing. And I want to make sure I'm not jumping the gun."

"Mick," Chester whispered. "What's said between us, stays between us. But for the record, I trust your decisions. You have never led us astray."

"I'm glad one of us trusts my decisions." He turned to stare at the far wall, the one separating them from the rest of the herd in the sleeping quarters.

The small bit of light the lamp cast across the main room flickered in an ever-changing dance of silhouettes. Shadows would ebb and flow, come into existence only to be quickly consumed. Mick found it soothing in a way, the quietness and serenity of this sterile room. He could not make any of the wall decorations out—many had been hung over the years—but he knew where everything was. A good majority of it was from his kids, their drawings. Works of art in his mind. What father would not be so blinded as to not think his child was the next Picasso? The one piece of artwork that he could make out despite the low light was also his favorite. Nate had drawn it at age six or seven; Mick forgot exactly, like so many other things. The drawing was a simple circle, colored yellow, with orange and yellow lines protruding from it. It took up the entirety of the page and glowed in the lamp's aura. Nate had told Mick at the time that since they did not have a real sun anymore, he'd made one for them, because Nate knew how sad Mick was. Just the thought made Mick fight back a tear. The simple innocence of youth could be so beautiful before the world came in and strangled it dead.

"Something happened today," Mick said, turning back to Chester. "And I'm not sure what to make of it."

A look of concern grew on Chester's face. He remained silent and listened.

"I met someone while I was out on my walk

today."

"Oh?"

"His name is Solomon." Mick quickly replayed his encounter in his mind so he could fully tell Chester the story. It was at that moment he remembered the bunny that Solomon had given to him. He reached up to the table to his left and grabbed his pack. He unhitched the buckle and removed the stuffed animal, handing it to Chester. "He gave me this. It's for the kids."

Chester took the stuffed rabbit and looked it over. "This little guy has seen better days." He handed it back. "I'm not sure the children will find much use for it."

He stared at the bunny on his lap, a reminder of the good soul he'd left with the wolves. "He showed me where food was. Or at least he tried to."

Chester perked up. "What, are you tired of canned meat?"

Mick laughed softly. Chester had a way with warming up a conversation. He had a certain purity that ran through his veins. Mick had spoken with him at length over the years. The topics varied, as did the hour at which they occurred, though rarely at this hour of the night. Their most recent discussion, maybe a month or so back, had been in regard to the meteorite that had caused the entire mess. The scientists had given Colossus a probability of hitting the Earth of 95 percent. There were those that clung to that other 5 percent, got on their knees and tried to pray away the doom that hurdled toward them unfathomably quickly. Chester had been in that 5 percent. By the time the population realized that the 95 percent was actually 100, it was already too late.

The elected leaders had chosen the never-ending profits of war over scanning the dark skies for things such as cataclysmic rocks. There was not enough money in the budget for both, they'd said. And as per the norm, they had chosen incorrectly. Even if they had detected it, Mick was not sure there would have been anything that could have been done to save the world from disaster.

"Where is Solomon now?" Chester asked, bringing Mick back to the present.

"I don't know." And that was the part that troubled him the most. For all Mick knew, Solomon was dead, smacked in the head one too many times.

"I needn't tell you this, Mick, but these times we live in are much different than the ones we grew up knowing. The problem, I find, is separating the feelings we grew up relying on from the reality we now inhabit, as they are constantly battling the other. And as much as we both wish it were true, you cannot save everyone, Mick. You've already done more than your share by taking care of all of us for all these years. Every group needs a leader if they are to be successful. And you have been a fine one. You saved me from that unholy band of thugs six years and seven months ago. If you hadn't come along when you did, I'm sure there would only be seven in this shelter, not eight. There are too many good deeds to be done but not enough good people to do them."

Of course Mick could not save everyone. But Chester made him think. Was there anything to save Solomon from? Mick had witnessed a small sliver of Solomon's world, a few minutes in a stranger's world. It was impossible for him to put together a view of Solomon's life from one simple interaction. However, the look of fear in Solomon's eyes as the Rubble King shouted for him to come out of the yellow house was very real. There was no way he could fake such a primal reaction. There was no mistaking it. Mick was sure there were others out there in need. Probably many of them. But he was no superhero. He was a man, ordinary in almost every facet.

"Well," Chester said, "what does your heart tell you?"

"To go after him. But I can't do that."

"Why is that?"

"That's the part of this whole thing that bothers me the most. Solomon wasn't alone. There was this guy who came to get him. He called himself the Rubble King."

"The Rubble King?" Chester repeated in a sarcastic tone.

"I know. It's a stupid name. And there was something really off about him. He brought some armed muscle with him, too." Mick snickered.

"Though I use that term loosely. He said he owned everything that I could see."

"So you did the right thing by coming back, Mick. It's a fool's errand to rush haphazardly into a situation without thinking it through. And I know you don't need reminding of how there are those that need you to stay alive. Two in particular."

Chester was right. But why then did it feel so wrong? Solomon aside, he knew he needed to return to the yellow house. If there was food there, and he had no reason to doubt that there was, then he had to get it. It was doing him no good to talk the night away. He had to try and force his mind to quiet down a bit. Sleep, in whatever quantity, is what he needed most. It would help to clear his mind.

Mick pushed himself back upright and gave his legs a minute to get the blood flowing. He then reached over to put the stuffed animal back by his pack. He caught sight of the vibrant red of the treasure box inside his pack. He had completely forgotten about it. Everything had sped up since he'd found it. Much more so than his typical days.

"What's that?" Chester asked as Mick removed the box.

"A treasure box the kids left for me the other day," Mick said. "I forgot about it. They haven't done this in years." He searched for a seam in the box where it would be easiest to open. "Remember they used to leave these things all over the place?"

Chester nodded. "That may be their best one

yet. I wonder where they found the red paint."

"Beats me," Mick said.

"Here. This may help," Chester said, taking a switchblade from his pocket and flipping it open with an amount of precision that seemed odd for a man of the cloth.

Mick reached out and grabbed the knife with a look of confusion on his face.

"It's quite helpful when opening some of the older cans. Sometimes they need a little nudge." He smiled.

"Fair enough," Mick replied. "I'll have to watch what I say to you from now on."

He cut the box through the word *open*, down the middle and with only the tip of the knife. He had no clue what the kids had put in there, and he did not want to damage anything with a careless swipe of the blade. He pried the top of the box open and looked inside.

"What did the kids leave you this time?" Chester asked.

Mick removed a white case about the size of his hand. Attached to it was a folded piece of paper with a printed message, something he had not seen in a long time. He read what was written. His eyes grew wide in surprise. It became readily apparent that this was not from the children.

CHAPTER 13

Robert returned the next day. He crept into the police station and sat down with those who were eating what they could, trying to avoid being noticed by King. Each day he listened to the men around him. And each day his resentment grew.

"Where have you been?" asked one of King's men across the dilapidated table.

"Out," was all Robert offered.

"Out where?"

Robert looked over angrily from the small portion of scraps he'd procured.

"Robert," King yelled.

Robert glanced angrily at the man who ruined his private moment. He scarfed down what remained of his pile and then walked over to King.

"I found out where that guy Mick is living," he said, swallowing what he could.

"Do tell."

"He went to the far side of town by the hills."

"Was he alone?"

Robert shook his head. "I saw two others. I think one of them was a guard or something. He was on the roof with a rifle. The other one was a woman he spoke with before entering a busted-up building. I had to stay far enough back so they wouldn't see me, so I couldn't hear what they were saying."

"Interesting," King said. It was one of the rare times that someone actually did exactly as he had asked. "You did well." Far better than his son would have done.

Robert smiled. He stood there looking at King as if waiting for something else.

"You can go now," King said, shooing him away with his hand.

Robert's face sank and he sulked away into the darkness.

While it was true that King had let Mick walk away, it was not out of the kindness of his heart. He sensed that Mick wasn't the type of person King kept around: mindless and subservient. He knew right away that Mick was headstrong and a man of moral fiber. And that disgusted him. Who else would try and save Solomon the dolt? He had been certain that all those types of people were long since gone. But now one had surfaced and walked into his life. He couldn't simply leave it at that, have this man wandering his streets. He could become a cancer if left unattended to. He had Robert follow him to see where the cancer lived so he could remove from it from his world.

King stood. "Clyde," he said into a crowd at the far side of the room. Clyde shot up and walked over. "We're going on a short trip to see our new friend."

**

"Where did you find it?" Sarah asked, eyeing the red box in Mick's hand.

He rotated the box slowly, while at the same time looking around at the group. "Outside the door," he said. "I figured it was one of those treasure boxes the kids used to make for me." He smiled. "Remember those things? I'd find the craziest stuff in there."

"I think we're a little old for that, Dad," Nate said as he brushed a tuft of hair from his eyes, pinning it behind his ear.

"Yes, Nate," Mick said, laughing to himself. "I thought so, too. But you can't blame me for thinking it. I half expected to find another collection of" —he paused— "drawings."

"Anatomically correct ones at that," Laurel added.

Nate blushed. "I didn't know," he said. "I drew what I saw."

"Don't you listen to them, Nate," Sandeep said. "It was a fine and accurate drawing."

"Says the man depicted as half man half elephant," Mick said. He then put the box aside and held up the white case in his hand. "It does this," he said, prying the case apart. The top piece appeared to be nothing more than a protective outer shell. He put that aside on the ground to his right. The other piece was more intricate. But for all of its delicate-looking features, the device seemed to be quite sturdy. It had a clear plastic tube at its rear, measuring close to a quarter of its length. A translucent blue, bubble-filled gel moved slowly inside the tube as Mick shifted the device in his hand.

"What is it?" Sandeep asked.

Mick handed it to him. "According to the letter, it's an immunization auto injector. Whatever that is."

Sandeep studied it at arm's length before bringing the object in closer. "There is no needle. This must be a high-pressure subcutaneous injection device." He looked up from the device to the confusion on the others' faces. "It basically pushes the liquid through the skin. No need for a needle."

"I could have used that at the hospital," Laurel said. "You'd be surprised how many people are afraid of needles."

"But what is that blue goop?" Greg asked. "And why would someone expect me to inject that into my body? I'll tell you all right now—it's not going to happen."

"I have a lot of questions, too," Mick said. He unfolded the piece of paper that accompanied the auto injector. "This was also inside the box. I've read it a whole bunch of times. It may be stranger than that little white thing," he said, pointing to the device in Sandeep's hands.

"Immunization auto injector," Sandeep corrected.

Mick nodded. "Right." He cleared his throat

and then read the letter after showing the group that it was typed out. "Dear Fellow Bostonians, We are a collective brought together before Impact, with the intention of restoring Earth to its former self. Our team has been working diligently to glue the pieces of our shattered world back together again. In our endeavor to improve humanity and restore what was taken, we have discovered a virus, one we believe will eventually finish the job the meteorites started. This virus is airborne, and, thusly, it is impossible to avoid. It is our belief that Colossus carried this pathogen to our planet and reacted with some subset of microorganisms to form what it is now. It is likely that many of you are already infected. It is also our belief that the virus, CV-1, has spread globally. At present there is no cure. We are working around the clock to find one, if one should exist at all. However, in the interim, we believe it best to immunize the population to stop it from spreading further.

"Please find an immunization auto injector included in this package. The injector contains enough serum for forty-five injections. Simply press the injector's tip, highlighted by a blue ring, against any exposed skin, preferably on either arm. Once against the skin, press the green injection button and wait three seconds. An audible beep will sound once complete. This procedure can be followed for each person needed. The device remains sterile between shots.

"We do realize you must have questions. They

will be answered in due time. However, now is the time to act to prevent those of you that have not been infected from contracting the virus. We will be in touch shortly after you have inoculated yourselves. With warm regards, Phillip E. Jones, MD, PhD, Executive Director, The Initiative."

Mick finished reading and passed the letter to Laurel. She looked a bit unnerved.

"Who the hell is The Initiative?" Greg asked.

Mick shrugged. "Your guess is as good as mine."

"The fact that the letter is typed is remarkable," Chester said, taking it from Laurel's outstretched hand. "Actually, it looks printed to be more accurate. Typewriters push the letters further into the paper. You can feel the indentation. I should know, being the oldest of us all. There were many days when my bottle of Wite-Out ran dry."

"What's Wite-Out?" Kathryn asked.

"You sure do know how to make a man feel old," Chester said, grinning. "We used it to correct mistakes we made while typing. There was no Backspace key when I first learned."

"What's a Backspace key?" Nate asked, showing that age no longer played any part in the world having passed them by.

Kathryn and Nate looked at one another and shrugged.

Sandeep handed the auto injector back to Mick. "Say this Initiative was able to find a computer and a printer, which I find highly unlikely, they would still need to power both the devices. I don't see how that's possible. You cannot fake power."

There was an uneasy silence in the room.

Mick's stomach churned uneasily; his mind swirled to the point of light-headedness. Who were these people? Better yet, where were they? They had clearly been watching them to know where they lived. It felt as if they had a million eyes on them at that moment. He figured they were somewhere within the city, which meant there was technology somewhere, too. The world was apparently not as primitive as they had been led to believe. This quick thought brought a multitude of others with it. Technology still existed. But was it contained to a small pocket of people? Were other parts of the world better off than they were? Had they been living in a nightmare unjustly?

"I don't think we should use it," Kathryn said. She gently took the device from her father's hand. She held it loosely and away from her body as if it was the cause of the virus and not its prevention.

"I'm with Kathryn," Nate said. He shook his head. "I can't believe I just said that." He looked at her with a smirk. She gave him a quick shove. Nate then looked to his dad. "You told us to trust nobody outside of our group, right? And this seems kind of shady to me."

"It seems shady to me, too, Nate," Mick said. "Listen, I'm not saying any of us should do what this letter is asking us to do. I want opinions, like yours." He looked around at the group one by one. "All of your opinions. This isn't something for me to decide. This has to be a group decision. We are a family. And our family sticks together."

"All right," Sarah said, now holding the letter. "I'll play devil's advocate. Say this is all true, and there is some sort of virus in the air that we didn't know about. The feeling I'm getting from that letter is that not everyone has the virus. Right? Why else would they want to immunize us?"

"That would make sense," Laurel added.

Greg said, "If it's even what they say it is. We don't know these people. We don't know what that stuff is."

"Right," Sarah replied, handing the letter back to Mick. "But to make things simple for the time being, let's assume that this Initiative group is who they say they are. And they do have our best interests in mind. Is there really much more harm we could do to ourselves that the planet hasn't already done to us?"

"We could die," Greg said. "That would be a pretty bad outcome."

"True," Sarah replied. "But wouldn't that be a roundabout route to get it done? It seems to me like they have a bunch of resources that we didn't think existed anymore. It would be a waste to go through all of this just to trick us into killing ourselves. Don't you think? They have to know what conditions are like out here, right? They must know."

"I have a hunch they know quite well how it is out here," Mick said. "They obviously knew where to leave the box so we would find it. The fact is, we have avoided the eyes of the others in the city by being hidden away up here behind the hill. But maybe there are some eyes we can't avoid."

"Yeah," Greg said. "Apparently we aren't as hidden as we thought we were."

"And that's my point," Mick continued. "They know we are here. That much is obvious. But how long have they known? How do they know? It's a bit unnerving when you start to think about it. We've been going about our business every day, ignorant to the fact that we have been watched this entire time."

"And that is part of my point," Sarah added. "If they wanted us dead, then they could have done it already and in a more direct way. If they are watching us, then they must know that Greg is up on the roof every day watching out for us. They must know that Mick goes out each day in search of supplies. They probably know more than we can even imagine."

"This whole thing is creeping me out," Kathryn said.

"You're not the only one," Greg said, standing. "You know how I feel about this. I have to get back up top. I don't like not having an eye up there. Especially now. That damn note got me all kinds of paranoid." He walked out of the room and toward the maintenance shaft that led to the roof. "You know where to find me." He then vanished into the inky darkness.

While Mick didn't say it, he felt the same as Greg did. The situation did not feel right in his gut. And this time he was going to follow that feeling. He took the injector back from Kathryn and replaced the hardened plastic cover. He then folded the note up and put them both back in the red box.

"We've survived this long without needing to inject ourselves with a foreign material. Let's not rush things now. I don't feel sick. And you all look fine to me. So let's just think on this for a bit."

The group appeared to be in agreement. A few nods and agreeing glances were thrown his way. However, the world Mick lived in had just dramatically changed. Somewhere there lived and worked a group of people with some semblance of the life he so dearly missed. Maybe there was hope yet.

CHAPTER 14

When King left unexpectedly, Solomon decided to use the opportunity to go down to the lower level and see Ms. Stella. He wished he had food to bring her. If only King hadn't shown up at the most inopportune instant, he would have had enough time to gather from the storage at the yellow house. Bring Ms. Stella back anything in terms of sustenance, something she desperately needed. Her frail frame withered more each time he saw her. He did not know how much longer she could hold out.

The next best thing he could think of was water. That he could bring her. He gathered the drops of water left in the heathens' cups for weeks when he was forced to clean their mess. Painstakingly, drop by drop, he filled the cup that he hid within a small dark hole in the corner of the main room. What the disgusting animals left behind was probably closer to sewage than water. But it was the best that Solomon could do. And it was something she needed. He fished all the loose particles that he could from the gathered drops of water, which happened to fill the cup about halfway. He then brought it carefully down to Ms. Stella.

"M-Ms. Stella," Solomon whispered as he

walked down the stairs. Her back was still pressed against the cold metal bars that held her captive.

She turned her head slowly to face him. "Solomon, my dear." Her smile was not enough to hide the pain that tore at her body.

"I b-b-brought you w-water," he said. "You n-need to d-d-drink." He held the cup through the bars.

"Always so thoughtful," Ms. Stella said before breaking into a small coughing fit. When it was done, she took the cup with her shaking hands. She then took a small sip. "Have you had any, my dear?"

Solomon shook his head. He would get water when he needed to. His concern was not for his health, but for hers.

"Please. Solomon. You must take care of yourself."

"N-n-no, M-Ms. Stella. I'm f-fine."

She looked back at him with disapproval on her face. He knew the look. He realized that it wasn't that she disapproved of him or his actions. Rather, she disapproved of how it never occurred to him that he needed to sustain himself, as well. He used to do the same thing when he was a teenager living in her care. Ms. Stella had very little money. What she did have was devoted to the children she cared so deeply for. As such, dinner was never anything to speak of. But it was enough. More so than he had ever been accustomed to.

Solomon had always eaten last. That had been

his own doing. He'd put his fellow orphans ahead of himself, never deeming himself worthy of more. Kids were kids, though. And not one of them had ever taken the time to notice his actions. But Ms. Stella had. She would sneak him extra when she could. She'd told him it was because of his selflessness and that his personal qualities would take him places someday. He was certain now that she did not intend for that place to be in an abandoned police station run by a group of lunatics.

Ms. Stella took another sip and then placed the cup down on the dirty floor. She looked lovingly into Solomon's eyes. "I'll ask you again, my dear. Please leave this place. Go and never come back. You still have your entire life ahead of you."

Solomon shook his head angrily. "I w-w-will never l-l-leave you."

"You must, Solomon. You are a fighter. A survivor. These creatures do not deserve to be in your company." Ms. Stella started to hack again, this time harder, to the point where it was difficult for her to catch her breath.

Solomon reached in through the bars and rubbed her back through her thin shirt until the coughing fit passed. Her back was more bone than skin now. Her spine jutted from beneath it like a tiny mountain range on a dying stretch of land.

She cleared her throat and sipped more water. "Is he still bothering you, Solomon?"

Solomon looked away. Ms. Stella was referring

to Clyde. It was one thing to allow the beatings to go on each day. It was another to remember how it used to be. The memories made Clyde's present acts of violence all the more painful.

Ms. Stella reached through the bars and put her delicate hand on top of Solomon's, like a withering rose petal on steadfast rock. "I'm so sorry, my dear. If I had known he would become such a monster, I never would have taken him in with all of us."

Solomon had had a different relationship with Clyde at one time. A good one at that. Shortly after meeting each other, they'd become inseparable. He had been Solomon's first true friend. Clyde had made Solomon feel normal during those first few years together. He'd never looked at him like he was any different than the other kids. He'd stick up for him when someone stepped over the line. They had played ball together, chased each other for tag, laughed at the same stupid jokes. Then something inside Clyde had changed, almost overnight it seemed. He'd become darker and more of a recluse. He had pushed Solomon away, along with the other children and eventually Ms. Stella. It got so bad that Ms. Stella had considered removing him from the house as he began to affect all those around him.

Ms. Stella had been certain that he was the one that stole their grocery money those weeks it went missing. And Solomon had seen him on more than one occasion talking to some of the local drug dealers that hid in the darker alleyways in the neighborhood. Then, close to two years after Impact, when the world teetered on its collapse, Clyde's father had come to get him. That man was King, although he had not yet anointed himself. Soon after, all within the orphanage realized that the meteorites were not the worst things that could happen to them. And when Ms. Stella had refused to abide by their delusional orders, she had been tortured and imprisoned. They'd threatened Solomon, promised that if he were to get out of line, she would pay the price.

Ms. Stella coughed again. She lowered herself to her side and curled into a ball. She was out of reach of Solomon now, too far into the cell. He felt as hopeless as always. Another minute went by before she was able to regain her composure, pushing herself back upright in exhaustion.

"Y-you're g-g-get-t-ting w-worse," Solomon said.

Ms. Stella closed her eyes and took a cleansing breath. "Don't you worry about me, my dear. I've been through worse than this."

That was a lie, words meant to put Solomon's mind at ease. He knew that. He watched as the light in her eyes faded more each day. She would not be around much longer. And when that happened, he would be alone again. Alone in a world that seemed to hate him even more than before. It made him angry to a point where he thought again about trying to steal the key from around Clyde's neck, run down here, and free Ms. Stella. Then they could both escape this hell together. But where would they go? She was too frail to travel any kind of real distance. And as soon as King found out they had escaped, he would surely hunt them down, if nothing other than to provide sport for his men.

"Solomon," Ms. Stella said. "You are a smart man. And certainly smart enough to understand that my time with you is coming to an end."

"D-d-don't s-say th-that."

She took his hand and grasped it as tightly as her weakening body would allow. "I wish it weren't true, my dear. But you need to prepare yourself for that eventuality. That is why I must ask again that you flee now while you can. Run as far away as you can. Never look back. Please, my dear. To see you in pain—" She stopped and began to sob. Tears slowly crawled down her face toward her quivering lips.

Solomon reached through with both of his hands and hugged her the best he could given the hardened steel bars that separated them. He put his head against the cold metal and thought back, very briefly, to a time when she held him and the world's problems seemed to melt away. When all it took was her embrace to let him know that at least one person on this giant ball loved him.

He then gently wiped away her tears.

"I m-m-met s-s-s-someone," Solomon said with his head still against the chilly metal. Up until that point he had forgotten about meeting the man in the alley. His mind had been so occupied with Ms. Stella.

Ms. Stella looked up and stopped crying. "Who did you meet, Solomon?"

Solomon thought for a moment. The man's name was elusive.

Ms. Stella had been in this position before. She knew Solomon had issues with remembering names. So she said, "Was it Mick?", using the man's name King had blurted out in his fit of rage earlier.

Solomon nodded.

"And was he a good man, Solomon?"

Solomon nodded. "I th-think so. He has k-k-kind eyes."

It was Ms. Stella who had taught Solomon to look into a person's eyes. She'd told him to see the person's intentions hidden in their eyes. She'd told him that some people lied, and it was difficult to tell a person's true intentions simply by their words. She'd told him that words were easily changed to form a lie. And that the only way to know a person's true worth was to peer inside them. So that is what Solomon did on the few occasions he wasn't staring down at the ground, averting his eyes so others could not see the pain that dwelled inside him.

"Where is this man now?" Ms. Stella asked.

Solomon shook his head angrily, remembering that King had showed up unexpectedly and ruined it all.

"It's all right, my dear. I'm happy to hear that you made a friend."

A friend Solomon feared he would never see again.

CHAPTER 15

Sid sat on the lab stool with his eyes firmly pressed against the customized electron microscope. He twisted the focusing knob with his right hand until finding the zoom he was looking for. He then looked up from the eye piece and rubbed his eyes. He needed rest badly. It would be time wasted to try at this point. His mind raced with thoughts and ideas, while his body begged for it all to shut the hell up. And he was stuck in between.

He looked to the small digital screen to his right that displayed an enlarged view of the microscope's view. The black stringy virus they referred to as CV-1 slithered all over the petri dish, darting and dashing, sometimes off the screen in its haste to find its next victim.

This lab was the most outdated of the five they had within The Facility. That was the very reason Sid had chosen it. He knew it was used sparingly, as everyone else wanted the newer equipment that the larger labs held, and therefore the foot traffic would be light. At least that was what he hoped. It's not like he was trying to hide what he was doing. Not that he really could even if he wanted to. Everything, aside from Phillip's own lab, was connected to disseminate information faster. But he needed to run these extra tests for his own peace of mind. Tests that were rarely run.

He'd had trouble focusing since Phillip had insisted on sending out those boxes full of what he paraded around as an inoculation. Sid knew the solution was not an inoculation, as purported in the note, and he had begun to have his doubts that it was a test, either. The blue gel that was sent out in the test kits had been designed by Phillip, tucked away in his private lab next to his office. Phillip had volunteered to create the test gel when the plan began to form. He'd insisted on it. Sid had had no reason to question Phillip's motives at the time. He was the most experienced man in the building. Who better to formulate the testing serum? But now things were beginning to unravel in Sid's mind. He'd begun to question things that he had not up until that point.

Sid had posted a copy of the bulletin that Phillip sent out on the wall in his room. He'd put it there to remind himself of what he was up against, what the unsuspecting people living outside the doors were in for. Some of it was true. There was an airborne virus. And most of the world was most likely infected. But to call the blue gel an inoculation was an outright lie. It was impossible to inoculate against a virus they barely understood. They had gathered bits and pieces of what made it tick, but not enough to do anything more than frustrate them with more questions.

This virus was like nothing they had

encountered before. It spread like a swarm of locusts, pulverizing anything in its path. But at the same time CV-1 seemed patient in a way. Once infected, a human might not experience symptoms for years. The oldest members of the population appeared the most easily infected. And they typically succumbed quicker than most.

The first to show symptoms of the virus within The Facility, besides the ill-fated Dr. Shaker, had been one of the engineers. Hank Loomis was the next to go. It had been quickly determined after a cell scan that the virus was not isolated to Dr. Shaker's lab. By the time they'd figured it out, it was already too late.

Sid removed the dish with the CV-1 virus on it and placed another below the microscope. This sample was from his own body, tissue taken earlier in the week. It showed more healthy cells than infected. He knew that ratio detrimentally changed every day. The black strings encased the blood cells and strangled them until nothing remained but a small dead pit floating in the solution. This was how the virus operated: suffocate a blood cell and move on to the next. The virus was methodical, killing cell after cell until the body began to break down on its own. By the look of his cells, Sid figured he had another four or five months to live.

He reached to his right and removed a small pipette filled with Phillip's blue gel. It was the first chance he'd had to get his hands on it. Phillip had not let it out of his sight since its inception. He'd had to stealthily take a single vial while Phillip was off doing his rounds of The Facility.

Again, he put his eyes to the microscope. He then dropped a bit of the gel onto the dish. The black strings of CV-1 instantly went into an agitated state, as if shocked by electricity. Some spun around in circles; others darted from side to side like rabid animals. He watched in horror as the black strands sped up their decimation of the cells. What would have taken ten minutes before, now took less than one. It was then that he understood what Phillip had done.

How could I not have seen this coming?

He began to frantically search for alternatives. While Phillip was misguided in certain aspects of his position, Sid hoped the conclusion he'd come to was not accurate. It couldn't be. It had to be something else, something he was missing. But then he thought of Dr. Shaker. It was too coincidental that Dr. Shaker's symptoms had drastically increased seemingly out of the blue. His body had failed at an exponentially quicker rate than they had seen before. It didn't make sense at the time. Sid had figured it was something genetic in Dr. Shaker's makeup. Now it made sense. Dr. Shaker built the auto injector prototype for Phillip's supposed test. He would have needed to test the mechanism with the actual gel to get the flow calibrations correct. The poor fool probably tested it on himself thinking it was harmless. Less than a week later he was dead.

Sid again looked over at the digital display. The virus had consumed all the blood cells present and had turned on themselves, one frantically trying to wrap the other in its suffocating grasp. The captive one would soon free itself and turn on another.

Sid stood from the lab stool, light-headed from the realization of what these people were about to inject into themselves and sickened by what Phillip had done.

CHAPTER 16

Robert led King and Clyde up the small hill on the outskirts of the city. They passed through a sagging chain-link fence at its top. King had chosen to keep this an intimate affair. No need to gather his troops for a show of force. Not yet. Plus, he did not need to hear any bellyaching about them being tired or cold. Poor babies. Maybe Mick would see it King's way from the start. At least that is what he hoped. For Mick's sake.

"Where did he go from here?" King asked Robert.

"Over there," Robert said, pointing to a building ahead of them, hugged between a series of smaller mound-like hills. He then nodded to the roof of the building to where Greg watched out over the exact space they needed to cover.

"All right," King said. "Stay close. Let's see how this goes. No one is to shoot unless I say so. Is that understood?"

Robert nodded. Clyde said nothing.

King then smacked Clyde in the head, a move that was turning into his modus operandi. "Did you hear me?"

"Yeah," Clyde said, rubbing his head. "Sorry."

The small group of men made their way from the fence toward the shelter.

A loud banging broke the breezy silence from above them.

Bang! Bang! Bang!

King looked up at Greg on the roof. He had a rifle in one hand. And with the other hand he beat twice more on the air conduit.

"We have company," Greg shouted into the vent, loud enough to carry on the wind. Greg then leveled his rifle against his shoulder and said, "Hold it right there, fellas."

King motioned for his men to stop. "Hello up there," he said. "We come in peace." King had always wanted to say that. But the right opportunity hadn't presented itself until that point.

"If you come peacefully, why the guns?" Greg asked.

"Have you roamed the city recently, stranger? Traveling without protection is nothing short of suicide."

"Well, you won't need them here," Greg said. "Not unless you give us reason to think otherwise. So why don't you go ahead and put them at your feet." Greg eyed them all while keeping the rifle pointed at King.

"I'm afraid we can't do that right now," King said. *Or ever*, he thought. But his true feelings would expose the person beneath the mask. And the play had only just begun. "You are the one pointing the gun at us. How do I know you mean us no harm?"

"You don't," Greg said. "But I didn't walk up

on your home. So I'm the one doing the asking. If you come in peace like you say you do, then disarming shouldn't be too much to ask."

"Maybe peace was the wrong choice of words," King shouted, inching closer as he spoke.

"Then what is the right word?" Greg asked, cocking the rifle. "Better hurry. My patience isn't what it used to be."

The door to the shelter opened, and Mick made his way outside. His rifle was at the ready the instant he exited the door.

"Ah," King said. "Good to see you again. Mick, was it?" Unlike Solomon, King always remembered a name. But he liked to keep others guessing. Make them speak more than they would have chosen to. Play the quiet fool while others lived it.

Mick inched closer over broken glass that crunched as he walked. "What are you doing here?"

"Come now, Mick," King said. "Is common decency really no more? Can't one person come to speak with another without all this unnecessary suspicion?" He laughed inside as he said it. It was fun to play someone that he was not.

"When it comes to you and me, yes, common decency is dead," Mick said. "You're not my type of people."

King made a shocked face, like he could not believe what Mick had just said. "Oh, Mick," he said. "Why must you hurt my feelings like that?"

"No offense," Mick said. "But I'm not buying

it. You and feelings are like oil and water. And you have no place here. So why don't you turn around and go back to where you came from."

"Like I told your friend up there," King said, looking up at Greg. "We came to talk. Nothing more."

"I can't see what we possibly have to talk about."

"I have a proposition for you, Mick. Something I offer to a few rare people. How would you, and whoever is here with you, like to be a part of my kingdom?" King smiled confidently. There had yet to be anyone he crossed that could not be persuaded to join his ranks, one way or another. His kingdom was the pinnacle of the new world. In King's mind there was only one correct answer to that question.

"You're serious?" Mick said with the slightest snicker. "What would make you think I'd ever take you up on that *offer*?"

King's expression went from cockiness to anger in an instant.

Insignificant fool.

"Why would you think I was anything but serious, Mick?" Just like at the yellow house, King let the hard *k* drip off his tongue with animosity.

"I find it difficult to take you seriously," Mick said. "I mean, you did dub yourself King of Boston."

"The Rubble King," Clyde corrected, seeming pleased with himself.

"Ah, right," Mick said. He looked up toward the roof at Greg, who still had the rifle trained on King's head. "Hear that, Greg? All hail the Rubble King."

Greg laughed.

Clyde took a step forward, past King and closer to Mick.

"Stop," Greg said from the roof. "Your next warning will be a bullet through your skull." Clyde stopped and sneered at Greg. He then looked at Mick, whose gun was also trained on him, before slowly slinking back.

"He usually doesn't miss," Mick said.

Neither do I, King thought, composing himself, suppressing the anger that normally would have burst free already. "Come now, Mick," he said. He realized that he should have brought more men. Next time would be different. "At least give it some thought. I have food and water. I can offer you protection."

Mick scoffed. "Like the protection you gave to Solomon?"

"Solomon is perfectly fine. I assure you. He is just as stupid and slow as when you met him the other day."

Clyde and the rest of the men giggled at King.

"That's funny," Mick said. He looked directly at Clyde. "He seemed a lot more intelligent than the bunch of you. And we have everything we need right here. We don't need you or your propositions."

King smiled to hide his growing anger. "Everything you need, huh? I wonder what else you have in there." He looked over Mick's shoulder toward the shelter.

Mick firmed up his grip on the rifle. "No more questions. Our conversation is over. I suggest you leave now. And don't come back. That way we won't have a problem."

The door to the shelter opened again.

"Daddy?" Kathryn said.

"Go back inside," Mick shouted, looking quickly over his shoulder and then back to King.

"Who is that?" Kathryn asked, seeming not to hear Mick's shout. She squinted from inside the destroyed outer shell of the shelter.

"Get inside, Kathryn. Now!"

"Oh," King said. "Lookie here, boys. Seems that our friend, Mick, has a daughter." King eyed her up and down and then looked back at Mick. "She's very pretty. She must take after her mother." He looked over Mick's shoulder again. "Come on over. We don't bite." *Much.*

Clyde snickered in his crude way. He then licked his slimy lips and tried to wink through his thick sports goggles, which just made his face contort in an even uglier manner than was the norm.

Mick inched forward. "One more word," he said. "Say one more word about my daughter, and it will be the final one you speak."

King held up his hands. "All right, Mick. But I

really think you should give my offer some thought. I will only offer it this once. And it is more than I give to most."

"The answer is no," Mick said. "It will always be no."

King's face reddened. He clenched his jaw and looked at Mick and then Greg. "Very well," he said. "I'm certain that we'll be seeing each other again soon."

"Don't come back here," Mick said. "I mean it. You are not welcome here."

King simply smiled and waved for his men to follow him back down the hill. He would have to get what he wanted through less friendly means.

CHAPTER 17

The more Sid thought about it, the more he felt betrayed. Phillip used them like puppets. Building bits and pieces of the accelerant and then combining them without anyone knowing what his true intentions were. Phillip had told Sid that the molecular stability agent he'd designed was for longevity testing of the vegetables. Sid had never questioned that because it made sense at the time. The hydroponically grown vegetables would last much longer if their decay was stabilized. He felt naive now that Phillip's true intentions were out in the open. It was all too apparent that his agent was specifically created for the blue gel, not the hydroponics. The clouds began to clear, and the truth shone down brightly. What irked Sid the most was that he'd had a hand in this. Unknowingly, of course, but he'd still played a part in Phillip's game of God.

He hurried down the white-walled main hallway, passing others going about their own business, surely unaware of what had been birthed in this very building. When he reached Phillip's door, Sid instinctively knocked, but he entered before being told to do so.

Phillip looked up from the tablet in front of him. "Sid?" he said. "Have you found something new?"

"You could say that," Sid replied, tossing down his own tablet in front of Phillip. On it played a video of what Sid had just recently found in the tiny lab. He watched as it replayed the CV-1 virus ramping up its attack after being dosed with the blue gel that Phillip had designed.

Phillip also watched the screen. He then stood from his chair, never one to stay in a position of being looked down upon. "And this is?"

"Don't play coy with me, Phillip. This is what you sent to the outside population. Isn't it?"

Phillip said nothing. He looked at the tablet again before gently tapping the red square to stop the video from playing.

"I knew this was not an inoculation. We all did." Sid then flipped the tablet toward him and quickly started another video. This one showed the end result of what the accelerant did: a gathering of dead shriveled-raisin blood cells. "But I never in a million years would have envisioned you as a cold-blooded murderer."

"A murder?" Phillip scoffed. "How dare you! Who are you to judge me?"

"I wouldn't dare judge you, Phillip. I don't think I could be harsh enough." He paused for a moment, feeling himself heating up inside. His anger brewed. But it would do him more harm than good to lash out. Phillip could snap his fingers and have The Facility's security team usher him into some dark corner of the building where few traveled. He understood the politics in play here, even without an official political structure present.

Phillip, too, calmed his demeanor. He stopped and buttoned the bottom button of this lab coat, which had sprung loose when he'd shot from his chair. "Sit," Phillip asked. He motioned toward the chair directly behind Sid. "Please. A shouting match will get us nowhere."

Sid wanted to storm out of the office. He knew this was going nowhere. But he had just started something he wasn't sure he should have yet. So he reluctantly sat.

Phillip again looked at Sid's tablet as it sat paused on the final image in the video. Ten or so dead blood cells stood frozen in time. Each cell had a stringy black strand of the CV-1 virus surrounding the entirety of it.

"It's an accelerant. Isn't it, Phillip?"

Phillip looked up from the screen. "Yes. It is." He offered no more.

"Why would you do something like this? What happened to you over the years? Where's the brilliant, ethical man I begged to come work for after the CDC?"

"There are bigger things than my intelligence or sense of humanity at play here. What we face is new ground, uncharted territory. There is no time to plan clinical trials. There is no FDA or CDC. There is not a single entity out there that can help us achieve the goal that is imperative to our survival. There is, as far as we know, only us left to save the world. And sometimes our hands need to get dirtier than we would like. The ethics you speak of are long gone."

"Speak for your own ethics, Dr. Jones. Mine have not wavered."

"Oh?" Phillip said. "You can't truly believe that?"

Sid thought for a moment. Maybe he had not been honest with himself. He shook the thought away. *No.* That was what Phillip wanted him to feel. He knew he had begun his game of manipulation. And Sid had almost fallen for it.

"I do believe that I have remained true to myself," Sid said. "I have always questioned any method that went against the very principles that we live by. Who are you to trick these people into speeding up their own deaths? Under the guise of a helping hand nonetheless. I find it despicable."

"Your misplaced sense of moral obligation will do nothing but slow down our hunt for the cure."

"If one even exists, Phillip. We don't know if it does. We don't know if CV-1 can even be slowed down. It's apparent that it can be sped up, though. Thanks to you."

"Thanks to us, I think you mean. You're an intelligent man, Sid. By now I'm sure you have figured out that your stability agent was used to keep the gel intact prior to injection?"

"I did," Sid said. "And you can screw yourself for bringing my work into your demented game."

"I assure you, Doctor, this is no game. And I

brought you into nothing. You knew before Impact what was needed of us. You fully understood the ramifications of living in The Facility. It was not me who brought you into this. You willingly came all on your own."

Sid stood from his chair. He balled his hands into fists to keep himself from doing something he would regret. He then walked to the large window that looked out from Phillip's office and into the largest lab in The Facility. There was a team of technicians buzzing around like a swarm of bees gathering honey. Except the honey in this instance was a blue gel.

"When I signed up for this assignment," Sid said, "it was under extreme circumstances. The world was about to end as we knew it. You told me our job was to find a way to rebuild."

"What do you think we are doing, Sid?"

"We are killing innocent people."

"That's where you are wrong. We are not killing anyone. They are already dying. It is our job to try and fix that. And the only way to accomplish that is by finding the immunity strand."

"Not by any means necessary, Phillip."

"Yes. By any means necessary is exactly what we must do. Do you think the virus is playing by these rules you impose upon yourself? Does it stop and consider the moral obligations before infecting our planet? You already know the answers, Dr. Roth. You simply need to come down off your high horse and see the world for what it is and not what it was."

Sid walked back from the window, slowly, thinking, before sitting back down on the chair. As much as he hated it, he realized that Phillip had a point. But having a point and being correct were entirely different things.

"Why didn't you tell us?" Sid asked.

"Because, Sid, I knew that this would happen." He fanned his arms out in front of him. "This whole battle of words we are having at the moment."

"Don't play that game with me, Phillip. You had no right—"

"I have every right," Phillip interrupted. "I am in charge of this facility. I am the decision maker here. Not you or anyone else. Me. And only me."

"Says who, Phillip? The government that no longer exists? The military brass that hasn't been seen or heard from in over six years? Who exactly is giving you the right to accelerate the deaths of these people?"

Phillip said nothing. He cocked his head a bit and removed his glasses, tossing them on his desk. He rubbed his eyes. "Sid," he said. "Listen, I respect your opinion—"

"Do you?"

"Let me finish," Phillip said, furrowing his brow. "But while I respect your opinion, I am under no obligation to agree with it. Furthermore, without structure, the entire Initiative will fail. Then it won't matter who did what, because we'll all be dead. And who will you preach morality to then?"

Sid said nothing. He simply stewed in the words that Phillip had just hung in the air.

Phillip picked up his glasses and pushed them back onto his nose. He reached over and picked up his tablet. After tapping a few digital buttons, he made a swiping motion and projected the tablet onto a television monitor that hung on the wall to his right. The screen showed a rough map of Boston's old city blocks in green lines. Scattered throughout the map were blinking red dots.

Sid looked at the screen curiously. He said nothing, however. It was still difficult for him not to storm out of the office. But he knew that would be exactly what Phillip wanted. He would not give him the satisfaction.

"These dots," Phillip said, "represent the targeted groups that have willingly taken the serum."

"Thinking it was for their own benefit, Phillip. You can pretty up a lie however you want. In the end it is what it is."

"Nothing is done for the individual in today's world, Sid. You are well aware that we work towards a collective betterment."

"So tell these people the truth. Let them decide if they want to put the accelerant in their veins. That they'll die so much quicker if they inject themselves. Then see how much better the collective feels with that knowledge."

Phillip stared at Sid for a moment. Their eyes locked on each other. He then broke his stare and tapped another button on the tablet. This one magnified a certain area of the map. The larger red blinking dots were replaced by several smaller blue dots, scattered in the same general area.

"These smaller dots represent each person within those groups that has injected themselves. I took the liberty to include nanotracking bots in the injection device so we could monitor where the process was."

Sid stared at the blinking dots. It then hit him that each dot represented a lie. A lie that he'd unknowingly contributed to.

Phillip continued. "If the infected person expires, the dot vanishes. If any dots remain in the next five or six days, then we may have found an individual with immunity to CV-1. And all of this will be forgotten."

Sid closed his eyes in disgust. How could things get to this point so quickly? He then reached over the desk and tapped a button on the tablet. The screen went back to the full map of Boston. The red dots were scattered all over the map, but most of them were within a few miles of The Facility. He noticed a large single green dot.

"What is the green dot?" Sid asked.

Phillip looked to the monitor. After finding what Sid was referring to, he said, "The green dot means it has yet to be used."

"Meaning they haven't shot themselves up?"

"Not yet, anyway. If the dot remains green much longer I will be forced to send one of our security teams out to do it for them. As you know, Sid, time is not our friend. We cannot wait too much longer."

If Sid had any say in the matter, that green dot would remain that way.

CHAPTER 18

Mick stretched out across his cot, thinking about what had transpired with King earlier in the day. The crazy man now knew where they lived—where their food, water, and supplies were. Mick's stomach knotted every time he thought about it. The relative safety afforded to them by living on the outskirts, hidden from most eyes, was now gone.

He had grown used to the way things were. A routine had formed over the years. Now everything felt different. And that pissed him off. But what bothered him the most was that King now knew that he had a daughter. Of the most inopportune times to come out of the shelter, Kathryn had picked a doozy. But it was hard for Mick to be angry with her. She didn't know who was out there. Greg had only warned them a few times like that. And not anytime recently that Mick could remember. Most of those warnings had turned out to be harmless stragglers that wandered too close to The Shelter. And Kathryn longed for company, for some semblance of how life used to be. Sadly, when that opportunity came, it happened to be the worst possible person that Mick could think of showing up.

The vibrations Mick had been feeling through

his cot for the past hour seemed to be getting worse. They denied him any chance of sleep. The one that rattled the shelter right then felt more intense than the others had. Something didn't feel right.

"It's a bad one," he heard Greg say from the main room, followed by the squeaky closing of the trapdoor that led to the roof.

Mick sat up in his cot and swung his feet to the ground. Another vibration hit the shelter and made the walls hum, similar to the one prior but shorter in duration. The floor buzzed like a swarm of invisible bees brushed the floor, tickling the soles of Mick's feet as they went.

He stood at the same time that Sandeep did. They met eyes. It was apparent that Deep felt a difference in the air the same as Mick did. They had lived in the shelter for so long that any abnormality stuck out with a vengeance.

"Sounds like a strong storm is passing through," Deep said, sitting back down to let Mick pass.

"It does, doesn't it?" Mick shuffled past him and into the main room, rubbing his eyes as they readjusted to the dim light of the lamp. "What's going on?"

"Storm snuck up on us," Greg said. "It's spread wide, too. The entire city's gone brown. I went to take a look, but it's too bad for me to stay up there."

They termed it "going brown" because no

matter how hard you looked at something, it all looked like the same brown nothingness. And this storm had brought with it extremely high winds.

Another vibration shook the structure above them, followed quickly by the unnerving sound of straining steel. Mick looked to the ceiling of the main room. He had been there during the initial renovation phase of the shelter to get the telecommunications conduits in place. The structure above had been secured with large metal pylons buried deep into the rock below them. Any vibration to the above structure traveled throughout the entirety of the shelter through the girders.

"Another storm?" Kathryn asked from the door of the sleeping quarters.

Mick put his arm around her. "I'm afraid so, honey."

"I hate these things," she said, giving him a little squeeze as another vibration ran the girders' length.

Mick did not much care for them, either. But like most things after Impact, they had little choice in the matter.

When the storms were severe, something that had only happened once or twice before, the skeleton of the structure above would seem to almost sing as the wind tore through it. It was strange for a storm to roll in as fast as this one, and for the singing to start so quickly after. That was what had Mick so worried.

Laurel, Sarah, and Chester came stumbling out of the sleeping quarters in unison.

"Is Nate really still sleeping?" Mick asked, noticing the absence of his son.

"He'll sleep through anything, Dad," Kathryn said. "I'll get him up."

Sarah passed Kathryn. "Don't worry, Katie." She used the nickname she had given Kathryn some years back. Sarah then gently brushed Kathryn's arm as if to reassure her that everything would be fine.

"I couldn't see much outside before I was forced in," Greg said as he double-checked the latch to the roof hatch. "The dust is thick right now. I can't even see the fires in the city. I haven't seen a storm like this in" — he paused to think — "well, ever, actually. This is going to be a bad one. The wind is already grabbing some of the heavier debris. Can't say I feel great about that."

Nate groaned and shuffled out of the sleeping quarters, Kathryn in tow. He plopped down on the chair to his right, pulled his sleeping bag over him, and fell back sleep against the cold wall.

Must be nice, Mick mused.

Another vibration jolted the shelter as the wind above picked up speed. This one Mick could feel travel from the bottoms of his feet and rattle his teeth. It resonated throughout the shelter as if a jumbo jet had fired up its turbines inside. The stack of plates they used for almost every meal came crashing down on the floor and shattered into a million pieces.

"Blasted things," Chester said, anger lacing his usually placid words. "Everybody watch your feet." He moved over to where the plates had dropped and bent down. Then Chester being Chester, he lightened up the mood despite the grim reality of the situation. "I'll have to run down to the store and grab replacements tomorrow." He smiled.

Then the storm's song became louder, closer to a howl, as if warning them what was to come.

"What's going on, Dad?" Nate said, now awake and standing. It appeared that this storm was enough to keep him awake, which said more than any words could.

Mick did not answer. Instead, he listened intently. The hair on his arms stood tall. His heartbeat increased. The storm did not sound like the ones before it had. This storm sounded harsher, more intense. The wind, rather than dying down between gusts, increased in velocity. There were no breaks, points where the storm subsided or simply stopped. The Earth seemed angry; it grumbled from deep down inside, intent on releasing its wrath.

"What the hell's that noise?" Greg asked. He looked toward the ceiling, at the thick metal beams as they seemed to sway in place.

The unnerving sound of the metal twisting and bending reached its climax. It strained under its own weight, fighting against itself to remain intact.

What was left of the structure topside, worn down from countless years of abuse, had finally given in.

And then came the crash.

Anything attached to the walls fell. The old florescent lights that had not worked since Impact came crashing down from the ceiling. Like popcorn, they burst on the dark floor one after another, showering all of them in thin glass and sharp plastic. The metal shelving that circled the room dropped from its anchors as if gravity had multiplied tenfold.

"Daddy!" Kathryn screamed.

He reached out and pulled her close. "Nate?" It was difficult to see anything. The lamp burned, but the room had filled with particulates from the crash. "Nate!" Mick listened as their only salvation they had known since Impact was ripped away as if a tornado hovered directly over them.

"I'm here, Dad," Nate said, coming up on his other side.

"Are you all right?" Mick asked. Nate nodded. His breathing was fast, his eyes wide with fear. "Stay beside me," Mick said. He then looked to Kathryn. "You, too. Stay next to me, okay?"

Kathryn was crying. He wished more than anything that he could help her stop, but she had every right to be doing so. Why should a fourteen-year-old have to suffer through more misery? Where was Chester's God now?

"Is everyone all right?" Mick shouted. It had become much more difficult to hear them with the insulated walls breached.

A sudden second crash sounded, much louder than the last and with far deeper repercussions. Whipping dust poured into the shelter's room. It bit at Mick's skin and blurred his vision.

Kathryn and Nate clung to his sides. Mick's heart raced. He was the one that cared for these people, protected them. And he did not know what to do. He had not planned for something like this. What is there to do when the planet you rely on for life wants to take it from you?

"Laurel!" Greg shouted. There was panic in his voice. "Laurel, I need you now!"

Mick could not make out much in the distance. He squinted, but the room was a mess. Dust swirled around as if they were outside. With Nate and Kathryn still clutching him, Mick slowly shuffled to the far side of the room where Greg was bent down.

Please, no.

"Laurel!" Greg shouted again.

"I'm here," Laurel said. "What's—"

A coursing numbness froze Mick in place.

Sarah.

Kathryn screamed. Mick instinctively cupped his daughters head and blocked her eyes. She shouldn't see what he did. No one should. *This can't be happening*, he thought. But it was happening. This was real, and there was no way to turn it off.

The last crash had brought with it one of the

large support beams from the structure above. The beam had crashed through the floor, what was once their ceiling, and landed across Sarah's now motionless body. She was alive, but barely. The beam had crushed her body as if it were made of papier-mâché, resting right below her chest. A thin line of blood streamed from each corner of her mouth.

"Help me get this off," Greg said, sliding down next to Sarah.

Sandeep and Chester went to the far side, while Mick joined Greg.

Greg quickly counted down from three. They all heaved with every fiber of muscle they had. The beam did not budge more than an inch, if that. Greg counted down again. And again they lifted in unison; this time the beam moved even less. When the beam came back down that tiny bit, it made Sarah scream. It was muted and sad, filled with pain. Her scream shot adrenaline through Mick's body.

Nate slid down next to Mick. Kathryn ran to the opposite side with Chester and Sandeep. Again, Greg counted down from three. And again, even with the addition of Nate, the beam stayed where it was: across Sarah, firm and unrelenting.

"Again," Greg shouted. And again they failed to budge it.

"Stop," Sarah said, her voice, soft and distant, mixing with the gurgle of blood from her throat. Her eyelids were halfway closed, and her eyes looked as if they wanted to roll into the back of her head. Despite the storm and the noise it brought, Sarah's voice echoed in Mick's mind.

"Stay with us, hon," Laurel said through tears, propping her head up as best she could.

Mick reached down and stroked her cheek with the back of his shaking hand. "It will be okay," he said, clearly lying to everyone within earshot. "We'll get you out of here. We just have to …"

Sarah's breaths became labored and uneven. She tried to speak again, but nothing came out of her parted mouth. A small trickle of blood dripped from her nose. The drop of blood crept slowly down her cheek. Before the drop hit the floor, Sarah was dead.

The metal girders above them continued to twist in the wind. There was little time to mourn; no time to feel what Mick could not help but feel. The shelter was falling apart. What had provided a life for them for so long had just taken a bit of it back. Their home, what was left of it, had become a tomb.

Laurel grabbed Kathryn and pulled her tight to her chest. They wept together, Kathryn sobbing to the point of losing her breath.

The herd sat around the beam, dejected and still. Mere hours ago they were all surviving in an inhospitable world; a world they'd thought they had finally figured out how to coexist with. Then that world had flipped upside down again, and their eight had become seven.

Another crash boomed, this one from the other side of the sleeping quarters. Dirt and debris flooded out of the doorway and mixed with the already heavy air where they were, pelting them with whatever could be pushed free.

Mick reached down with the gentlest touch he could and closed Sarah's eyelids, which had already begun to build up a small layer of dust.

I'm so sorry I let this happen, Sarah.

He felt the tear roll down his cheek and did nothing to stop it. He was sure there would be more.

Mick looked to his left. The dirt and debris from the last crash cleared. In its wake, he realized that the sleeping quarters were gone, lost beneath tons of twisted metal. And then the stark reality of their situation hit him. Behind the sleeping quarters was the food store. Their water, fuel, and food. Their survival was no longer a guarantee.

"Sandeep," Mick said over the storm's fury.

Sandeep stared at Sarah, catatonic and still. His darker skin had paled.

"Deep," Mick said louder. Still nothing. He reached across and grabbed his arm. Deep looked over at Mick, his eyes blank. "Deep," Mick said again. "I need the tarp behind you." Sandeep remained still.

Greg got to his feet and rushed behind Sandeep. He handed the tarp to Mick and helped him unfold it.

As dangerous as it seemed inside, Mick knew that they could not go outside; the storm would eat them alive. He made a decision. Since the beams had already crashed down, at the very least the roof above them could not fall for a second time. So he figured the area below them was probably the safest place to be. He did not know if it was the right decision or wrong one, or if one even existed that could be so clearly labeled. All he knew was absolute sadness and fear.

He waved Laurel and Kathryn to his side and beneath the tarp that rested over their position, including the body of Sarah and the beam that had taken her life. They would ride out the storm with her. All eight of them together for the final time in the hope that there was an end to the storm at all.

One thing was for sure. If they did make it through this, they would come out the other side in shambles.

CHAPTER 19

Inside his room, Sid shoved a few things into a backpack in a methodical, almost thoughtless way. A few light garments, the cellular scanner he'd used when they first began to track the virus's degenerative process, a few protein bars should he need them, and a mobile tracking device to locate the group that had yet to doom themselves to a quick death.

"I'm sorry, Sid," Alex said from the chair he sat rigidly in, "but I can't support this."

Sid looked back. "I'm not looking for your support, Alex. I told you about this so you'd know where I had gone."

"You're going to catch something out there."

"It can't be any worse than what we all caught while in here."

"Well, how are you going to explain this to Phillip?"

"I'm not."

Alex paused as if trying to wrap his head around what Sid was saying. "So how are you going to get outside then?"

"Alex," Sid said. "Did we let the little things stop us back in medical school? Remember how Professor O'Brien fawned over his prized possession. That skeletal model that belonged to

Harry Houdini?"

"I remember it well," Alex said. "And do you remember the trouble we got in when we were caught?"

"I do." Sid stopped to recollect. They had snuck in through the skylight in Professor O'Brien's classroom. Down a knotted rope, which they'd then used to hoist the skeleton back up. Pretty impressive feat for two dorky med students. If it wasn't for that security guard who got their license plate, they might have made a clean getaway. "We should have taken your car," Sid said. "My old Jetta didn't do us any favors by backfiring when it did."

"Sounded like a gunshot. It scared the crap out of me."

Sid nodded. "Terrible timing. The point I'm trying to make is that we didn't let the fact that the front doors were locked stop us back then."

"There's a big difference here, Sid. You do realize that, right? You're not stealing some prop this time around. Much worse things can happen to you."

"Of course I realize what I'm doing, Alex. All I'm saying is there is more than one way out of this place. And when I leave, it has to be without Phillip's knowledge. I don't trust him."

"Why risk your life for a group of strangers? Who's to say they don't kill you when they find out?"

Sid stopped packing and sat down across from

Alex on a thin plastic chair. "Because this group of strangers have, for whatever reason, escaped the immediate grasp of Phillip's accelerant. If there is any chance for me to prevent them from becoming victims, I have to take it. I can't turn a blind eye to what Phillip is doing."

"We're all victims, Sid."

"Stop it, Alex. We aren't victims of anything but selfishness. We live in here protected from what's out there. If CV-1 didn't make it through our air scrubbers, we wouldn't even be having this discussion. We'd still be ignoring the glaring truth that's outside. We were supposed to help rebuild. All we've really done is ignore the people we were supposed to help. And I'm sick of it."

Alex turned his gaze to the ground.

"I don't mean to throw all of this on you," Sid said. "But this is something I have to do."

Alex looked back up, resolutely. "Then I'm coming with you."

Sid paused. "You're a good man, Alex. But you can't come with me. If you really want to help, figure out if Phillip is hiding anything else from us. When Phillip asks you why I left, just play dumb. Pretend like it came as a shock to you, too. That way you can still do your work without drawing his suspicions."

Alex took stock of what Sid said. He then nodded. "All right. That's what I'll do. But for the record, I think this whole thing is a bad idea."

"Duly noted, my friend."

Sid zipped his backpack closed and shouldered it. He realized this would be a one-way trip.

CHAPTER 20

It was the first time the kids had really had to deal with death. Aside from having to tell them about their mother's passing when they were four years old, Mick thankfully had not had to cross this bridge all that often. The kids had been through a couple of deaths in the family before, but only as babies. They remembered their mother, of course—vaguely, but they did. They only had to ask "When is Mommy coming back?" a couple of times before it really sank in. But kids were the most resilient of them all. They bounced back. They forged on and created a new life with what they still had. Yet, in a cruelly ironic way, it was something that seemed to fade as a person aged, becoming weakest when it was needed the most.

While this was the children's first time watching a person die, sadly, it was not Mick's. It felt the same though: losing someone you love. It did not matter in what manner they were loved. Sarah was the closest thing to a second daughter he would ever have. Over the past years, Sarah had had as much of an influence on his kids' lives as he did. In some respects probably more. She was around during the days while he was out. She was a motherly figure for them while he obviously was not. Now that part was gone, forever, like so much else. He could not help but feel as if he had done something wrong to permanently endanger those he loved. It felt like the universe punished him.

They waited the storm out beneath the tarp. The lamp had shattered when the roof fell, so it was darker than normal. That was probably for the best. Most of them cried at some point. None of them wanted to leave the shelter. This was their home. But they knew that staying was not an option.

The hardest part was saying good-bye to Sarah. They had no choice but to leave her body behind. The beam was far too heavy to move. The group even tried, in vain, to move it a few more times after she had long been gone. Mick felt they owed that much to Sarah and, in reality, a whole lot more. In some twisted form of logic, at least her final resting place would be where she'd felt most comfortable in an existence that provided very little of it.

The group said their good-byes, some of them together, others alone. It was a moment that Mick hoped to never have to repeat, but one that he swore to never forget. He was especially angry because there was no outlet for what he was feeling, no single person he could confront. Let him throw a punch or kick something over. Let him take his revenge on this world that had tormented him, stolen from him, refused to back down at any point to let the light shine through, if even for just a minute. At that moment he hated the world for all those reasons and an infinite amount more.

The world suddenly felt very intimidating. There had always been a place to leave from and come back to. Now they had neither.

They were foodless, waterless, and hopeless. At least Mick's rifle had survived the storm's onslaught. At that point, anything was better than nothing.

Chester insisted on giving Sarah a proper burial. That meant reading from his book, praying by her side, and cleansing her spiritually, or so he said. Mick had no problem with any of it. And while he did not believe any of what Chester did had any effect on her, he felt it was best for everyone to remember the person Sarah was rather than how she'd died. Chester spoke briefly of Sarah, how selfless and caring she was. How her passion for life would never falter even under duress. How she'd changed all their lives for the better. All of it true.

Laurel really had not said anything since the storm passed. She stayed as busy as she could gathering whatever was salvageable.

"How are you holding up?" Mick asked. He put his hand softly on her back. Laurel and Sarah had been inseparable at times, being the only two grown women in their group. Kathryn learned things from them that she could never possibly learn from Mick. Some for obvious, natural reasons, while others were more subtle and passed down within the ranks of womankind.

Laurel did not turn to Mick. She kept her eyes on what was left of the table and sifted through the dirt, stone, and metal. "I'll be fine, Mick," she said. Her voice dripped with sadness. She took a large gulp and, he assumed, tried to push the feelings back down.

"Are you sure you'll be okay? You haven't stopped moving since the storm passed."

Laurel stopped sifting and took a deep breath. She then turned to Mick and patted her chest as she tried in vain to hold it back. She shook her head slowly, as if she was trying to negate what had happened by simply thinking it away. And then her eyes flooded with the tears.

"Why, Mick?" she said, sobbing. "Why her?"

Mick put his arms around Laurel. He squeezed her tightly. He did not have an answer for that. Why any of them? Why did they have to continue to live only to watch others die?

He stroked the top of Laurel's head as she cried harder. She gasped for air at times, and he held her tighter during them. He wanted to cry with her, to fall to his knees, dejected about life as he knew it. He could not, however. He knew his role. It was that of father and shepherd. Be it fate or something else, Mick was there to help guide his herd. And he would do just that no matter how deeply the circumstances pained him. But guide them to what? Where were they to go now? How would they survive without all that they lost? Each time he thought of it, his head numbed.

Laurel forced herself to stop crying after a few more minutes. She wiped her eyes and looked up at Mick. She smiled. Not out of happiness, Mick could tell, but out of acceptance for things she could not change. She went back to gathering what she could.

"What are we going to do now?" Greg asked.

Mick was not sure. "Give me a minute?" he said, nodding his head in his kids' direction.

"Of course," Greg said, understanding. "Take your time."

His children sat huddled in the only corner left of the shelter that was free from topside debris. They sat side by side. Kathryn had her head buried in her knees, while Nate watched Mick walk over from behind tired-looking red eyes.

"How are you guys holding up?" Mick asked. He went down to one knee in front of them. He realized he would need to be strong. He would need to exude a confidence that he did not have. Sometimes being a good father meant shading reality in a better light to help others that weren't as well prepared to cope.

"What are we going to do now, Dad?" Nate said. His body looked limp and unmoving, as if he had lost the will to continue. Mick could not let him fall into despair—either of them. For as difficult as it was, he knew his children needed their father. They needed a strong figure to tell them that everything was going to be all right, even if that was a complete and utter lie.

Mick took a breath. "We're going to be fine, Nate. It's what we've done for the past ten years, and it's what we'll continue to do."

"But we have nothing now, Dad."

"That's not true, Nate," Kathryn said, mutedly, her face still buried in her knees. "We have each other. Sarah said that was always the most important thing. That we have each other." And with that she began to weep softly.

Mick moved in between them on the ground. He sat atop a few jagged pieces of debris. The pain reminded him that he was still there, in the present. He put his right arm around Nate and his left around Kathryn. He pulled them in to his body as tightly as he could and closed his eyes. A family bond, while intangible, was something powerful enough to see them through the worst of times.

Children were not the next logical step after marriage. Mick was sure that was how many married couples saw it. Because that was how he'd seen it initially. But after having children, he'd realized they were not a logical step, but rather the ultimate gift. Their smiles, which unfortunately were fewer and farther between nowadays, could heal his pains in an instant. And their pure souls gave him reason to hope for a better tomorrow. They showed him how it felt to be unequivocally loved. It was for those reasons, and a million others, that Mick would force them to see the light no matter how dark it became.

Mick squeezed Kathryn a bit tighter. "You're right, sweetie. We do have each other." He kissed the top of her head. "But I can't sugarcoat this, guys. This is a bad situation." He looked over at the black ratty tarp that hid Sarah's body. "Losing Sarah …" He gulped to push back down the feelings that so desperately wanted to show themselves. Saying those words made it so permanent.

He continued. "Sarah will always be a member of our family. And just like Mom, we'll never forget her." Kathryn looked up at him. Her eyes were red and puffy from a night of crying. Mick took his hand from around her back and pointed to his head. "They live up here now, in our memories, our dreams. That is something that can never be taken away." Kathryn's quivering lips tried and failed to form a smile.

"That's great, Dad," Nate said, now looking him in the eyes. "But seriously, what are we going to do now?"

"We'll figure that out together, Nate."

Nate looked away, put his head against the wall, and sighed. Everyone dealt with pain in different ways. Nate felt Sarah's loss just as heavily as everyone else. Mick understood that this was simply his way of dealing with things for now.

"I love you both more than words could do justice. You don't deserve this pain. And I wish more than anything that I could take it away." He gave them each a kiss on the head. "I promise you that we will make it through this."

Mick stood. "Can I have everyone's attention, please?" The words just seemed to come out. They sounded so businesslike, as if he were about to begin some bimonthly sales meeting. Mick had no idea what to say, but he knew something needed to be said. The herd needed unity.

The group members stopped whatever they were doing and turned to face Mick.

Mick paused and looked at each of them. He then gathered his feelings, the ones he could grasp at the moment, and said, "Sarah is gone. Our home is gone. There is nothing we can do to change either of those things. And that sucks. It just sucks." He looked down at the tarp over Sarah. "Sarah certainly didn't deserve to die, especially in the way she did. And I can't tell you how deeply I will miss her. How we all will miss her." He looked back from the tarp, more resolute to stick all of this back in the universe's face. "But we can't dwell on the things we can't control. You know as well as I do that this world doesn't allow for that anymore. So what we need to do is concentrate on us. We are all a family and have been for a while now. Grieving is important. To remember is even more so. We will push on. We will survive. And we will do it together as we always have."

"We're with you, Mick," Greg said. "Always have been. Always will be."

The rest of them agreed in their own ways.

Once he got the words out, a sort of finality

came over him. It was now time to move on, to find something in a world with nothing to offer. Then it rushed back into his mind, as if Sarah's ghost pushed it there. The red box. The inoculation to the virus. He reached into his pack and removed the box. He unfolded the letter and read it again.

We will be in touch shortly after you have inoculated yourselves.

He did not understand how they would be in touch, or who they even were, but the herd was out of alternatives. He realized the group needed to make a difficult choice. And now was the time to do it.

He turned to the group and held the red box in his hand. "I hadn't given this much more thought because of everything that's been going on. But now." He paused. He glanced over at the tarp again. It would do them no good to wallow in despair. Sarah would not have wanted it that way. "I think we should inject ourselves."

"Mick," Greg said, "I still don't think that is such a good idea."

"I understand your reservations, Greg. I share the same ones. But the note specifically said that they would get in contact with us once we had inoculated ourselves."

"Anyone could have written that note, Mick," Greg said.

"I know," Mick said, nodding. "But this note wasn't written. It's printed, as Chester pointed out. And that means there are things that exist that we thought didn't. I think we have to take our chances on this one."

"Like I said before, if they can print, then they have some form of power," Sandeep said. He hadn't said anything since Sarah had died. "I agree with Mick."

"Yes. Things like power," Mick said, nodding his head. It was good to hear Deep's voice again.

"It doesn't feel right, man," Greg said. "Can't they pick us up, or whatever they plan on doing, and then give us the choice to inject some blue stuff into our veins?"

Mick shrugged. "I don't think we have much say in the matter."

"It's a leap of faith," Chester said, appearing from the back of the room. "Sometimes we must all make decisions that make us feel uneasy at the time."

Greg said, "So you're okay with putting that stuff in your body?"

"Not necessarily," Chester said, slowly lowering himself onto a small pile of rubble. He took the Bible from beneath his jacket and placed it on his lap. "I realize that most of us that are left on Earth probably have a difficult time believing in a divine being." He patted the Bible twice before looking toward the sky. "But as a man of faith, I believe you must practice what you preach." He grinned, realizing his choice of words rang true. He then rolled up his sleeve. "I will be the first. If this is part of the grand plan, then so be it."

Greg said, "Chester. No."

Chester held up his hand and smiled. "I am fine with this, Greg. I have faith that this is the correct path for us at the moment. Of course, it's not that we have many others."

Mick wanted to question him further. To tell him how silly faith was in the place they now inhabited. But then it occurred to Mick that having faith and being religious were not necessarily intertwined all the time. He could have faith in his decisions, in himself. He could have faith that the world was not out to get them, that maybe by thinking differently, they could alter their lives' trajectories.

Mick removed the hard outer shell and pressed the green button on the injector's side. The device beeped three times before sounding a longer single tone.

A pleasing female voice sounded from the device. "Please press the tip of the auto injector firmly against your skin. Wait for the solid tone to stop before removing the auto injector."

Chester smiled and held his arm out. Mick pointed it toward his own wrist and pressed it firmly against his own skin.

"Mick," Chester said.

"Chester. Thank you for being brave. But I'll be the guinea pig. I simply have to have faith."

Chester nodded very slightly.

Kathryn rushed to her father's side. Her saucer-size eyes were wide with fear.

Mick took his other hand and put it around her. "Don't worry, sweetie. It didn't hurt." He wasn't lying. In fact, he barely felt a thing as the auto injector pushed the blue gel beneath his skin and into his bloodstream.

The rest of the group looked at Mick. Apprehension on some of their faces. Curiosity on the rest.

"Do you feel any different?" Greg asked.

Mick thought and felt before answering. "Not really," he said. He looked down at his wrist. The auto injector left a very faint red circle.

"Device ready," chimed the auto injector. Mick looked around at the group, unsure of what to do or say at the moment. Chester again volunteered his arm. This time Mick obliged. He waited for the long tone before removing it from Chester's arm.

"How do you feel?" Mick asked him.

"Same as you, I suppose." Chester rubbed his arm. "Amazing little device. I didn't feel a thing."

Injecting himself was one thing. But now that he had done the same to Chester, it felt different.

Sandeep was next up. "I guess I'll be number three. I always did like that number."

Mick looked at Sandeep. Doubt clouded his mind.

"What's wrong?" Deep asked.

Mick said nothing. He simply shook his head, lost in a momentary thought. It had all seemed so clear when left with no alternatives. But now he'd taken decisive action. He had leaned on faith, something he had no right to lean on. The gong of guilt rang and reverberated throughout his body.

"Mick?" Sandeep said.

"I'm sorry, Deep. Just having second thoughts, I guess."

Greg said, "It's a little late for those." Mick looked over, alarmed. But Greg smiled. "I'm just giving you a hard time. Listen, you're right. We don't have any choices left. And this seemed to come to us when we needed it most. I'm not saying this is from God"—he looked to Chester quickly and then back to Mick—"or anything besides good fortune. But we have to play the cards we're dealt. And I'm hoping our hand is full of aces and not jokers." Greg then rolled up this sleeve. "I'll go after Sandeep."

"Count me in," Laurel said, rolling up her sleeve, too.

But what about the kids?

"We're in, too," Kathryn said. Nate was now by her side.

"We trust you, Dad. If you think this is what we should do, then so do I," Nate said.

He wanted to faint at that moment. He didn't know if this was what they should do. And the word *trust* seemed a heavy one. Should they trust his instincts? Hell if he knew.

Mick nodded. He thought as he injected each member of his extended family. Every injection felt like he was sentencing each of them to death. When all the injections were finished, Mick carefully placed the hard plastic case back on the outside of the auto injector, closing it slowly to prolong the finality of what he had just done. He then put it back into the red box, which he slipped into his pack.

"So now we just wait?" Nate asked. "Isn't that what the note said?"

"It said that they would be in touch," Mick said.

"What does that mean?" Laurel asked.

Mick said, "I have no idea what it means. If these people ..." Mick paused, trying to remember the name of the group without having to dig out the note.

"The Initiative," Deep interrupted. "I believe that is what they called themselves."

"The Initiative. Right. Thanks, Deep." Mick gave him a quick pat on the shoulder. "Anyway, the gist I get from the note is that they will know when we inject ourselves. So I'm guessing they must have the technology to find us."

"Okay," Greg said. "But who knows how long that will be? And we have nothing left. No water. No food. Nothing."

Mick had the answer to that. "I already gave that some thought. I didn't have time to tell any of you this." He then looked to Chester, who looked back and nodded. "But I found someone when I was out scavenging the other day. His name is Solomon. And he led me to a yellow house near the crucifixion zone. I wasn't able to confirm it, but he told me that there are supplies there."

"Mick," Greg said, startled. "You shouldn't be going around those parts of town without me. You're lucky you made it back alive."

"I wish that wasn't true. But you're right. I was lucky. And stupid for even going there. Unfortunately, that was also where I bumped into that crazy guy that came looking for me yesterday. But what's done is done. And at least something came out of it."

"The Rubble King," Greg said, thinking back. "That guy was an asshole with a capital A."

"That's putting it mildly," Mick said.

"So, we're going back to the house where you saw this guy?" Kathryn asked.

Mick looked at her over his shoulder and nodded reluctantly. Like most of his ideas lately, this one did not seem like the best one on the surface.

"Oh," she said, pondering Mick's response.

"So let's go," Greg said. "Who cares about that guy? We'll take care of it." He cocked his rifle that had been damaged superficially by the storm, but still in working order.

"It won't be that easy. It's not just him and his two buddies that came calling yesterday. You should have seen the look in Solomon's eyes when they showed up at the house. It was fear. Real fear. The kind you can't help but show when you feel it."

"Okay," Laurel said, following along. "Who is

Solomon again?"

"I don't really know anything about him. He doesn't say much. I could tell the world hadn't been kind to him, though."

Nate asked, "Do you think he's one of them?"

"No," Mick said. "I don't think so. He didn't seem to want to leave with them."

"So they took him?" Greg asked.

Mick nodded. "Sort of. He voluntarily left with them. But he didn't want to. I could see it in his eyes. They must be holding something over him."

Mick had no idea just how right he was.

"Let's gather what we can from The Shelter," Mick said. "Anything useful and easy to carry. Once we get that settled, we'll head out for the yellow house."

CHAPTER 21

"See you for the lab meeting tonight?" asked a young woman in the hall as Sid hurriedly rushed by.

"See you there," Sid lied.

He tried to keep as cool as he could on his way out. *Keep calm*, he kept telling himself. *Don't act like anything has changed.* Of course, that was easier said than done. Alex knew the truth. But that was because Sid wanted him to know. He needed him to know. And he trusted Alex. But Sid knew it wasn't as simple as that. He was an integral part of the executive research team. His experience was needed. His ideas and experiments were constantly probed. Phillip would know he had left as soon as he opened the secondary door. And then there was no turning back.

Sid flashed a few more smiles to those he passed in the sterile white hall. He then quickly banked right and into the men's bathroom. No sooner had the door swung shut when the toilet flushed. Followed by broken whistling, as if done through dry lips.

The stall door opened. "Ah, Sid," Phillip said. "I didn't hear you come in."

Of all the people, Sid thought, frozen in the moment. "Ah," he spit out. *Say something.* "I just got here." He realized it was stupid but hoped it would suffice.

Phillip smiled and walked over to the bank of sinks. "I'm sorry about earlier, Sid. No one ever said science was easy." He waved his hand beneath the soap dispenser. It burped out two foamy piles into his hand, which he quickly lathered in the steaming water. "I should have been more open from the start about what I was doing. I have a bad habit of keeping things inside. It was my fault for not clueing you in. And for that, I apologize."

Sid leaned against the stall behind Phillip. His immediate reaction was to debate Phillip, not to let him off that easily. And Sid fully understood that Phillip was trying to tell him what he wanted to hear. Phillip no doubt wanted this to be swept under the rug as quickly as possible. But things had become clearer since finding out about the accelerant. Sid wasn't there for that, however. He'd come there to leave. And what he said now was meaningless.

"It's all right," Sid said. "We're all under a lot of pressure."

Phillip turned off the water. He shook the excess water from his hands and then reached below the paper towel dispenser, which promptly ejected one clean sheet. "I'm glad you aren't angry, Sid," Phillip said as he dried his hands. "It's important we all stay on the same path. You'll see. In the end, what we've done will be celebrated throughout human history. We are on a cusp of a new age."

Sid bit his tongue. Phillip appeared to be bordering on maniacal now. *A new age? Celebrated throughout human history?* This was what power did when put in the wrong hands. It corrupted the already misguided.

"I'll see you at the lab meeting later?" Phillip asked.

"See you there," Sid said again.

Phillip tossed the paper towel in the trash and left, whistling.

Sid closed his eyes and took a breath. That was way too close. And certainly not what he had expected to find waiting for him in the bathroom. But it was good in a sense. It took him out of his comfort zone. And that was where he needed to be once outside the protected walls of The Facility.

He went to the farthest stall against the bathroom's back wall. He put his bag down, which thankfully Phillip had not questioned. Why he needed his bag while using the bathroom was not something he could answer on the fly. He then removed a small clear plastic case with different size screwdrivers in it. For all the high-tech gadgets located within the walls of The Facility, the plumbing maintenance was located behind a rather archaic piece of painted plywood, affixed by six screws. The only reason Sid even knew about this was because one of his source pipes for clean water ran through this wall. A leak had ultimately led him there a little less than a year ago.

After he removed each screw, Sid would pause and listen. The last thing he needed was more company. The sixth screw fell into his palm and he pushed the plywood off to the side. A labyrinth of pipes was now exposed, twisting in on itself, weaving and bending out of sight far into the wall. Below the pipes was a grate. This was what he had come for. The maintenance crew who had been summoned to fix the leak after Sid tracked it down had told him that it led to the boiler room two stories below The Facility's main level. He had never envisioned needing to go down there until now.

Four more screws and that grate came off. He then lowered himself into the opening. He listened again. Thankfully no one had to heed the call of nature while he was doing this. He wasn't about to wait around for that to change. Sid slid the plywood back over the opening the best he could. He then slid the grate back over his head.

The climb down the narrow ladder was quick. The underbelly of The Facility knocked and clanked to the point where he could not hear himself think. However, he did not need to think. He needed to act. He had memorized The Facility's schematics before even attempting this. He understood there would be others down there, mechanical engineers, namely. But they would be few and far between. The maintenance crew was not nearly the size of the research team.

Down a long pipe-filled tunnel he went.

Yellow banners that read "steam" lined his right side, white "sterile" was written in the blue banners on his left. This was the way out.

Whoever designed The Facility had taken its evacuation very seriously. The obvious way out was through the two large main doors that kept the outside out and the inside in. They were rarely opened and also in plain sight. And when they were opened, it was always under proper procedural guidelines with a full security detail. But what if those doors malfunctioned? That was a question apparently posed and answered by way of this second emergency exit. The one Sid now neared.

The hallway ended abruptly and emptied into another one that ran perpendicular. He slowly peeked from behind a gathering of valves. Seeing no one, he darted quietly out and to the left. At the end of this hall stood a menacing door, two stories in height and large enough to drive a truck through.

This was it. As soon as Sid put in his exit code, others would know right away. The Facility's security system was sure to rat him out. He again checked behind him, nervous about the whole damn situation. Closing his eyes, he made sure this was what he wanted. By doing it he would permanently change his life, and most likely for the worse. But would it really? he wondered. He certainly could not live here any longer. Not knowing now what Phillip had hidden from them all. So there was really no choice to be made. It had already been made for him. He was just speeding it along.

Sid reached out and entered his twelve-digit exit code. *What if my code doesn't work?* He hadn't thought of that. How could he overlook something so obvious? What if Phillip was one step ahead of him already?

There was only one way to know.

He pushed Enter.

"Disengage lock?" appeared on the small security monitor next to the keypad. A green *yes* flashed next to the more foreboding red *no*.

His bag began to beep. He reached in and removed the mobile tracking device he had "borrowed" from Phillip's lab. The last remaining large green dot blinked several times and vanished. It was quickly replaced by a small blue dot. One by one more of the smaller dots blinked into existence, seven in all.

Dammit. I'm too late.

His heart sank. This meant that the last group had injected themselves with the accelerant. His mind pleaded with him to hit the flashing red *no* on the screen. It would do him no good to leave now. There was still time to salvage what he had here. But his gut told him otherwise. His dusty sense of morality made him aware that there was always hope.

With a shaking hand, Sid reached out and tapped *yes*. Flashing yellow lights burst into action.

The walls became bathed in their light. Surprisingly there were no sirens or audible alarms, just the lights and undoubtedly a security warning to those that monitored such things. The door's strong steel pins slid free, and the door swung open. Sid looked behind him one last time before vanishing into the darkness beyond.

CHAPTER 22

The storm that passed through the city had wreaked havoc on the old police station. The already crumbling roof had caved in midway through the storm, taking with it Solomon's only way out of the station undetected. When the roof collapsed, it also destroyed King's prized food storage room. King's men had tried to dig out what they could, but it proved to be a futile effort. For each brick or bucket of dust they removed, two more would take its place. This put King in a particularly sour mood.

"Clyde," King yelled from his faux throne. "Where the hell are you?"

The main room of the police station had survived the storm without much damage. One of the boarded windows had burst open when it was at its most ferocious, spilling piles of dust beneath it until the plebes were ordered to fix it. As such, the room was cloudier with dirt than usual. This, too, made King angry. He liked things to be as tidy as possible given the conditions, and now his base of operations was an utter mess.

"Clyde!"

Clyde came scampering from the back of the building, rubbing his eyes.

"Didn't you hear me calling?" King asked.

"What were you doing?"

Clyde did not answer right away.

King knew from the look on his face that he was trying to formulate a lie, but his simple mind lacked the power to do so quickly enough.

"Spit it out," King commanded.

"I was in the back," Clyde said.

"Doing what?"

"Um, cleaning."

King lurched forward with catlike precision and quickness. He smacked Clyde across the face with the back side of his hand. When Clyde looked back up, he did it again, harder.

Clyde was not so quick to look back this time. His lip bled and began to puff where King's largest ring had met its mark.

King then reached out and pulled Clyde in closer. "You are lying to me. And I do not appreciate being lied to, especially by my dear son. So I will ask again." He inched Clyde closer. So close that he could see his own reflection through the haze of Clyde's sport goggles. "What were you doing?"

"I was sleeping," Clyde said, wincing.

King held him still. He let Clyde stew a bit in fear before releasing his grip. Clyde stumbled backward and off the faux throne, tripping over his own feet and onto his back. King then readjusted his rings from the displacement that Clyde's face had caused. A rude imposition to say the least. He walked past Clyde, stirring his own thoughts, before stopping at the far wall.

"You sleep when I tell you to sleep. Do you understand that?"

Clyde nodded quickly.

"Now get up."

Clyde stood. The trickle of blood dripped down his face and made a few wet marks on his dirty shirt.

"We have a problem, Clyde. While you were sleeping," King said, allowing it to sink in for an extra second, "we lost our supplies." It then occurred to him that they had just moved the new supplies from the elderly couple's home. He hated wasted energy. And that entire day had been wasted.

"I'm sorry, King."

"I don't need you to be sorry," King said. "What I need is to find a new supply, and to do so quickly. I have had a feeling for a while now that the boy may know where to find one. I think he is hiding something from us."

Clyde perked up a bit.

"Go see what he knows," King said. He turned his back to Clyde and began to walk out of the room. "Use whatever means necessary to get me the truth."

CHAPTER 23

The first thing Sid did after exiting The Facility was toss his white lab coat. He stuck out among the grime like a bright marshmallow on a bed of dark chocolate. His intention was to draw as little attention to himself as possible. And a rogue scientist seemed to do the exact opposite. He went so far as to smear dirt across his face and rip a few small holes in the flannel shirt he had stolen from one of his colleague's lockers. This would, he hoped, allow him to travel freer on the outside, blend in more with the people they had ignored for so long.

He ogled the destruction that surrounded him. Pristine white walls and organically grown food had been his life for the past ten years. Sid had not been outside since shortly after Colossus, taking some readings that the team would later use as a baseline. And even then it was not for long, just long enough to do what he had to and return. But now he was in the midst of it. He'd thrust himself headfirst into the very world he had been ignoring all these past years. And what he saw saddened him deeply. The guilt he had felt earlier became magnified.

He climbed over toppled concrete support columns and through walls of bent rebar, all the while thinking about the people who had lived in the outside world night and day since Impact. He had not spent an overabundance of time thinking about them until that point. Out of sight, out of mind, he figured. But now everything was in sight and clearer than it had been in a while.

The wind gusted quickly. Sid turned his back to it to try and shield his face. This was not the wind he remembered. It shifted quickly again, like it had a mind for mischief, reversing its direction and blowing directly on Sid's face again. His open mouth gathered a light coating of dust before instinct shut it. He spit, gagged. The wind soon stopped. Sid coughed the remaining particles from his mouth. Punishment, he figured. The world was punishing him now that he was within its grasp, no longer safe within The Facility's walls.

He reached into his bag and removed the tracking device. A few button presses brought the large red dot that he needed to find. He tapped the red dot, which then zoomed in to seven blue dots. *Good*, he thought. Same number as before. At least none of them had had any sort of adverse reaction and expired immediately. But did it really matter? Phillip said the patients had five or six days after injection before they died. Sid still had time. But what exactly did he have time for? To find them? Then what? There was no cure for CV-1. And now these unsuspecting people had hastened their own deaths. And he was going to be the one to tell them that.

Ahead of him, past a line of cars that appeared frozen in a permanent traffic jam, stood a small group of people huddled closely together. He checked his scanner. There were no dots where these people were. Meaning they had not been included in the initial groups that were given the accelerant. Phillip had been careful when selecting his initial groups. At the time, Sid and his colleagues had believed these specific people were chosen because they offered a group mentality with characteristics that Phillip thought would be best suited to administering the serum. Now that he knew the truth, Sid figured Phillip simply chose the groups at random with no true value to his selections. All the initial groups appeared to be the ones closest to The Facility. It would make things easier for Phillip.

The group of four people kept their eyes locked on Sid as soon as they noticed him. While he'd done his best to dirty himself up, he was a far cry from their ragged appearances. He made his way through more of the rubble, tripping over a few fragments here and there, his legs not used to anything but flat polished floors. He looked over at the group again and then quickly looked away. They appeared cautiously curious of him. He had not given much thought to his own defense in his haste to leave The Facility. It hadn't even occurred to him. And the more he thought, the more things he realized he'd failed to take into account before leaving. But once he had found that Phillip had sullied his principles, nothing else seemed to matter but trying everything he could to make it right.

The blue dots remained stationary on the tracker. And thankfully they were not more than a couple of miles from The Facility. That was pure luck that the ones closest to him also happened to be the group that injected themselves last. It was kind of a silver lining, if he looked really hard for one. He wished he could gather all the dots on his screen and tell them all what had happened and how they had been deceived. But he did not have time for that. Sadly, he would not be able to save them all. He didn't know if he would be able to save any at all.

Covering those two miles seemed to take far longer than he had envisioned it would have. But he finally made it to the base of a small hill. He checked the screen again to confirm. Seven small blue dots. They were somewhere up there all right. He placed the tracker back in his bag and began his ascent.

Even though the air was cool, and a strange type of frost mixed with the unending dirt and dust on the ground, he found himself sweating very lightly. It was nervousness; he knew that much. Now that these dots were about to transform into people, the situation became all the more real. How the hell was he going to explain to them what he needed to? *Hey, I'm from a secret place that infected you to speed up your death?* There was no way around it. He was the devil's messenger.

At the top of the hill he turned toward the closest building. It seemed to be nothing more than a pile of steel and concrete, with large shards of glass sprinkled about. *This can't be the place*, he thought. He pulled the tracker out again. This was the place all right. He was directly on top of the red dot. He tapped the dot and six blue dots appeared directly below him. The seventh appeared to be on the move. He looked around to try and make sense of what he was seeing.

The door to The Shelter slammed shut.

Sid froze in place. He squinted through the hazy air, toward where the sound emanated from. The outline of someone become crisper, less of a silhouette and more of a human form. It looked like a woman.

"Hello," Sid said. He put the tracker away and walked toward the shelter.

Laurel turned around. She said nothing, but rather eyed Sid with distrust.

"I'm a friend," Sid said.

"That's funny," Laurel said. "I don't have many friends now. And those that I do, I tend to remember. And I don't remember you." She inched back toward the door leading underground.

Sid laughed nervously. "Sorry. I mean, I'm here to help."

Laurel looked at him. "Help with what?"

Sid thought about it. He thought of the note that Phillip had sent out. It would put him in company he no longer chose to be with, but he hoped they would recognize the meaning behind it.

Sid said, "I'm from The Initiative. And we have some things we urgently need to discuss."

CHAPTER 24

Solomon sat hunched in a corner of his cell during the storm. They had thrown him in there so quickly when the hard winds began to blow that they had completely forgot to shackle him. Not that it mattered much. Having his hands free simply gave him a place to rest his head while riding out the storm. But it was nice to not be bound.

He thought for sure the walls were going to fall in on themselves when the winds were at their worst. The dust was forced through the barred windows of his cell and into a sloping brown mound. Somewhere, in the back of his mind, he'd hoped the roof would cave in and pancake its way down until they were all dead. It would solve so many problems in so little time.

"Get up, boy," shouted Clyde as he stumbled down the hallway.

He fumbled for his keys like he always did. Even if Clyde had ten fingers, it would take him just as long. A small-brained man doing a small-brained task. He then unlocked the cell and stepped in.

Solomon, however, was not in the mood. He stood as Clyde neared, unwilling to relent today. There would be no beatings, no harassment. Clyde had picked the wrong day to mess with him.

Clyde picked up his pace suddenly and pushed Solomon against the wall.

"King wants to know where you been hiding your food?"

Solomon said nothing. He knew his silence said more than his words ever could.

Clyde kneed Solomon in the balls. "I asked you a question, boy."

Not a flinch. Solomon was prepared. No matter what Clyde chose to do to him, Solomon would not give in. He was adamant.

"B-bump y-you lip, d-did you," Solomon said with a smile, looking at the bloodied lip King had recently given him.

Clyde went to knee him again, but Solomon shifted his legs to protect himself. That made Clyde angrier. He pushed Solomon up against the wall again, banging his head against the brick.

"Where's the food, boy? Tell me."

And then something just snapped inside Solomon. Today was no different than any of the days prior. The brewing seed of anger had just grown too large to stay contained. It needed to blossom regardless of Solomon's desire. It burst into the moment with a ferocity.

Solomon grabbed Clyde by his shirt, under Clyde's own grip on his shirt, and pushed him enough for Clyde to skip back a step. Clyde's face took on a look of surprise. This was the first time Solomon hadn't just accepted the beating. This was uncharted territory for him. Territory that felt so right. Solomon then ran full speed across the cell and into the opposite wall. He rammed Clyde against the brick. Debris spit into the air around them in a puff of disobedience.

Clyde sank to the ground with his back to the wall. "You'll regret that," he said, shaking off the cobwebs that banging his head against the wall had introduced. He then stood and sneered at Solomon before darting back in his direction.

Solomon stood fast, unwavering. When Clyde was within arm's reach, Solomon picked him up by the neck with his unusual strength, off the floor so his feet had an inch of air below them.

Clyde's face was a mix of confusion and fright. "What—are you—doing?" he asked in short bursts. His face turned from his typical pasty pink to a dark purplish red. He tried in vain to pry Solomon's hands free.

Solomon stared straight into Clyde's eyes. He then leaned in closer, their noses almost touching. Solomon had been waiting for this day for what seemed like forever. He did not care about a single thing at that moment. The rest of the world, his jail cell, his mind, all went white with rage. It was only the two of them now. The filthy cockroach that slithered on King's every command and Solomon. The tormentor and the tormented. And it felt glorious to know that he had finally taken the upper hand.

"He'll," Clyde said softly. "Kill." His words carried little tone to them, more of whispered air.

"Her."

And then, just as quickly as he had picked him up, Solomon dropped Clyde to the floor with a thump.

Clyde grabbed his throat and gasped for air.

Solomon simply stared down at him. He felt like that was it. He had made up his mind that Clyde would die by his hands this day. His putrid life would end, and the world would rejoice. But as Solomon stared into Clyde's hate-filled eyes, he knew he could not give in to his emotions. Clyde was right. If Solomon killed him, then King would kill Ms. Stella.

Clyde adjusted his goggles and slopped over a patch of his greasy hair that had become lodged under them. He then stood, but at a distance from Solomon.

"You'll pay for that, boy," Clyde said.

Solomon took a step toward him. Clyde backed away a step. For as "stupid" as King and his goons thought Solomon was, he knew full well that the cycle of torment had been changed in that instant. Solomon would no longer allow himself to be beaten. And he felt as though Clyde also now realized that.

"What's taking so long?" King asked, appearing from the darkness outside the cell. "I gave you a simple task."

Clyde looked over, still red in the face. Much to Solomon's surprise, he said nothing of what just happened. He'd figured Clyde would love nothing more than to tattle on him. But at the same time it would make Clyde look weak in King's eyes. It was a double-edged sword that played to Solomon's advantage.

"We were just getting to that," Clyde said, rubbing his red neck.

King turned to Solomon. "Well, boy? Where is the food you've been storing away like a little squirrel?"

Solomon shook his head, but he already knew that his eyes gave him away.

King smiled. He moved closer to Solomon, his lips next to Solomon's left ear. He whispered, "There are worse things than death. Would you like me to show you?" King waited for a response but none came. "Actually, maybe we could start on your little friend in the basement? Would you like to see that?"

"N-no," Solomon said, anger lacing his words. "D-d-don't t-t-touch—"

Clyde interrupted, "Spit it out already."

King spun around and backhanded Clyde across the face. "You are working my last nerve today." He held up his index finger and turned back to Solomon. "What happens next is up to you. I will tell you this once, though: I am not playing games right now. Where are the food and supplies you have been gathering on your little"—he paused—"excursions from this castle?"

Solomon thought for a second. He had to tell King what he wanted to know. Clyde was one thing; King, however, was another.

"Y-yellow house," Solomon said.

"What yellow house?" King asked.

Clyde then cleared his throat. King turned to him suddenly, forcing Clyde to flinch.

"The house we found him at the other day was yellow," Clyde offered.

"Ah, yes. The house where we met our new friend, Mick." King stopped and thought. "So that's what you were doing there, boy. Maybe you're not as dumb as I thought." He then tapped him twice on his cheek with his palm and waved for Clyde to follow him out the door.

Clyde did as requested. He locked the door behind him and sneered at Solomon. He then made a throat-slashing sign and vanished into the darkness.

Solomon was not done with him yet. That was a certainty.

CHAPTER 25

Phillip gathered the entire scientific team in the largest of The Facility's conference rooms. He stood at the front of the room, behind a cherry wood podium, and stared out furiously as the last of the lab coats entered the room. He signaled to one of The Facility's security personnel to close the door in the rear of the room.

"May I have everyone's attention please?"

The room hushed in an instant. They had all been talking about Sid leaving. Word had spread quicker than Phillip had hoped it would. He had not had a chance to squelch it in time. So now he would need to address what had transpired head-on and hope that it ended here.

"As some of you may know," Phillip said, "one of our colleagues has decided to leave the security of The Facility. I do not know his reasoning. Though to say that reason played a part in his decision would seem like folly at this point. There is no logical reason to leave The Facility. What is outside these walls is nothing more than a painful reminder of what the meteorites destroyed." He looked around at the faces that stared back at him intently. "As you all know, we rarely open the doors for fear of contamination."

There were a few hushed giggles that died

down too quickly to tell where they came from. But Phillip knew what they were laughing at. They had already been contaminated. Thankfully, to his benefit, the people within these walls still believed the virus was brought in from the outside because of poor air filtration. If they found out the truth, it would be sure to spark rioting. Or worse, a lynching.

He waited for the room to fall silent before continuing. "Once a person voluntarily leaves The Facility, they surrender all rights to return. Dr. Roth made his decision. He must now abide by the consequences. I will not further risk the stability of The Facility over egregiously wayward personal decisions."

The room remained quiet until he attempted to wrap up his pleasingly short spiel. "Very good," he said. "Let's all get back—"

"Dr. Jones," interrupted a woman near the middle of the room. She stood before being addressed. "I've known Sid for years. He doesn't strike me as the type to just up and leave for no reason."

This was exactly what Phillip had hoped to avoid.

"Yes," Phillip answered. "Dr. Barron, is it?"

The woman nodded. She smiled slightly, seemingly pleased that Phillip remembered her name. That in itself was a surprisingly difficult task. The people inside The Facility never changed. But there were enough of them that he had fits trying to remember everyone. And that was only because he had to. If given the choice, they would all wear numbers across their lab coats so he could refer to them more easily. He had far too many important things to remember. Names should not have to be one of them.

Phillip continued. "This has come as a shock to me, as well. Sid, as most of you know, was on my executive science team. I relied on him for a great many things." That was not totally accurate, but he figured it was best to play up his relationship so he did not appear to be in any way associated with Sid's decision. He would plant a seed of doubt in everyone's head to prevent any further escapes. "His departure greatly weakens our ability to find a cure for CV-1. I had the greatest amount of respect for Dr. Roth. But he has selfishly left us all in our time of need. I don't think I need to remind any of you how important it is that we find a cure?"

He again looked over his audience. They looked at one another. Some nodding, others whispering.

"But Dr. Jones," continued Dr. Barron. "How did Sid even get out of The Facility without you knowing?" She looked around the room. "Actually, without any of us knowing? It's hard to miss the doors when they open."

That question burned him. He pursed his lips to prevent a flurry of anger from escaping. How dare she question him? Who was she? A nobody, that's who. Not even recognizable beneath his shadow of greatness.

He composed himself. "There is a second exit from The Facility located beneath us. But before anyone gets any ideas, I have put both the main doors and the secondary exit that Dr. Roth used to es—" He caught himself, pausing for a moment. "Both doors are now under administrative lockdown."

"Lockdown?" someone said from the audience. There were more murmurs, louder this time. Less caring of who heard what.

Phillip held his hands up to quiet them down. "Please. Everyone. It is simply a term used by the system."

"So we are free to go if we choose, right?" said someone else.

Phillip looked to see who was saying what, but the stationary audience had begun to shift in their seats as if a tide of anger had started coming in.

"Well," Phillip said, "not exactly."

"What does that mean, Dr. Jones? Not exactly?"

"It means the doors will not open for the immediate future."

"How long is that?" someone else said.

"Until order is restored within our walls," Phillip said.

"You mean until you feel like it," another voice said loudly so everyone could hear.

"People, people," Phillip said. "Do I need to

remind you of the dangers outside? Why must you fight to leave? I am merely concerned for your well-being."

"It's called freedom, Phillip." This time it was Alex that spoke up. Another of his trusted group of executive scientists. "And once you take it away, it's all anyone will want."

Phillip sneered at Alex. How dare he join the masses in revolt?

"No one has taken anything from anyone," Phillip said.

"Then we are free to leave?" Alex said.

Phillip found himself getting angrier by the minute. Who were these people to question him? He provided them a life the rest of this ragged world would kill for. Selfish bastards, the lot of them.

"Is that what you want?" Phillip asked angrily. "Do you want to leave, Alex? To eke out a miserable existence while you wait to die? You should know better than most what little remains outside our walls."

"You did not answer my question, Phillip," Alex said. "Are we free to leave if we so choose?"

The room fell silent.

"Yes, Alex," Phillip said. "Of course you are free to leave. This is not a prison."

Alex took off his white lab coat and let it fall to the floor. He then picked up a bag by his feet.

Phillip laughed. "Yes, Alex. Very funny. You actually had me there."

"I'm not joking, Phillip. You say we are free to go. Prove it."

The rage within Phillip boiled his blood to the point where he felt he may explode from the pressure. *Insolent idiot!*

Alex simply continued to look at Phillip, waiting for his answer.

"If that's what you want," Phillip said.

"Yes. That's what I want."

The room broke into a flurry of conversation. Some tried to get Alex's attention, but he remained focused on Phillip. He slung his bag over his shoulder and headed toward the door to the conference room, where he was stopped by one of the security personnel. They both then looked back at Phillip.

This was it. Alex was truly leaving. Phillip did not have time to think of the ramifications of this move. He only knew that he had been put in a position where he could not possibly win. If he denied Alex his request to leave, then he would be seen as a liar, and everyone else within The Facility would know they were not free to go. But if he let Alex walk, then others would be sure to follow. He could not have a mass exodus. Not now. Not when he so desperately needed to find the cure to erase the mistakes that were made.

Phillip nodded to the security officer. None of the options seemed good, but he had to choose one.

The uniformed man stepped aside and let Alex leave. The entire room watched as he walked by the long wall of glass and toward the two enormous doors at the end of the hall. Alex stopped when he reached the doors and waited.

"If you'll excuse me," Phillip said, dashing from the room. He walked purposefully down the hall toward Alex. He was still in plain sight of everyone in the room and therefore needed to remain tactful for appearances' sake. But there was no one close enough to hear what he had to say.

"You have a lot of balls, Alex," Phillip said, stopping next to him. "After all I've done for you."

Alex said, "I know what you've done, Phillip."

Phillip had expected a fight. For Alex to lash out. That was his intent. To show that Alex was a loose cannon and that he was the collected one simply trying to help fulfill a colleague's desire. But what Alex said made his legs weak. What did Alex know? He prayed it was the one thing that no one but himself could ever find out.

"And what is it you think that you know?" Phillip asked, trying to keep his composure. "I'm curious."

Alex smiled at Phillip. He then looked to the large doors.

Phillip paused. "Very well." He then walked over to the access panel to the right of the doors. He punched in his code.

A female voice said, "Access restricted to Dr. Phillip Jones. Please enter executive unlock code."

Phillip waited. He turned back from the panel. He caught sight of the conference room as he did.

The wall of glass was stacked with scientists and the like as they peered out. A few had spilled into the hall behind them, trying to get closer to add audio to the drama taking place.

Alex walked closer to Phillip. He said, "Others will find out what you've done. And when they do, they may not choose to be so passive."

Phillip kept his eyes locked on Alex for another few seconds before turning his attention back to the keypad. He angrily tapped the twelve-digit unlock code.

The female voice sounded again. "Access granted."

The same yellowish lights that traced the secondary set of doors that Sid had left through began to flash. The metal pins slid from inside the walls to the recesses within the large doors. A moment later the two doors parted, swinging inward slowly.

"Have a nice life," Phillip said with a smirk.

Alex walked out of The Facility without uttering another word.

Phillip turned to the crowd that had gathered. "Anyone else want to leave? The doors are open. Now is your chance to test your freedom." He waited and watched. People looked around for who was next. No one volunteered. Some even shrank away from their positions in the hallway, fearful, no doubt, that they would be pushed out for looking at Phillip the wrong way.

"Very well," Phillip said. He entered his code

again and watched as the doors closed and locked.
He hoped his secret had just walked out the door.

CHAPTER 26

"Mick," Laurel said. She exited the stairway and into what was left of the shelter. "We have a visitor."

Mick looked up from his position on the floor. His kids had fallen asleep against him, Kathryn to his left and Nate sloppily to his right. With Sarah's death still fresh on everyone's minds, and the fact that soon they would be leaving the only home they'd known for the past ten years, he figured it was best not to wake them.

The Herd decided it was imperative to find food and supplies. With all of theirs lost to the storm, it had to be one of their first priorities. But they were all worn thin in every aspect possible. When even the slightest chance for rest came, they needed to take it. Mick understood that. So he wasn't about to take it back from his children.

He carefully slipped out from between them. He then walked the few steps toward Laurel and their new visitor. The confusion he felt seeing someone new must have been evident on his face. Laurel offered the answer before Mick had a chance to form the question.

"This is Dr. Roth," Laurel said.

"Sid, actually. Please just call me Sid."

Laurel looked at him and then back to Mick. A

smile cut her face. "He's from The Initiative."

Mick perked up. "That was quick."

Sid seemed confused. "I'm sorry. Quick for what?"

"Your note. It said that you would be in contact once we had injected ourselves. We just did that a couple of hours ago. That's a pretty good turnaround time in my opinion." And he was overjoyed to know they existed in the first place. "And it couldn't come at a better time." He looked around the destroyed shelter and at the tarp.

Sid took a breath. "We need to talk."

"We are talking."

"No," Sid said. "I mean, we have something important to talk about. The reason I'm here."

The others heard that and slowly gathered around.

Mick said, "Everyone. This is Sid. He is from The Initiative. That group from the note. He has something he needs to discuss with us." Mick turned to Sid. "The floor is all yours." What little of the floor could still be seen, anyway.

Sid said, "As I was telling ..." He paused and looked to Laurel.

"Laurel," she said.

Sid smiled. "As I was telling Laurel here, I *was* part of the group known as The Initiative."

"Was?" Mick questioned.

"Yes," Sid said, nodding once. "I was part of the group up until a few hours ago. Our group was formed by the United States government, in secret, to be their proxy after Impact. We were to study the aftereffects of the impacts on the Earth. And maintain a scientific chain of command in the eventuality the world was impacted on a global scale. Once the damage had been determined, we were to outline restoration projects to get things such as the power grid and the Internet back to where they were prior to Impact. But no one ever thought the Earth would become this." He looked around. "Not in a million years did anyone envision the meteorites doing this kind of damage."

Greg said, "So now that there is no government, who calls the shots?"

"Dr. Phillip Jones. He is the man in charge of The Facility."

"The what now?" Greg asked.

"The Facility. That is where the Initiative is located. I know. It's a bunch of silly code names. But the intent was anything but silly. The Facility was initially built as a research center before anyone knew about the meteorites. It was the perfect repurposing at the time since The Facility already had a lot of the equipment we needed."

"Is this facility a submarine base?" Mick asked, remembering what Sarah had said the other day. Sadness then swept over him as he thought about their last conversation. He missed her terribly already. But this wasn't the time to grieve. "And does it have some kind of nuclear power or something?" He thought that was what Sarah had said.

"No submarines," Sid said. "The Facility is landlocked. And not far from here. But it does have a large-scale prototype fusion generator. It has worked surprisingly well since Impact."

"Wait," Sandeep said. "How far is not far?"

"About five miles from here."

"Five miles?" Mick said. "Wow." To know there was indeed a secret base a mere five miles from them all this time put his thoughts into overdrive. All those times they needed something and it was right there. Then came the animosity. They had gone without for so long because, in their minds, there was no choice in the matter. But to know there were others a few miles away that lived the life that had been taken from them was infuriating.

"So this fusion reactor means you have power, right?" Laurel asked.

"Yes," Sid said.

Laurel processed that. She asked, "Well, what else do you have?"

"The Facility is fully equipped with a great deal of what the world had pre-Impact."

"Like refrigerators?" Laurel asked.

"And running water?" Mick added.

"Yes," Sid said. "We have both."

"Indoor plumbing? Heat?"

Sid nodded. "Yes. We have all of that, too."

"It appears we made the correct decision, Mick," Chester said. "All that worrying about nothing." He looked to the sky. "Thank the Lord! He has come to us in our time of desperation."

Mick smiled back at Chester. It did appear that way. Sarah passing and the shelter being destroyed were two of the worst things that could have ever happened to them. But now it appeared that fate had finally smiled on them.

Mick said, "So when do we leave for this 'Facility'?"

Sid took a large breath. "That's what I came to talk to you about. No one was ever going to come and get you," he said.

"But the note—"

"Most of that note was a lie."

"I'm still not following you," Mick said. "You are from The Initiative, right? And you did come after we injected ourselves like the note said you would."

"Yes. I *was* part of the Initiative. And I did come after you injected yourselves. I tried like hell to get here before you did it, though."

The room fell silent. They waited for Sid to elaborate.

Sid took a breath. "What you injected into yourselves was not an inoculation. The gel was an accelerant." He held up his hands quickly. "But I assure you that I was deceived just like you."

"What, exactly, is it accelerating?" Sandeep asked.

"You have the CV-1 virus. We all do. It's not just the people on the outside. Everyone inside The

Facility has it, too. Our air purifiers failed to protect us."

"That doesn't answer the question," Mick said. "What does this blue gel do?"

"It speeds the virus in our systems."

Greg shot past Mick and pinned Sid up against the wall. He got nose to nose with him. "Tell me why I shouldn't kill you right now." He then turned to Mick. "I told you that stuff was bad news, Mick. I told you."

Sid said, "I left The Facility as soon as I found out what was really going on. We were told the accelerant was a test to search for an immunity to the virus. I was lied to just like you. I'm just like you."

"You are nothing like us," Greg said.

"So did you bring an antidote to get this gel out of our systems?" Sandeep asked.

"There is no antidote. There is no cure for the virus. That's what we were searching for."

Nate and Kathryn were now awake and listening. The enormity of what Sid told them hit home when Mick saw their faces. He'd injected something into his kids that was going to basically speed up their deaths. His worst fear materialized in an instant. Done by his own hands.

"How long do we all have?" Mick asked through his clenched jaw. He was angrier than he could remember ever being. To play with his life was one thing. But to play with his kids went beyond infuriating. But he knew it was misguided to unleash his anger now, especially on some scrawny scientist with a newfound sense of obligation. Just when he'd thought things had turned for the better, they couldn't have possibly gone any worse.

"Like I said, I tried to get here before you injected yourselves," Sid said before being cut off by Mick.

"How long do we have?" Mick asked.

"At most, five days. But it's probably closer to four at this point."

Mick sank to the floor, defeated. *Four days?* Everything he had worked so diligently to maintain over the years had just been destroyed.

"I didn't have enough time to study the accelerant," Sid said. "As soon as I found out what it really was, I left and came here. I wanted to stop you from injecting it. I promise you." Sid looked around, panicked. "I know it doesn't mean much, but I left everything I knew behind to try and help. Please believe me."

Greg shoved Sid one more time against the wall, grunted, and then let him go. He punched the concrete wall and walked away toward the tarp.

"Are we going to die, Daddy?" Kathryn asked. Her face had become pale. And her legs wobbled. Nate reached out and grabbed her tight.

Mick looked at his kids. His eyes welled up. His lip quivered the slightest bit. A sickening light-headedness overtook him. How could he say no at that point? It was evident the answer was yes. But here was his little girl, asking the man who had always protected her if she really only had four days to live. An all-consuming blackness draped over Mick.

"There's still hope," Sid said. "That's why I came as soon as I found out. It may not be much, but it is something."

"What are you getting at?" Mick said.

Sid reached into his bag. He removed a device that looked similar to the auto injector. This one was black with a flat, circular tip. "This is a cellular scanner. I can use it to gauge the virus's progress in your bodies."

"And what good will that do?" Laurel asked. "So I can see what's killing me?"

Sid said, "Our original thought was to find a natural immunity to the virus. It happens all the time with other viruses and diseases. Certain cellular makeups are immune to certain virus strands. If we were to find the immunity to CV-1, I could synthesis a possible cure."

Mick shook his head. "So why has it come down to this?"

"Because this virus is like nothing we've ever seen. We believe that it was introduced by the largest of the meteorites, Colossus, thus the CV-1 tag. Whatever the meteorite brought with it interacted negatively with another less harmful earth-borne virus. We're not sure there is an immunity. But it's our only chance."

"So scan us already," Greg said from the back

of the room.

Sid nodded. He powered on the cell scanner. A few beeps and the screen lit. "Who's first?"

"How about yourself?" Mick said. "I'm not putting these people through any more without first seeing what it is."

"Okay," Sid said. "That sounds like a good idea." He held the flat end of the device against his skin. He then held down the button on the device's handle. A green line traveled up and down the screen. Each pass was something like a radar screen, showing small round cells mixed with longer stringy cells. He nodded toward the screen. "The longer shapes you see is the virus. See how they are moving towards and attaching to the round shapes?"

The group gathered around for a better look.

Sid continued. "The round shapes are my blood cells. The virus works by killing them off. Basically strangling them to death."

"And this crap we injected ourselves with speeds this whole thing up?" Mick said dejectedly.

"Unfortunately. Yes." Sid took the cell scanner from his arm. "I can show you."

Mick understood. He rolled up his sleeve and held out his arm. Sid then placed the scanner on his skin and repeated the same process. This time the screen had many more stringy virus cells and many less healthy blood cells.

Sid said, "You can clearly see the difference only a few hours have made."

"What's going to happen to us?" Sandeep asked bluntly.

Sid removed the device from Mick's skin. He paused, seemingly looking for the correct way to say it. "Your body will begin to break down from the inside. You'll experience an increasing sensation of weakness, followed by organ failure. Your lungs will be the first to deteriorate. And then—" He stopped.

"And then we die," Greg said. "That's just great."

Sid bowed his head momentarily. He then said, "But like I said. There is hope. If one of you shows no sign of the CV-1 virus, then you are the road to a cure. The accelerant wouldn't have an effect on you because it would have nothing to accelerate."

"So that thing you have there," Greg said, pointing to the cell scanner in Sid's hand, "that will tell you if one of us is immune to this thing?"

"Yes," Sid said.

Greg rolled up his sleeve.

Sid then scanned Greg. It was clear as the sky once was that Greg carried the virus. He then scanned Laurel, followed by Chester and Sandeep. They, too, were infected.

"I'm scared, Dad," Nate said before being scanned. "I don't want to die."

Mick pulled his son to him. He then did the same for Kathryn. He kissed them both on the heads and then nodded for Sid to scan them. When done, Mick hanged his head and kissed them again, resting his head on theirs. They lived as a family and they would soon die as one.

"I realize this is a morbid thought," Mick said. "But we don't have many options at this point. What about Sarah?"

"Where is Sarah?" Sid asked.

They all looked to the tarp at the back of the room, lifeless and still.

Sid followed their glances. He said nothing.

Mick said, "She died in this past storm. Can you scan her?"

Sid nodded and made his way to the tarp. He very carefully pulled aside enough of it to gain access to her bloodied arm. He scanned and then turned, shaking his head.

"Now what?" Greg said. "We just wait around to die? This really sucks."

"No," Sid said. "There are others that were sent the same package as you. Those groups injected themselves well before you, though. Days before in some cases." Sid pulled out the tracker. "This is how I found you. Each dose contained a nanotracker. And this is how we will find the others. Maybe, just maybe, one of them has what we need."

CHAPTER 27

Mick snuck out first while the rest of the group was finishing up with their final good-byes to both Sarah and their home. He wanted his final good-bye to Sarah to be a bit different from the others. He went to one knee and pushed away the dust where Sarah tended to her pseudo-garden. He took the time to thoroughly remove as much as he possibly could, down to the cracked soil, as he had seen Sarah do time and again. It came as no surprise that nothing had grown there. But he wished, in some mystical, Chester-type way, that something had sprouted from the infertile land. A transcendent sign from Sarah that she was in a better place.

He stood from the garden and gave it one final look. He then gazed up the hill where he had spent countless hours of his time. Maybe the billboard had found a way to survive the storm. He had not given it much thought lately. Not with everything that had been going on. Even from where he stood, he could always see the billboard's outline among the haze. But as he'd feared, this storm had been the one to finally win the long-waging battle. It seemed so trivial to be upset about an inanimate object. But somewhere buried deep inside him, everything compounded upon itself, and this was just one more addition. One too many.

The rest of the group members made their way out of the shelter over the next ten minutes.

Mick wanted to trust Sid. He really did. But there were too many red flags to fully commit. He could not shake the fact that Sid was part of the lie that was ultimately speeding up their deaths. But at the same time, he was also the only one who could help them. It was a terrible situation that seemed to have no right choice to make within it. So Mick put off making a decision on Sid for now. They needed to get away from the shelter and find those other groups.

Sandeep, ever the teacher, took the opportunity to question Sid about his life, The Facility, their science. His scientific mind was able to look past Sid's hand in all of this.

"And your team truly believes they have a cure for cancer?" Sandeep asked.

"Not my team, necessarily. But the oncology team thinks they found a cure. They derived it from genetically modified radishes of all things. It's a radical change from what I had seen them working on. But they did make more progress in the ten years since Impact than they had in the fifty years prior. There were no political hoops to jump through. No government agencies to worry about. Our science was unimpeded, so to speak. "

"See what that gets us?" Greg said, walking past the two. "A deadly virus. It doesn't matter much what other diseases have been fixed. We'll all be dead soon. Then nobody will have to worry about nothin'."

Sid turned, "We didn't create the virus. We were trying to eradicate it."

"That's true," Alex said, walking up the hill from behind the group. "*We* didn't create the virus."

"Alex!" Sid said. "What the hell are you doing here?" He walked over to him and hugged him, patting his back.

"I came to help," Alex said.

"I can't believe you left. How did you get Phillip to open the doors?"

"Oh, man. You should have seen it. I made a big scene in front of everyone. You know how he hates that." Alex smiled. "I left him with no choice but to let me out the front door. It was either that or he'd look like the liar he is in front of everyone."

"I would have loved to see it," Sid said.

"This someone else from The Initiative?" Mick asked.

Sid nodded. "This is Dr. Alex Cole. We've known each other for what seems like forever. I trust him without reservation."

"Well," Greg said, walking past them both and toward the hill, "I don't trust either of you."

Alex looked to Sid. "I'm assuming they know about the accelerant?"

Sid nodded.

Alex then leaned in closer. "Listen, I have some disturbing news."

"What could be worse than what we already know?"

"How about the fact that the virus wasn't introduced by Colossus? It's man-made."

"What?"

"I never would have known if my tablet hadn't died. One of the tech crew gave me a loaner while he repaired mine. He was in such a hurry that he didn't notice that the tablet was still logged in as someone else. Conveniently, it was Phillip who had used it last."

"So what did you find?"

"Like I said, the virus was man-made. And the man who made it was Phillip."

"Wait," Mick said, overhearing the muted conversation quickly ramp up. "So this stuff inside us was not just more bad luck?"

Alex shook his head. "I'm sorry. It turns out our boss was more evil than any of us thought."

"But why?" Sid asked. "Why would he do something like that? It doesn't make any sense."

"That I don't know," Alex said. "I dug around as much as I could before the tech came back. He was frantic. He must have realized what he had given me. I played stupid. I didn't need Phillip finding out that I knew until it was too late for him to do anything about it."

Greg said, "So let's go pay this Phillip guy a visit."

"It won't be that easy," Sid said. "There's no way he's going to let us back into The Facility. And the others inside The Facility won't complain. Phillip will paint us as infected and a risk to all their lives. And The Facility can't be accessed aside from the two sets of doors."

"And those are now on admin lockdown," Alex said. "Only Phillip has the authorization to open them. And I don't think he's about to do that."

Mick paused and thought about the situation. Knowing where the virus actually came from made no difference in their situation. They were all still infected. The minutes were still counting down. And there was still no cure. Mick did not have the luxury of hate at the moment.

CHAPTER 28

The herd walked down the hill like a procession of sullen elephants, numb, muddled in their own thoughts about everything that had so quickly transpired. Each second felt more precious. Each breath held in a bit longer for fear it could be the last.

"Where are we going, Mick?" Laurel asked as they carefully traversed the hill down toward the remains of the city.

"Our priority, obviously, is to locate the other groups. But we need supplies first. Let's head to that yellow house I told you all about and see what's there. We'll be quick about it."

Mick made the decision to go left, down by the Charles River, and loop back around to the yellow house. It was best to draw as little attention to themselves as they could. When the Rubble King and his crew had left Mick, they'd headed back the way he had originally come, down by the old police station that Solomon vanished into. And he wasn't about to go parading by there.

The trip to the yellow house was uneventful. For that Mick was thankful. After the night they had been through, and what they had lost, the last thing any of them needed was more strife. The herd filed down the road, checking all the windows and rooftops as usual.

Chester scurried up next to Mick as he stopped the group at the house, number eighty-eight.

"Is this the place?" Chester asked.

Mick nodded.

"I know this house," Chester said.

"You do?"

"Yes. This was Stella Murphy's house. Not sure it was one hundred percent legal, but she ran an orphanage out of it. The neighborhood embraced her. And her kids loved her. She was a wonderful woman. I'd come here once a month to bring the children toys that my parishioners had donated. They always loved to see me coming."

The picture that Solomon showed him flashed in his mind. The lady in all the pictures must have been Stella Murphy. And Mick assumed that made Solomon an orphan. It also explained why Solomon had such a love for this house. His mind wandered to the memory of Solomon's fright when King had shown up.

Mick said, "Do you remember a young kid named Solomon?"

"Oh," Chester said. "The man you met the other day?" Chester thought for a moment. "I don't recall his name. But this was a very busy house. Overcrowded would be putting it lightly. Stella committed her life to helping those children find some glimmer of hope in their otherwise dreary lives. She spent every penny of her savings to raise those kids." He paused and sighed. "I can only imagine what happened to all those young lives after, well, the meteorite and everything."

Greg walked up to the door and attempted to look through the same windows that Mick had when he'd first came here. The blinds were still drawn. Everything looked the same except for a larger amount of dust attached to everything.

"It should be open," Mick said. *Or at least it was last time*, he thought.

Greg looked back at Mick and nodded. He then slowly opened the creaky door. He peaked his head inside. "All clear," Greg said, waving them in.

One by one, the group entered the house. Mick closed the door behind them, taking a look out of the front door's window to make sure they had not been seen entering. He could not see anyone among the dust and nothingness, but he realized that did not mean they were alone.

Nate looked to Chester and said, "Did you tell Dad this place was an orphanage?"

"Yes, Nate. This is where people without hope tried to find some."

Nate slowly nodded and looked around. "Seems like a good place for us then, huh?"

Chester patted him on the back. "Indeed."

Without his head racing with questions about Solomon, Mick could now fully take in just how tiny the house was.

"How many kids did you say lived here?" Mick asked Chester.

"Hard to say. The number changed all the

time. Kids were coming and going. But I'd guess no less than fifteen children at one time."

"In this house?" Mick said. He found it hard to believe. They were only nine of them in there now and it felt confining.

"Stella made the most out of her situation. It was something she taught her children, too. Like I said, I spent a good amount of time here when I was able to. She ingrained in the children that it didn't matter what you had in life. What mattered is what you made out of your life." He walked into the living room and stared at the wall of pictures, fixing one that was terribly crooked. "She was a good woman, Mick. One of the best."

"Was?" Mick said. "You don't think she is still around?"

Chester turned from the wall of memories and faced Mick. "No. I doubt it very much. She loved this house, as tiny as it is. She would never leave unless she was left with no choice." He eyed the interior quickly. "I can only assume she has passed on to the next life. God rest her soul." He signed the cross.

Mick caught sight of the picture of Stella with Solomon. He had not noticed at the time, but Solomon was smiling in the picture. It was impossible to tell, of course, but he seemed genuinely happy standing next to the woman. A far cry from the expression of the man he had encountered only days ago. Where was he now? Was he all right? Did King harm him? All of these questions with no answers. No matter how hard he tried to focus, his attention, rightfully so, kept going back to their own bleak ordeal.

Sandeep walked down the stairs, closing a door behind him that separated the upper floor from the floor they were now on. A large puff of dust spit from the change in air as the door closed. "The upstairs is a mess," he said. "Part of the roof fell in. No use going up there."

"All right," Mick said. "Let's get what we came for. I don't want to spend more time here than we need to."

Mick pushed past the group and back into the hall. He walked into the dining room. The rug was just as Solomon had left it. He bent down to lift the rug, making his back crack. It seemed that turning fifty had flipped some imaginary switch in his body. His bones had cracked more in the past few days, and his arms and legs had ached more than usual. The joker in him made light of the situation. At least he would not have to deal with that much longer.

He flipped the rug over to reveal the trapdoor that Solomon had shown him a couple of days before.

"In here," Mick said, signaling the group.

Greg exited the smallish kitchen. He stood beside Mick and looked down at the trapdoor. "This is it?"

Mick nodded. Now that they were at the yellow house, Mick felt gun-shy about opening the trapdoor. He knew in his heart that Solomon was good. He'd seen it in his eyes, and the eyes never lied. But who was to say that someone did not come back after they'd left? What if this door was now very literally a *trap*door?

There was no time for second-guessing. Mick bent down and lifted the surprisingly heavy door. He then peered into the hole in the floor. "I can't see a thing." It would do him no good to feel around a dark room.

Mick turned to Sid and Alex. "You wouldn't happen to have a flashlight?"

"No," Alex said. "Sorry."

"Neither do I," Sid said. "I didn't put much thought into my packing."

Of course not.

Sandeep appeared from behind Mick. He looked over his shoulder and into the dark pit. He seemed mesmerized by the dark hole, but Mick had seen that look on his face many times before. He knew what he was thinking.

Sandeep said, "This was once an orphanage?"

"That's what Chester said, anyway."

"Hmm," Sandeep said. "I may have a solution." He looked unsure. "It's a bit of a stretch, but I did this experiment with my kids in school every year. They always got a kick out of it. Like magic. But that was then. And this is the now, without the tools we probably need."

"Listen," Mick said. "Nothing is off the table at this point. What do we need?" He had learned not to question Deep when he was on to something. Just help out when he could and let the science teacher do his work.

"Since this house was once an orphanage, I assume the children had crayons. See if you can find some."

"What are the other things you need?" Mick asked.

"I will also require some steel wool and a nine-volt battery."

"Oh, that's it?" Greg said sarcastically.

Sandeep smiled. "And a cup of hot coffee if you happen upon it."

Greg smiled back. "All right, guys," he said to the rest of the group. "You heard the man. Let's find the impossible."

Alex said, "I see where you are going with this. Inventive idea."

The herd fanned out and began to ransack the house. Much to Mick's surprise, Nate found a box of crayons, or what was left of the box, anyway. The cardboard had almost completely deteriorated, but it held within it two crayon pieces, one yellow and one blue.

The steel wool was the next item found.

"Will this do?" Chester asked as he came back into the house from the rear deck. He'd found a small swath of steel wool, about the size of his thumb, beneath a pile of rusty metal chairs on the back deck.

Fate seemed to be smiling on them for a

change. When Sandeep had first told them the items he would need, Mick deemed the idea dead from the start. Where were they going to find these things? But they did. Somehow, someway, his idea was taking shape. Whatever that idea was. The battery, however, was nowhere to be found. That came as no surprise to anyone in the house. None of them had seen a battery in what seemed like forever.

Sandeep turned to Sid and Alex. "Those tracking devices of yours. They would not happen to use a nine-volt battery?"

Sid said, "No. Sorry. I wish in this instance they did. But they run on rechargeable lithium fusion chips. They wouldn't be much good for this. No discharge."

As it turned out, they were looking in the wrong direction for the battery. Mick watched curiously as Kathryn brought a backless chair from the kitchen into the room adjacent to the dining room, where they all now stood watching her. It then became clear to him. A smoke detector hugged the ceiling, surprisingly still intact. Kathryn slid open the battery compartment and popped the nine volt out.

"Will this work?" Kathryn said, turning with a smile.

"Nice job, sweetie. How did you know?"

Kathryn carefully stepped down from the chair with Mick's helping hand. "I don't remember much from before the meteorites. But I do remember you cursing around the house with batteries in your hand trying to find which smoke detector was beeping."

"Good job, kiddo."

Kathryn handed the battery over.

"That's unreal that we found everything Sandeep needed," Nate said. "That never happens to us. Like, ever."

"Maybe the tides are turning, Nate," Mick said.

Sandeep quickly got to work. He brought the three items over to the metal kitchen sink. He then brushed the debris off the steel wool. A small coating of rust painted the metal sink red and brown.

Sandeep handed Mick the yellow crayon. It happened to be the larger of the two. "Mick, I need you to hold this." He then broke off the tip of the crayon so the paper was exposed at the top. "If this battery somehow still has anything left within it, we may just have your light. As you would say, keep your fingers crossed." Deep then put the steel wool in the metal sink, took a breath, and brushed the terminals against the wool. Nothing short of a miracle—the steel wool ignited on the third try, enough for Sandeep to blow on it, kindling the flame just enough for the next part. "Quickly, Mick, this will only last for a moment."

Mick understood what he was to do. He pressed the crayon against the dwindling embers of the lit steel wool. Sandeep blew the glowing wool again and the crayon lit.

"Amazing," Mick said.

To which Sandeep replied, "No, Mick. Science."

Mick then handed the unlit second crayon to Chester. "In case we need it." He was surprised this worked in the first place. Having a backup plan seemed like a good idea.

With the burning crayon lighting his way, Mick slowly descended the stairs to the basement. He knew he needed to act fast. His makeshift light was already on borrowed time.

"Stay here," Mick said to the rest of the group.

The flight of stairs consisted of simple wooden planks, rickety but preserved. He crept down, ducking his head beneath the floor that quickly became the ceiling. The crayon candle, or crandle, as Mick had started mentally calling it, provided just enough light to find his way through the basement. He moved slowly across the dirt floor, careful of his steps and his head. The perimeter of the room was flanked by wooden shelving units, rotting and moldy in spots, covered in long-abandoned cobwebs in others.

"What do you see?" Greg asked.

And that was the thing. There was nothing down there. No food, no water, nothing at all. Simple emptiness punched him in the gut.

"Still looking," he shouted back. He was not about to spread the bad news without first being absolutely sure about it.

But why would Solomon tell him there was food and water there if there wasn't? Was Mick so wrong about him?

Then a bone-chilling scream sounded. It was Kathryn.

Mick dropped the crandle in his haste for the stairs. He did not remember climbing them. He only knew that when he emerged from beneath the house, he found they were no longer alone.

CHAPTER 29

"Drop your gun," Clyde said. He held a knife to Kathryn's throat. She was on her knees and crying. "And be quick about it."

Mick immediately complied. He did not want to, obviously, as now he, too, was at this cretin's mercy. There was little choice in the matter. He was not about to play with his daughter's life. But he knew full well that dropping the gun did not prevent that.

"Daddy," Kathryn said through tears.

Mick held up his hand. "It's going to be all right, honey." He then looked at Clyde. He wanted nothing more than to spring across the floor and rip the little rat's head off with his bare hands. He wondered why Greg would let this happen. How did this one small man get past him? But then he looked over Kathryn's shoulder and noticed Greg sitting down in the hallway; his hands appeared bound. The rest of the group was gathered with him, corralled by many more men, some with rifles such as his own.

"I did as you asked," Mick said. "Now let her go."

"That's not up to me," Clyde said with an evil grin.

"Well, well, Mick. We meet again," King said,

emerging from the kitchen's darkness. "I believe the last time you visited this house, I told you not to come back here." King seemed to ponder his own thoughts. He turned to Clyde. "I did say that?"

Clyde nodded. "Sure did."

"And then they so rudely kicked us off their hill the other day," King said. "Very inhospitable."

"We had no choice but to come back." Despite the situation, Mick had enough presence of mind to keep the facts to himself. There was no need to empower this lunatic with anything more than he already had.

"No choice?" King said. "Was someone holding a knife to your throat?" He laughed, looking over at Clyde.

Mick looked down at his daughter. Her innocence was being tainted each second she was forced to endure this. Her lips quivered. Her cheeks were wet with tears. Mick mouthed, "I love you" while King and his men were caught up in their own laughter. But there was nothing that Mick could do. He was at their mercy as much as that burned him from within.

"It just breaks my heart," King said, "that you have to go through this. But are you certain you didn't come here to take my food?"

Mick couldn't help his eyes from widening. He tried to hide the surprise, but it was impossible.

"Ah," King said. "Now the truth comes out. So not only are you rude to guests but you are also a thief. Not very becoming, Mick."

Mick looked to the dark hole he had just climbed out of. He then looked back at the Rubble King.

"I'm sure you are wondering where all the food went?" King asked. He moved closer to Mick so they were almost nose to nose. He tilted his head to the side a bit and sniffed. "Is that fear I smell?"

"Listen—"

King wound up and clocked Mick on the crown of his head with the butt of his pistol.

"Silence!" he screamed. "How dare you tell me to listen? You are the one who will listen." He grabbed Mick by the shirt and kneed him in the ribs. A hot pain shot the length of his spine as Mick fell to his knees. It quickly became more difficult to breathe.

"Dad," Nate yelled from the hallway.

Mick held up his hand while still looking at the floor. He did not want him to see the pain he was in.

"I'm fine, Nate."

King turned to get a look at Nate. "Ah," he said. "You also have a son."

Mick looked up. Pain in his eyes. "Stay away from my kids."

"Or what?" King laughed. "I don't think you are in a position to make threats, my friend."

King backed away from Mick. He brought his face in close to Kathryn. His lips and her cheek had only a hairbreadth between them. "Isn't this a nice little family you have here. Maybe my son here"—he looked to Clyde—"and your daughter will hit it off." King laughed. "Then we would be family, Mick. Wouldn't that be great?" He moved away from Kathryn and back to Mick. "But where's Mommy?"

Mick sneered. The anger almost pushed him off his knees.

"Oh," King said, seeing he had pushed the correct button. "She didn't make it. What a pity."

"Shut up," Mick said.

"What a shame. These poor children growing up with only you to guide them. They must be lacking in some areas, huh?"

"Leave my family out of this," Mick said.

"But I did not bring your family into this," King said. "That was your doing. You are the one who put them all in danger by bringing them here. I am simply protecting my property. In the eyes of the law you are at fault."

"What law?"

"My law, Mick. The only law that matters."

"Boston ain't yours, man," Greg shouted from the hall. No sooner had he finished than one of King's men rammed the butt of his rifle against his temple, knocking him out cold.

King said, "What your sleeping friend there fails to realize is that Boston *is* mine." He stole a quick glance at Kathryn. "Everything will eventually be mine. And there is nothing you can do to stop that, Mick. Not a single thing."

"We'll leave," Mick said.

"I'm afraid that is no longer your choice."

"We took nothing," Sandeep said from the hallway. "Please. Just let us go."

"That's only because there was nothing to take," King replied without taking his eyes off Mick. He bent down on one knee so he and Mick were face-to-face. "Are you wondering where the food went? Hmm?" he said. "Well, I'll tell you. You see, Solomon was kind enough to fill me in about his little stash of food he had been hiding from me." He shook his head. "It took a little"—he paused—"convincing. But he eventually gave in."

"What did you do to him?" Mick had originally feared that he had been double-crossed, but it seemed Solomon had met with King's evilness, too.

"You can relax. For what it's worth, he'll be fine in a few weeks. Nothing time can't heal." He smiled crookedly.

"Please," Mick said. "Let my daughter go."

King arched his eyebrows and looked back. "I don't think you are in a position to make requests, Mick. And I have grown tired of this conversation." He turned back calmly and smiled, before winding up and hitting Mick in the head again with the butt of his pistol. This time the blackness of unconsciousness enveloped him.

CHAPTER 30

A warm sensation brought Mick back from the darkness, like a morning shower splashing on his face. But the rankness of the water forced his thoughts into the now.

"Wakey, wakey," Clyde said.

Mick cracked his eyelids. The world was blurry and gray. He was lying on the floor on his back and staring at the ceiling. His hands were bound behind him. He looked up to see the same man who had held a knife to his daughter's throat now urinating on his face.

He rolled to his side and spit to rid his mouth of the animal's dark urine. Clyde continued to empty his bladder on Mick's face, squealing in delight as he did.

When Mick turned, Clyde arced his stream of urine to compensate.

"It looked like you could use a cleaning off," Clyde said.

Mick spit what he could out of his mouth. The rancidness of what had just happened began to seep into his skin much like the piss that dribbled down his face. What the hell was going on? What had he gotten them all into?

"Where are my kids?" Mick asked. He spit again. The dark-yellow urine, a sure sign that

Clyde was dehydrated along with the rest of them, seemed to dry on his skin in an instant. It was all Mick could smell. He gagged.

"Your kids are dead." Clyde laughed.

Mick flailed in place. Red-hot rage shot to the surface. "I'll kill you," he said. "I'll kill you!"

"Oh, relax," Clyde said. "Can't anyone take a joke anymore?"

"What?" Mick said. He could barely catch his breath he was so livid. "What the hell are you talking about?"

"Your kids are fine," Clyde said. "For now."

What kind of twisted idiot would say something like that? Mick tried to calm his mind down. "Where are they?"

Clyde swung his leg back and kicked Mick in the side. A shooting pain traveled Mick's right side. "You don't get to ask questions."

Mick clenched his jaw and stared at Clyde.

"Now, Clyde," King said as he entered through the open cell door. "Is that any way to treat our guest?"

Clyde snickered. "I suppose not."

King shooed him away. Clyde scampered out of the room like the good little dog he was. King walked casually over to Mick and sat down next to him on the floor, careful of the wet spot of piss next to him.

"I wish it didn't have to be like this, Mick."

"It doesn't."

"Unfortunately for you, Mick, it does. You see,

I gave you your chance back at your place. I came to unite our groups." King sniffed the air in front of Mick. "You smell awful. You really should consider taking better care of yourself."

"Screw you," Mick said.

"Aren't you the brave one?" King smiled. He cocked his head as if admiring Mick. "But you should watch your tongue with me. I don't play as well as some of the others."

"Where are my children?"

"They are here. And I give you my word that they are unharmed. However, my generosity has its limits."

To hear the words from Clyde meant nothing. Mick thought he was a few cards short of a full deck to begin with. But this King guy, as arrogant as he was, seemed less insane.

"What do you want?" Mick said. He spit again to clear the last of the piss from his mouth.

"I want all your supplies, Mick."

Mick laughed out of pity for everyone involved. "We don't have any. Why do you think we were at the yellow house? People don't care to sightsee much anymore."

"Come now, Mick. You must know that lies will get you nowhere."

"I'm not lying. The storm took almost everything from us. And then you took the rest."

King stared at Mick for a moment. He eyed him carefully, studying his face. "You're telling the truth. Aren't you?"

"Why the hell would I lie?"

"Well," King said, pushing himself back to his feet. "It appears we are in a strange predicament. I will have to give this some thought." He turned around and began to walk toward the cell door.

"Let me see my kids," Mick shouted. Whatever secured his hands seemed impossible to break out of. Some kind of wire.

King stopped but did not turn around. "No," he said before vanishing into the darkness.

Mick squirmed. He tried to free his hands. They did not budge in any way. Suddenly Solomon appeared from the other side of the hall, opposite of where King had gone. He entered the cell, carefully looking around. He had a new black eye since the last time Mick had seen him. But Mick was happy to see him. He was alive and well.

"Solomon," he said.

Solomon hushed him with his index finger to his lips. "I c-can't f-f-free you. He w-will know."

Mick understood. "Have you seen my children?"

Solomon shook his head. "N-not yet. I know w-w-where th-they are."

"Are they all right? The rest of my group, are they safe?"

Mick clearly heard footsteps coming his way. Solomon apparently had, too. He bolted from the cell and back into the hallway without saying another word.

CHAPTER 31

Solomon hurried down the back stairway. He knew this was a risk. He was not supposed to be down there. King had warned him more than once. And with King already on the warpath, this seemed like an extra-foolish idea. But this situation was different. There were kids involved. He could not in good conscience think about his own well-being at a time like this. He would always protect children like Ms. Stella had protected him.

He exited the stairway, hugging the shadows where he could find them. He had been down there so many times that he knew where to stand to stay invisible. After confirming it was clear, Solomon stepped out into the bit of light available. Ms. Stella was not in her usual spot. She had found the energy to move to the opposite side of her cell closest to the cell next to her.

"Ms. Stella," Solomon said. He went to the front of her cell and down to one knee.

"Solomon, my dear." She seemed more upbeat than usual. Though her frame appeared more meager than he was used to. Maybe it was because she now sat beneath a strand of light that crept through the cell's barred window. He was used to conversing with her from her shadowy part of the cell. "We have new friends," she said.

Solomon looked at the other cells, three besides the one Ms. Stella had been held captive in. One of the cells held a smallish woman and two men. The men appeared cleaner than the rest. The cell next to that held three men; the largest of them had a bloodied head. The cell adjacent to Ms. Stella held two teenagers. Solomon figured those were Mick's kids.

"Y-y-your f-father is w-worried," Solomon said, past Ms. Stella and toward the kids.

"Dad," Kathryn said with a note of elation. "Is he all right?"

Solomon nodded. He was well enough. That was the best they could hope for at the moment.

"Can you get us out of here?" Chester asked from the cell to Solomon's left.

Ms. Stella answered the question for him. "The monsters holding us all prisoner do not obey any sort of rules." She cleared her throat. "As I was just telling you before Solomon arrived, I have been down here for the better part of eight long years. They don't care about me, or anyone for that matter. I am nothing more than a pawn in their twisted games. The longer I stay alive, the longer they can hold Solomon captive." She looked over at Solomon. Love filled her bloodshot eyes. "I beg him daily to leave me. But he refuses time and again. He is too good at heart to do it. It pains me more each day to see him tormented."

"Where is Mick?" Chester asked.

Ms. Stella again spoke, looking at the children.

"Your father is most likely upstairs. Close to King."

Solomon nodded again. "He is in m-m-my cell."

"Why are we here in the first place?" Sandeep asked.

Greg said, holding his head, "Don't try to make sense of crazy, Sandeep. We're here because that King guy is crazy. And he's surrounded by crazy. This whole damn thing is crazy."

"Unfortunately," Ms. Stella said, "you are correct. You will not get anywhere with them by reasoning. They will use you like they use everyone and everything else. And once you run out of usefulness …"

The room grew silent as everyone came to their own conclusions.

"We can't just sit here and wait," Greg said.

"It appears we don't have much of a choice, Greg," Chester replied. He then looked toward Solomon. "Mick told me about you, Solomon. He said you were the first good person he had met in a very long time."

Solomon felt the same about Mick. In fact, even though it had only been for a few minutes, he knew these people that Mick associated himself had the same type of good nature. If Ms. Stella liked them, then so did he.

Heavy footsteps on the stairs hushed the room.

Solomon darted from sight and back into the shadows, watching, nervously waiting.

Clyde tripped over the last stair and went

headfirst into Ms. Stella's cell, catching himself at the last moment on the bars. He then pushed himself back off like nothing had happened. He fumbled for his keys once he'd stopped in front of Ms. Stella's door. "King wants to see you," he said to Ms. Stella.

"Well, tell him I don't want to see him," Ms. Stella replied in the most serious of tones.

"You don't get to decide that, bitch," Clyde said. He found the correct key and unlocked the door. The door creaked open. "When King calls, you come."

"You may come," Ms. Stella said. "But that is because you are a weak man with no morals, Clyde. Whatever happened to that poor boy I rescued all those years back?"

Clyde laughed. "Rescued? I didn't need your rescuing, bitch. You basically kidnapped me."

"Have you become so jaded that the truth now escapes you, Clyde? Has your mind been so poisoned that there is no way to save you?"

Clyde walked over to Ms. Stella and looked down at her. "Save me?" he said, pointing his middle finger toward his chest. "It's not me that needs saving, Stella." He chuckled, his fat jiggling. "Say good-bye to your new friends. You won't be seeing them again."

Solomon remained in the shadows, silent. He had seen the way Ms. Stella was treated. Clyde and King had no respect for her. But it felt different this time. While he was still a captive of the building, the captivity of his soul felt undone in a way. His decisions and actions did not need to pass through a filter any longer.

Clyde reached down and grabbed Ms. Stella forcefully by her frail arm and heaved her up to her feet.

Ms. Stella winced in pain at the sudden jolt.

"Leave her alone," Nate said.

"Shut your mouth, boy," Clyde said. "I'll be back to see you soon."

Ms. Stella spit what little saliva she could muster as Clyde. "You're a monster."

Clyde reacted instantly. He punched her in the face.

Ms. Stella crumpled to the floor.

The rage came over him again, and Solomon could not hold back what had built up inside him any longer. The years of torment. The years spent captive. The utter filth that surrounded him. The lack of respect for not only the elderly but for a good soul such as Ms. Stella. It was too much. Consequences were no longer included in this thought process.

Solomon darted from the shadows like an angry bull. Before Clyde knew what was coming, Solomon ran into his back at full speed, knocking Clyde clear off his feet and headfirst into the brick wall in front of him. He moaned in pain.

Solomon dropped to his knees by Ms. Stella's side. "M-Ms. Stella," he said, brushing a tuft of bloody hair from her eyes. She had a small laceration above her right eye from Clyde's punch. Her eyes were open, but the life behind them seemed dimmer than it had been a moment ago. "I—I'm s-s-s-sorry."

"Solomon, my dear." Her voice seemed distant. She reached up to his face but had no time to touch it.

Clyde grabbed Solomon by the neck and hoisted him up. He then punched Solomon multiple times in the back of his head. Each punch brought a quick flash of bright light to his sight.

But Solomon was driven by something deeper than rage. Something that seeped from his very fiber, morphing to an unyielding hatred that would never be stopped again.

Solomon turned and grabbed Clyde by his neck. His thumbs pressed firmly against his trachea. He stared deep into Clyde's eyes. He looked for something good. Any kind of gleam that would make him stop. Something that reminded him of the child he'd once considered a friend. He saw nothing worth saving.

Clyde's feet dangled over the floor. Solomon's grip was unrelenting and strong. This was for all the kicks to the back. All the punches to the head. All the torture he put Ms. Stella through. This was for all that and a multitude of things more.

Clyde gasped for breath. He tried to pry Solomon's hands off, but they would not budge.

"Please," Clyde whispered with the breath he had left. His goggles formed white circles where they touched his bloodless face.

But Solomon was past caring. He was determined to make that the final word that Clyde ever said. Until Ms. Stella spoke.

"Solomon," she said in the softest, most caring of ways. "Let him go, my dear. This is not who you are."

Solomon looked back quickly at Ms. Stella, who had struggled to her feet. She held on to the cell bars for support.

Solomon turned back at Clyde. His face was now a hue of purple he had not seen before. He released his grip, and Clyde tumbled to the floor. At that moment Solomon had no idea what to do with the rage that tore through him. So he yelled. At the top of his lungs, he yelled. Like a mother bear protecting her cubs. He cared not who heard him.

Ms. Stella slowly came over to his side. When she reached him, she put her scrawny arms around him the best she could and hugged him with all the energy her body could muster. She put her head on his chest and wept for the pain that tormented him so deeply.

"Watch out!" Kathryn screamed.

It was already too late. Clyde had pulled a gun from his waistband. While still on his knees, he pointed and fired, hitting Solomon in the side. Solomon and Ms. Stella fell to the floor in unison. Clyde pointed the gun at Solomon's head, but Ms. Stella was in the way.

"Move bitch," Clyde wheezed, still trying to find the air that Solomon had taken from his lungs.

"I will not let you hurt him anymore." Ms. Stella forced herself to her knees. "There comes a time, Clyde, when a person can no longer be given leniency because of their mental condition, or who they once were. If you choose to be who you are now, then you must deal with the consequences."

"There's nothing wrong with me," Clyde laughed. "You're the ones with problems. I'm fine. You can't see that. So that makes you all crazy."

Ms. Stella swayed on her knees. Her head hung heavily as if it were forged from lead.

"Get up," Clyde said to her, waving the gun. "I said, get up." He walked closer to lift her from the ground.

In a motion that seemed overly energetic for her age and shape, Ms. Stella lurched forward as Clyde got within arm's reach. She then reached down to Clyde's boot and removed his dagger, one he always kept in the same spot, one Ms. Stella had eyed every day he came to hurt her. The very dagger he had poked and teased her with over the many years.

Before Clyde could react, Ms. Stella stuck the dagger upward and below his rib cage. She pushed it again, farther into his body with the little power she had left, until only the hilt remained visible.

Clyde's face froze in shock, his mouth open. He dropped the gun and then quickly followed it to the ground. "You bitch," he said exasperatedly.

Ms. Stella had punctured a lung with her thrust. Clyde lay on the dirty cell floor like a fish out of water nearing the end. His breaths became more labored and further apart. They all watched silently until the breaths stopped coming.

Solomon, despite having been shot, rushed to Ms. Stella's side as she toppled from her knees and onto her back on the floor. "M-Ms. S-S-S-Stella." He cupped her head on his. It was only then that he realized what had happened. The bullet that had thankfully missed Solomon's arteries had not done the same for Ms. Stella when it exited him and entered her.

She smiled sweetly. "My dear, dear Solomon," she said. She caressed his cheek as she had when he was a boy. She then coughed and heaved. Solomon steadied her the best he could. The patch of red beneath her grimy shirt began to grow rapidly.

"N-no," Solomon said. His eyes welled with tears, something he could never remember happening before. "I—I—I'll g-get h-help." He shook his head angrily. "M-M-Ms. S-S-Stella. N-n-no."

"I can help," Laurel said. "I was a nurse. Get me out of this cage."

Ms. Stella grabbed hold of Solomon's arm. She looked at him through fading eyes and said, "No one can help me now, my dear." She smiled a truly genuine smile. "I am eternally grateful for having had a chance to know and love you over these years. My life would have no meaning without you, my dear. You are a beautiful man both inside and out. And don't you dare ever let anyone make you believe otherwise."

Tears flowed more freely down Solomon's face. "P-please d-d-don't go," he said. "Please." He kissed her forehead. "I sh-should have k-killed him w-w-when I c-c-could have."

Ms. Stella hushed him. "Solomon," she said through obvious pain. "A life as pure as yours does not need a death to soil it. My dying wish would have always been that you would have a chance at freedom." She coughed again. A small bit of blood coated her teeth. "You have that freedom now. I love you, Solomon, with all my heart and then some. Go with these people and live your life. Live, Solomon." She winced and then let the word *live* travel one more time from her mouth atop her final breath.

Her arm fell limply from Solomon's face.

Solomon sat completely still. Ms. Stella's head on his lap. Numbness and anger fought the other for dominance. The only family he had ever known was gone.

CHAPTER 32

King sat atop his faux throne and rifled through the groups' belongings. When he reached Mick's bag, he stopped.

"What do we have here?" King said, removing the red box. He eyed the top, pressing down the two flaps to once again spell *open*. King looked up from the box and toward Mick, who was still bound and down on his knees in the main room. "I see you already did as the box crudely instructed you to. What did you find, I wonder?"

Mick stayed silent. He was not about to share anything. All his mind could focus on were his children and his group. He had not given the accelerated virus running through his system as much thought as he probably should have. But for all he knew, it wouldn't matter soon.

King opened the box and removed the auto injector. He eyed it, shifting the hard plastic case in his hands. He then put it back in the box and removed the note. "What do we have here?" he said again, unfolding the note. His eyes widened further with each second that passed.

When King finished reading the note a second time, he grabbed hold of the case again. He pulled off the case, exposing the auto injector. "Have you used this, Mick?"

Mick stared through him in disgust.

"Fine," King said. "Be that way." He turned toward the back of his faux throne. "Clyde," he yelled. But Clyde could not respond. "Clyde!" he yelled again, sustained and angry. When Clyde did not come scampering as per the norm, King summoned Robert over. "Go find Clyde," he said. "And be quick about it."

Robert went to leave the main room. He stopped when he neared the stairs leading to the basement. Clyde had appeared. His lifeless body was being dragged up the stairs by Solomon. Each step a new place for his head to bounce off. When he reached the top, Solomon continued forward with Clyde in tow. A streak of blood followed the body through the main room, past Mick, and up to the faux throne, where Solomon dropped it at the feet of Clyde's father, King.

King stood. "What the hell have you done, boy?" He looked down at his dead son.

"W-w-what I sh-sh-should have d-done a l-long t-t-time ago."

The group, now free of their prison, followed Solomon up the stairs from the cells and emptied into the main room.

"Guards!" King shouted. His men poured from various doors that lined the main room. All of them were armed. And their numbers far surpassed those of Mick's little beat-up group.

Once Mick's group had been secured, King turned his attention back to Solomon. He looked down at Clyde as he stepped off his throne. "What a pity," he said. "Such a young vibrant life. So much promise." He then began to laugh maniacally at the top of his lungs. He laughed and then laughed harder. And then, as quickly as he'd begun, he stopped. "And you did this, boy?"

Solomon stared at King.

"You certainly are full of surprises lately, aren't you?" King said. "To tell you the truth, I didn't think you had it in you."

Mick turned to see his children at the top of the stairs. They appeared unharmed. The relief he felt was absolute. He flashed the smallest of grins possible to avoid detection. Those who looked at Mick reciprocated. While they had no idea what was to come, at least they would find out together as they always had.

"Robert," King said. "Bring the boy over a chair. He must be tired from his ordeal."

Robert did as King requested. He brought over a wooden chair and put it behind Solomon. He then forced Solomon to sit against his will, pushing down on his shoulders until he relented.

King then waved a few of his men over that were not attending to the rest of the group. He looked down at Clyde's corpse. "He was really starting to get on my nerves." He looked to Solomon. "You did me a favor, really. And my nerves thank you for it." He then snapped his fingers at the large group of men to his left. "Get this out of here," he said, pointing to Clyde's corpse, shooing him one final time. "I don't care what you do with it."

The two men that came running looked to each other, then down at Clyde, then back to King. "Now," King said. The men wasted not a single second more. They hoisted Clyde into the air and left through the front door.

The situation became all the more unpredictable now. Clyde and King were far from a normal loving father and son. But Mick could not imagine how one man could be so utterly cold and uncaring. If he felt nothing while seeing his son's corpse, then what chance did any of them stand of reaching him through reason and understanding? It was at that moment that Mick understood if they were ever going to free themselves, their tactics would need to change.

Another man ran up the stairs from the basement. He hurried over to King. He whispered something to him. King's eyes grew wide. He then nodded very slightly.

"Now it makes sense," King said. He looked at Solomon. "Clyde kills the woman. You kill Clyde. An eye for an eye."

"M-Ms. S-S-Stella," Solomon said.

King raised an eyebrow.

"Sh-she h-has a n-name."

"*Had* a name," King corrected. "And to you she did. To me she was nothing more than a waste of my air." King took a deep breath. "Feels better already around here."

Solomon shot up from the seat. Robert, who was standing behind him, quickly pushed him back down. Robert then patted his shoulder as if to help him understand he was wasting his energy. When Solomon started to push himself back up, Robert waved another of the men over to him after finding out how strong Solomon really was.

Solomon winced as they pushed him back down. The bullet wound refused to be forgotten.

Noticing the pain, and then seeing the blood spot on his side, King said, "It appears as if Clyde got in one good shot, huh?" He smirked. "Not good enough, though. I told him his time would come if he continued to be so amateurish.

"So what happens now?" King continued. "Do I kill you all and go about my day?" He thought for a moment. "Or do I kill some of you? Decisions, decisions. Maybe I could save a select few of you for other things." He smiled over toward Kathryn and Laurel.

Laurel pulled Kathryn in tight against herself. "Stay away from her."

"I do what I want, bitch!" King shouted. "Now mind your tongue. Or I will mind it for you."

He walked slowly around the room, his demeanor again calm. "You know, I'm surprised by myself," he said. "I think I must be becoming a better man. Typically I would have killed you all by now."

He then casually made his way back to his throne. He picked up the red box and again removed the auto injector. He decided to paraphrase the note. He would divulge only what he deemed his men worthy of knowing.

He held the auto injector over his head and waved it slowly so all the others could see. "This," he said, "is what salvation looks like." He pried the auto injector free of its hard outer case. He turned his attention to Mick, who swayed slightly on his knees. "I'll ask again. Did you use this, Mick?"

Mick looked up. "You think you're so smart. Why don't you tell me?"

"Mick, Mick, Mick. Always the hero." He walked over and backhanded Mick across the face. Mick fell to the ground. "Things don't need to be this difficult, you know."

Mick spit blood from his mouth and onto the dusty floor. "You're the one making things difficult."

"On the contrary," King said. "I am the one who offered you an olive branch. Have you forgotten already?"

"I remember you threatening us."

King shook his head in disgust. "I let you live, Mick. If you call that threatening, then you are wrong. The first time we met, I let you walk away. With one simple rule: that you don't come back. I don't think you're a dumb man, Mick. You've done well to survive this long. So I assumed you knew that I am not the type of person that jokes."

Greg shouted from the back of the room by the stairs, "What gives you the right to decide who lives and dies?"

King did not take his attention from Mick. "Because I'm the one with the power," he said. "I am the Rubble King. And the one with the power gets to make the decisions. Is this a new concept to you?" He removed a pistol from the holster on his waist. He then walked at a quick pace toward the rest of the group.

He put the silver barrel of his pistol beneath Greg's chin, pointing up. "Now," he said. "Wouldn't you agree that I am in a position of power at this moment?"

Greg said nothing. He stared down the bridge of his nose at King. Greg tried to play his part. To remain unbreakable and stolid. But all the room could see that having a gun pressed against your chin is something that mere bravado is incapable of disguising. Sweat beaded on Greg's forehead.

King continued. "The thing is, I don't even need this crude weapon. I am more than capable of ending your life in a multitude of ways. Some more creative than others." He leaned in closer to Greg but kept his voice loud enough for everyone to hear. "I use guns because they're efficient. They allow me to exercise my will and move on. I have greater things at play than emotion. I have a kingdom to protect." He again laughed loudly, crazily.

King then removed the gun from Greg's throat. With one decisive motion, he brought the barrel of the gun up and off the side of Greg's head, inches from where he had previously been hit. Greg fell to the ground unconscious. King then fired off two rounds into Greg's chest.

"No!" Mick screamed. He fought to free himself, but it was no use. The wires that bound him were tied tightly enough to limit his movement.

King then turned his attention to Kathryn. He moved in closer to her. He let the tip of his pistol brush against her tear-soaked cheek.

She closed her eyes, shivered.

Laurel stood strong. She stepped in front of Kathryn. Her eyes were red with rage. "Don't you touch her." She looked down at Greg and then back to King. She was visibly shaking and afraid, but resolute to the core.

King turned his attention to Laurel. "You're a brave little woman," he said. "Are you not afraid to die?"

Laurel stiffened her posture. "Screw you," she said. "We all died ten years ago. You can't possibly do any worse than that meteorite."

"Well, see, you just don't know me well enough yet. I can do much worse." He turned from Laurel and began to walk back to his throne. "Much, much worse. But I think I've made my point for today. And I have grown tired of this. If the rest of you want to live, you better keep your mouths shut unless I tell you otherwise."

CHAPTER 33

Mick sat on the dirty floor, his mouth bleeding and his hands bound. To first lose Sarah to the storm and then watch as Greg was brutally murdered shut him down in a way he had not ever felt before. It all seemed like a nightmare he had no chance of waking from. In that moment, for only a minute, he thought selfishly of himself. It would all be so much easier if he was dead. If those bullets tore through his chest rather than Greg's. The pain of loss and the pain of living would both be gone if that were the case.

That minute came and went. And Mick thought of his children. How must this be affecting them? No one was equipped to deal with what was happening. The innocence of children, even of those in their teenage years, was too raw to recover to its former state before a traumatizing event. And their entire lives seemed to be one traumatic event after another. If they somehow made it out of this, and he knew that was a big *if*, the scars inflicted on his children would be permanent and deep.

"Since you refuse to answer my question, Mick, I'll go on the assumption that you have injected yourselves," King said. "And, after reading the note, it turns out this is some kind of inoculation to a virus we didn't know existed in the first place? And you were going to keep it all to yourselves? You know, Mick, that's really selfish of you."

Sid stepped forward, out of the shadows of the group. "We just recently discovered the virus."

"And you are?" King said.

"Dr. Sid Roth."

"A doctor," King said. "How civil of you." King waved his hand. "You were saying?"

Sid took a small breath. "We all have this virus. It's been in the air for some time now. We believe it originated from the meteorites."

"And this virus," King said. "What does it do to us, exactly?"

"The CV-1 virus attacks the body from the inside. It will eventually lead to organ failure and ultimately death."

"And this," King said, turning the auto injector in his hand. "What does this do, exactly, if we already have the virus? I'm no doctor, but I understand what inoculations are meant for. You can't inoculate against something you already have."

"That's true," Sid said, obviously lying to those who knew better. "But that," he said, pointing, "can prevent it from spreading further inside you. We developed it at The Facility to slow the spread."

King interrupted, "The Facility?"

This time it was Alex who spoke. He, too, stepped from the back. "The Facility was built prior to Impact. All was not lost as most thought."

King stared at the group. His gaze was powerful and unwavering. He said, "And this blue stuff is my way into this 'Facility'?"

"Yes," Sid said, now furthering his tall tale. "The only way they are going to let you enter is if you show degradation in infection rate."

Mick watched as the entire thing unfolded before his eyes. Sid was more resourceful than he'd initially given him credit for. Each time he looked back to King, however, he wondered if he was buying what Sid was selling. King was ruthless. And Mick was sure he was crazy. There could be no doubt about that. But King also appeared to be intelligent and calculating. A dangerous mix. If King sensed that Sid was lying, then Mick feared they would all die without a second thought. Right there. Right then.

King stood. "I have to say that I am a bit torn on this," he said. "What has the world come to when one man can't trust the next? But what better way to test than to experiment. Wouldn't you agree, Doctors?" He looked to Sid and Alex. "Hold him down," King commanded Robert and the two others that were near.

"King," Robert said. "He's in pretty rough shape. I don't think—"

"That's right, Robert. You don't think. I do. Now roll up his sleeve. Or would you like to join Clyde outside to talk it over?"

Robert relented and nodded for the other two to help him hold down Solomon.

When King turned to grab the auto injector, Robert leaned down quickly and quietly whispered, "I'm sorry," in Solomon's ear.

King pressed the auto injector against Solomon's exposed skin, waited for the long tone, and then removed it after the injection. He backed away from Solomon and studied him as if he were close to exploding. He continued to watch, as did everyone in the room, until he was satisfied.

"Well now," King said with a smile. "It appears that the boy survived." He placed the device down and clapped three claps. "I guess you are good at something, boy. Good for you. You should feel proud. If that bitch was still around, I'm sure she'd say the same thing."

Solomon spit at King. It was nothing to speak of, however. More of a spittle of wet air.

"Come now," King said. "Are you *still* upset about that old woman? You need to get over things, boy. She isn't coming back."

Mick watched silently from the floor. He saw the fire in Solomon's eyes from all the way across the room. The timid man he'd met in the alley, hiding in the Dumpster, was no longer there. It seemed he'd been replaced by the tarnished soul they all were forced to become over the years. Solomon no longer had Ms. Stella to lean on. And King no longer had Ms. Stella as a pawn. Their game of chess was nearing the end.

King reached down in front of his throne. He picked up Clyde's large key ring, which had fallen when the corpse was removed. He tossed it to Robert. "You've just been promoted. Take them all back down to the cells. And get that," he said, pointing to Greg's body, "out of my castle."

CHAPTER 34

Mick ended up in the same cell with his kids, who freed his hands from the ropes and hugged him profusely. Chester, Sandeep, and the two scientists were put in another cell. And Solomon and Laurel were put back in Ms. Stella's cell. This reminded Solomon of how drastically things had changed and how deeply he already missed her.

"I can't believe this is all happening," Chester said. He looked paler than usual. "Why would he kill Greg like that?"

"Don't try to make sense of it," Mick said. "He's obviously not all there. That's what worries me the most. We need to get out of here."

"But how?" Sandeep said. He walked over to the bars on the windows. He got on his toes and peered out. He then tried to move one of the bars. It did not budge, still as strong as the day it was put in place.

"I have no idea," Mick said, wincing. He tried to get to his feet but could not quite manage it. His kids helped ease him back down to the floor.

In a lucky twist of fate, the goons had put Laurel in with Solomon. She tended to Solomon's gunshot wound, which had thankfully missed any organs. The bullet had exited cleanly from his body, only ripping through a small section of his side. She tore the bottom portion of her shirt off and used it to help stop the bleeding. The wound would need to be sewn or cauterized to heal. But this was the best she could do with what she had.

Sandeep broke into a sudden coughing fit. He bent over and put his hands on his knees. He then spit a small amount of blood on the floor. He stared down for a moment. He looked back up with an uneasy expression on his face.

"I must have breathed too much dust in," Deep said.

Sid said, almost reluctantly, "I'm afraid that is one of the first signs that CV-1 is ramping up inside you. Your lungs will be the first organ to deteriorate."

Sandeep said nothing. He stood there, soaking in what that meant. He was the first to show signs. And he was smart enough to understand that he was probably going to be the first one to die because of it. He nodded slowly in acceptance before lowering himself back down to the floor. Chester moved closer to comfort him.

"The rest of you are going to start showing signs soon," Sid said. "Expulsion of blood means your body has gone into full-out defense mode. And it's losing."

Sandeep looked up. "How long do I have?"

"A couple days at most. I am truly sorry."

"It's not your fault this is happening to us all," Sandeep said. "You came to help us. It's more than most have done."

"No," Sid said. "I don't deserve your compassion. I helped all of this happen. I am just as guilty as everyone else."

"No," Alex said. "This is on Phillip. Don't blame yourself, Sid. We were all duped into believing him. At least we tried to make things right. That should count for something. Right?"

"None of that matters right now," Mick said. "The blame game is not going to help us get out of here."

"Even if we did escape, where are we trying to escape to?" Chester asked. "We are all going to start coughing soon. And that means we are all going to die soon." He signed the cross and looked to the ceiling. "Whether we die here or there, what does it matter?"

"Stop that, Chester," Mick said.

"No," Kathryn said. "Chester's right." She looked at her dad. "The truth is the truth, Dad. You can't protect us from that."

Mick did not know if there were words to say at that moment. He simply stared back at her. There was that trick of the light and, although the words came from his fourteen-year-old, he saw only his four-year-old. No one at either age should have to accept such a morbid reality as they were now faced with.

While the group talked among themselves, Solomon listened. When Laurel finished bandaging him the best she could, Solomon said, "W-what d-d-did he p-put in me?"

"Something that is going to make you die quicker," Sid said bluntly. "Much quicker."

"S-s-so I w-will die s-s-soon?"

Sid nodded empathetically.

"G-good," Solomon said. He had had it with this world. It had never given him anything but grief and heartache. And now that Ms. Stella was gone, he had nothing to live for.

"Don't say that, Solomon," Kathryn chimed from her cell. "We haven't known you long at all. But I can tell you're a good person. You belong with us."

"And we look out for each other," Nate added. "You're part of the family now. Don't worry. Dad always figures something out." Nate looked to his father.

And then Nate began to cough just as Sandeep had: a rough, hacking cough that convulsed his body. He did not spit up any blood. But all who heard him knew what it meant.

Mick reached over and rubbed Nate's back. The thoughts that screamed through his mind were unbearable to entertain. He knew soon they would all start to cough. And when they did, the time they had left was nearing an end.

CHAPTER 35

Robert brought the scientists back up on King's command.

"What does this thing do?" King asked them as he held the cellular scanner in his hand.

Neither spoke.

"Would you prefer we do this the hard way?"

Sid looked at Alex. He said, "It's a cellular scanner."

"And what is a cellular scanner used for?"

"We can see how far the virus has spread within someone by using that."

"Show me," King said. He handed the device over to Sid.

Sid powered the device on. He then waited for the software to initialize, which took only a few seconds. He held the flat tip on his skin and waited. A moment later the images he had grown so accustomed to seeing were digitized on the screen. Many elongated black strands were equaled by what remained of his healthy blood cells.

King stepped off the throne and next to Sid. He gazed at the display. "What is that?"

"The black objects are the virus. The white ones are my blood cells."

King watched as one of the thin black strands wrapped itself around one of the round blood cells.

It squeezed a bit at a time until the blood cell was half the size it had been. He then rolled up his own sleeve and held out his arm. He said nothing, but the gesture could not be misconstrued.

Sid took the scanner off his arm and placed it on King's. He pressed the Sequence button again. The same image was displayed, only with a few more virus strands present and a few more dead blood cells floating by them.

King took his arm away. He turned his back to the scientists and walked to his seat, rolling his sleeve up while he did.

"So it's true," King said. "We are all infected."

Sid nodded.

King reached into the red box and removed the auto injector. "And this will slow it down?"

"Yes," Sid said.

King studied the auto injector, stuck on the deep blue of the gel inside the chamber. He then looked to Sid. "Why are you here?"

"Because you had him bring us up," Alex said, looking at Robert, who stood behind them, listening.

"Don't be a wiseass," King said. "You should know by now that my patience wears thin easily. Why are you here, as in outside your little utopia you've been living in?"

"We came to gather those who took the serum," Alex lied. "Like the bulletin said we would."

"And how do you know who took it?"

Sid pointed over King's shoulder. "That other device is a tracking unit. We use it to determine who has been inoculated."

King looked back and then reached for the device. He took the liberty of turning it on with the single button present on its handle. A few beeps later and the tracker was lit with small blue dots. King was quick with observing.

"I see seven dots."

Alex nodded. "Those are the ones in the cells downstairs with us."

"Why do you not show up as dots?"

Sid took no time replying, already in a lying mood. "The dots only represent those that have inoculated themselves with this batch. This was specifically designed with nanotrackers inside so we could find those that had taken the injection and bring them to The Facility."

"And what's to stop me from taking you two to this 'Facility' and using you as my way to enter?"

"We could take you there," Alex said. "But they would never let you enter. Not for either of our lives. They would never risk contamination."

King pondered his options. He turned to Robert. "Did you notice the boy downstairs?"

"He looked fine," Robert said. "Aside from the bullet wound."

King said, "And once I take this, the virus will stop spreading within me?"

"That's correct," Sid said.

As much as King appreciated being the ruler of his band of misfits, he longed for something better, for the creature comforts he had not had the pleasure of feeling in too long. And to have a new land and people to eventually rule over excited him.

"Inject me," King said, handing the auto injector to Sid. He again rolled up his sleeve. "But listen very carefully. If you double-cross me, it will be the last thing you do."

Sid did not hesitate. He held the device to King's skin and waited for the high pressure to deliver the accelerant. He took the device off when done.

"I didn't feel anything," King said. "Are you sure it worked?"

"It worked. These were designed for minimum discomfort. You wouldn't feel much."

"How long until this works?"

"It can take up to five days," Sid said. "But you should begin seeing signs in a few days. Things will begin to change quickly."

King stared down at the small red ring left by the injector. "When do we leave for this 'Facility' of yours?"

Sid thought on his feet. "They won't even consider opening the doors unless the scans come back positive for virus progression halt. They have ways of telling."

Robert then stepped in front of the scientists and rolled up his sleeve. "Me next," he said.

Sid went to inject him.

King stopped him. "No," he said. Robert turned back. "I will decide who gets the injection and when they get it."

"But, King," Robert said.

King removed the gun from his waist holster. He pointed it at Robert's head. "This is my kingdom. Do you understand?"

Robert backed away slowly.

"Now," King said. "Take these two back downstairs. I have some thinking to do."

CHAPTER 36

Day turned to night and back to day. None of them slept. All of them worried. Mick suppressed a few coughs. He found it especially difficult considering the two people he wanted to hide it from leaned against him in the same cell. He needed to be strong for them.

Robert exited from the stairs. He apprehensively looked over the room before approaching Sid. "If you repeat this, I will deny it."

Sid stood and walked over to the bars. "Okay," he said. "But what is this about?"

Robert looked over his shoulder at the rest of the group. He then walked to the stairs and peered up to make sure he was alone with them.

"Me and some of the guys were talking," Robert said. "We don't want to die out here. I was a plumber before all of this stuff happened. I'm no killer. I just go along with what King says to stay alive. And when he told you not to inject me, well, it made me think about my priorities."

"And what are your priorities?" Mick asked.

Robert turned. "Keep it down," he said, checking toward the stairs again. "I want to come with you."

Mick had spent the entire night trying to devise a plan to free themselves. He thought it was a lost cause. Now this? He could not help but feel this sudden turn in events was a little convenient.

"How do we know King didn't send you down here to toy with us?" Mick asked.

"You don't," Robert said. "But what other choices do you have? None of us want to be living here. If there is some place better than here, then that's where I want to be."

Sandeep had another coughing fit at that moment. This one was louder and longer, and it produced more blood from his lungs.

"Is he all right?" Robert asked.

"What do you think?" Mick answered.

"Is he coughing because of the virus?"

Sid looked at Sandeep and then back to Robert. "Yes," he said softly. "That is what will happen to you. It will happen to all of you."

Robert's eyes grew wide with fear.

Mick saw an opportunity. All his faulty plans involved using force to escape. That was why none of them worked in his mind. He had not thought of persuasion. He'd never thought of that as a valid option until that moment.

"And then what do you think will happen?" Mick said. "Do you think King is going to stick around and take your temperatures? Feed you chicken noodle soup and tuck you in? Come on, man," he said. "You've seen what he is capable of. You know how little he cares about anyone but himself. His own kid was killed and he couldn't care less. He's not right in the head."

"Just stop," Robert said. "I know what you're trying to do."

"And what is that?" Mick said. "Have I said anything untrue? Or are you just having a hard time accepting what is right in front of your eyes? We are all going to die. So tell me. What exactly am I trying to do?"

Robert soaked in what Mick said. He then reached into his jacket, after again looking toward the stairs, and removed the cellular scanner. He handed it to Sid.

"Test me," he said. He rolled up his sleeve and held it through the bars.

Sid went through the routine. The image displayed was the same as all the others. Robert clearly had the virus. And he longed for the very thing that would kill him quicker.

"Damn," Robert said after seeing his blood. "Isn't there anything you can do?"

"How about you do for us first?" Mick said.

Robert turned. "Do what?"

"Get us out of these cages."

Robert shook his head. "I can't do that," he said. "I'm a dead man if I let you out."

Mick stood, wincing more as he did. He then coughed quickly. It was too violent to stop from coming out. He took a second to compose himself, reassuring his kids that he was all right.

"You're a dead man either way. You let me worry about that douche bag upstairs. Just get us out of here."

"Okay," Robert said. "Let's do this." He removed Clyde's key ring and fished along the row until he found the cell key. He opened each cell only after checking the stairs one final time.

Mick coughed again, in chorus with Sandeep.

Sid walked past the group and scanned Sandeep with the cell scanner. The resulting display was dire. He then approached Mick and repeated the procedure. Mick, too, was closer to death than life. He scanned them all one by one. Each had telltale signs of an accelerated virus.

But when he scanned Solomon everything changed.

Sid looked up from the screen. He took the device and popped out the fusion chip from the battery pack. He waited a minute and put the battery chip back in. A hard reset was in order.

"What is it, Sid?" Alex asked in a whisper.

Sid said nothing. He waited for the cell scanner to finish its boot sequence. "Come on, come on," he said impatiently. He then scanned Solomon again. "I can't believe it."

Alex looked over his shoulder. "It can't be," he said. "Are you sure?"

"You just watched me reset it," Sid said.

"Can someone please explain?" Mick said. "We don't have a lot of time here."

"Actually, we may have more time than we thought," Sid said. "There is no trace of the virus in Solomon's system. Not a single strand."

"How is that possible?" Sandeep asked. "We

all saw him get injected."

"Yes," Sid said. "But injected with an accelerant specifically designed to work with the CV-1 virus. If the virus is not present, as in Solomon's case, then it's harmless. After an hour the solution will flush from his system."

"I'm n-n-not d-d-dying?" Solomon said.

"No," Sid said. "In fact, you're the key to saving everyone. You are the most important person on this planet right now."

Mick knew Solomon was special. From the first second he'd set eyes on him, he'd known something was different about him. It was nothing he could feel. Just something he knew in his heart. There was still a small glimmer of hope to hang on to. His children could live. They all could. But they did not have time to simply hang on hope.

"You guys can make a cure then?" Mick asked.

"I think so," Sid said. "But we need to get back to The Facility. We need the instruments there to extract and synthesize a cure. There is no way we can do it out here."

"Wait," Robert said. "I thought the stuff upstairs was to stop the virus or something?"

"Not exactly," Mick said. He understood he had no choice but to trust that Robert would not go telling King about what was transpiring. "Are you still in with us?"

Robert looked around at the group. He appeared utterly confused. Finally he nodded. "I'm in. What do I need to do?"

Mick thought for a moment. He then said to Robert, "Be quick and quiet about it. Tell those you trust that change is coming."

CHAPTER 37

The instant Robert started back up the stairs, Mick wondered if he'd made the right decision. Even without Greg, their group could have overpowered Robert. They could have easily put him in the cell. Left him behind while Mick worked out a plan. The problem was that he had no plan. He was winging it now. And they did not have the luxury of time.

He turned to Solomon. "Whatever happens, I want you to know that I'm really glad I met you in that alley. Stella was right," Mick said, reaching out and touching Solomon's arm. "You need to live your life, Solomon. So how about we start that now?" Unlike the first time Mick had tried to be tactile, Solomon reached up and braced Mick's arm back.

Solomon almost smiled, but he said nothing.

Mick then turned to the rest of the group. "Okay. Here's how this is going to go down. We have to pull out all the stops now. Our bodies are failing. Our time is running out. But now we have hope." He turned and shot Solomon a glance. "And hope is what I will use against King."

The group appeared to have a bit more life to them, even though, in reality, it was the exact opposite.

Mick went up the stairs first, stopping when he reached the top. He peeked from within the shadows. King sat on his throne. He held the auto injector in his hand, rotating it, mesmerized. Robert was to their right and had silently gathered a group of those he thought shared the same desire to survive that he did. Mick figured he would have to persuade the others. He committed this moment to one of both absolution and necessity. He fully understood there would be no do overs. This was the point where things either changed or ended.

Mick calmed his mind. He took a short, cleansing breath. *Let's do this.*

He leaned out of the shadows and into the main room.

"Is this the life you all want?" Mick shouted. His voice echoed off the walls.

"How in the world did you get out?" King said. He stood from his throne and reached for his gun. "Robert. Do you care to explain what this is all about?"

There were a few clicks from his right. Robert and a few of the other men held their rifles toward King.

"What are you fools doing?" King said.

"We want to hear what he has to say," Robert said. "Don't we?" He looked around at the group he had gathered. They slowly nodded in agreement. Those that Robert had not let in on the surprise appeared to go with the flow of the situation. For now.

King laughed. "You're serious?"

Robert nodded tentatively.

Mick figured they were all seconds from a gunfight.

But King surprisingly relented. "Very well," he said. He sat back down and waved his arm. "Speak your mind, Mick."

Mick moved farther into the main room. He watched King as he went. The rest of his group eased out behind him. He instructed his children to stay within the stairwell. If things went south, then at least they would be afforded some protection from ricocheting bullets.

"Is this what you all want?" Mick said. "To live in squalor? To wonder if today is your last on this planet?" Mick looked around the room as he spoke. "There is a better way," he continued. "A way to change all of it."

"How?" someone said from the darkness behind Robert.

"There is a place not far from here that has power. They have running water. They have everything we all thought was gone."

"Yeah, right," someone else said.

Mick strained to see who said it. He moved back a bit toward Sid and Alex. "These two men are from a place called The Facility. It's located a few miles from here."

"Unlikely," King said. He turned to his men. "Do you really believe this garbage? A secret facility a few miles from here? We have searched everywhere in the city. We know everything around here. Have any of you seen this place?"

Lots of heads began to shake.

Sid said, "You wouldn't be able to find it even if you looked. It was built specifically to remain hidden. We have been down there for the past ten years trying to find a way to rebuild."

"So you know how to do that?" another voice chimed in.

"No," Sid said. "Not yet, anyway."

"So why are you here then?" asked another of King's men.

"We are here because all of you are infected with a virus," Sid said. "We all are, actually."

Mick said, "We are here to offer you another way." He looked toward the gathering of men to his right.

"Another way to what? Die?" King said. "I don't believe you will have many takers on such an offer." He turned to his men. "But what say you? If you want to take this man up on his offer, then so be it. I don't need you here if you don't want to be here. But there is no coming back to my kingdom once you leave. Once you find out this little fairy tale is just that, you're on your own and no longer in my good graces."

"Why don't you explain to *your* men how you injected yourself?" Mick said.

"What I did was for all of you. I injected myself to preserve leadership. Without me there is nothing."

Mick laughed. "I don't think even they believe that. Everything you do, you do for yourself. You have made that one point very clear."

King stood. He stepped from his throne and neared Mick at a quick pace.

"What are you trying to do, Mick? Huh? You want to turn my men against me? Walk out of here with my army behind you? It will never happen."

"It's true," Robert said. "He injected himself with what he thought was a way to stop the virus from spreading inside him."

King paused. He looked down at the fading red circle on his arm. He then looked at Robert. "What did you just say?"

Robert shied away for an instant. He then stiffened his back and said, "What you put in yourself was not what you thought it was. And thank you for denying me it. It turns out that you may have just saved my life."

King looked from Robert to Sid. Fire in his eyes. "What did you inject me with, you little shit?"

Mick turned to King's men. "You are all expendable to him. Each and every one of you. This man sees no value in your lives."

"What did you inject me with?" King screamed, furious that his question had gone unanswered. And more so that he had been duped.

Mick answered. "The injector has an accelerant in it. It supercharges the virus."

King laughed nervously. He shook his head. "No," he said. "That can't be. This is part of your plan. Make me doubt myself, my decisions. I have to say, I didn't see that angle coming. Well done, Mick. Well done."

"I have no plan," Mick said. "Your own greed and callousness finally got the better of you."

King turned his attention to Sid. He stared through him in anger. He pointed his gun toward Sid. "Get it out of me now," he said. "I warned you what would happen if you double-crossed me."

"That's impossible," Sid said. "I can't remove it."

"Make it possible!" King shouted.

"N-no," Solomon said. He stepped in between King's gun and Sid. "N-no m-more."

"Solomon," Mick said, almost under his breath. "What are you doing?"

"Oh. Isn't that sweet?" King said. "You've turned the boy into a man."

"Solomon," Mick repeated.

Solomon looked to Mick. "It's all right," he said without a stutter, then turning his attention back to King. "L-l-leave them b-be," Solomon said. He then slowly walked to the side of King. "If y-you l-leave them, I w-will let you t-take m-m-me."

"Take you where, boy? I don't want to take you anywhere."

"Solomon, no," Mick said.

"T-t-to The F-Facility."

"And why would I want to do that?"

"B-because I a-a-am th-the c-cure."

King pointed the gun at Solomon's head. He

looked toward Mick and the group. "What is he talking about?"

"Solomon. Why?" Mick said.

"Someone better answer me quickly," King said, pulling the hammer of the pistol back.

Sid spoke. "Solomon is somehow immune to the virus. We think we can create a cure from his antibodies."

"So you can get this out of me," King said.

"I'm not sure," Sid said. "But it's the only hope we have."

King smiled at Mick. "How things can change so suddenly. Eh, Mick?" King then reached out and brought Solomon in front of himself. He put the barrel of his gun in Solomon's back. He then nodded to Sid. "You're coming with us."

"I don't think that would be wise," Sid said.

"I was not asking, Scientist. You will take me and the boy here to your 'Facility.'"

"I understand what you're saying. What I am telling you is if they see me back there, they will kill all of us on sight," Sid lied. "Phillip told me as much. So if you want to die quickly, then take me."

King pondered the lie. "All right then." He pointed to Alex. "You'll take us then. And don't say no or he dies." King pushed the gun harder against Solomon's back.

"There has to be another way," Mick said.

"The only way right now is my way," King said. He nodded to Alex. "Now, Scientist."

Mick nodded to Alex for him to comply. The

only thing to do at that moment was let one of the most villainous people he had ever met walk away with their only hope. And that was just how he wanted it.

CHAPTER 38

Like a three-car train, Alex led the way, while King walked Solomon along with the help of his gun. They weaved in and out of debris on track toward The Facility.

Solomon walked silently with the gun to his back. His mind was stuck on a constant loop of all the fond memories he had of Ms. Stella. He tried to remember her sweet smile from before the meteorites hit—a time when he'd thought his world had started to change for the better. But the one image that became unshakable was that of her lifeless eyes as they stared up at him from his lap.

He was happy that Clyde was dead. No use trying to convince himself otherwise. Clyde was rotten to the core. And the man who now held a gun to his back was the catalyst that started the darkening within Clyde. Solomon was sure of that. They shared the same blood, the same issues. A wretched father and his wayward son.

"Are we almost there?" King said like a child from the backseat.

Alex stopped for a brief moment. He looked around and then nodded left. "It's this way. We're close."

A few minutes more and they stopped again.

"This is it," Alex said, turning to face King.

"I'm not sure if they are going to welcome me back with open arms."

King ignored what Alex was saying. He looked at where they had stopped. "Where is this grand 'Facility' you spoke about? All I see is a lot of nothing."

"Like I said before, you wouldn't have found it."

Alex squeezed in between a few cars, past a downed light post, and up to a leaning parking meter. He turned the broken change dial on the front of the meter until the large red Expired tag fell out of sight. He then turned the dial again until the green Paid tag rose from within it. When he did, a keypad flopped down from behind the dial. He entered a long string of numbers. He then backed up to where King and Solomon stood.

"You may want to move back a bit," Alex said.

The ground shook. The piles of debris in front of the group began to part. A steel entryway encased the thick doors of The Facility. What was once hidden now towered in plain sight.

"Now what?" King said.

"We wait."

CHAPTER 39

It was Solomon's idea. One that Mick was initially reluctant to accept. But Solomon was insistent. So Mick simply took his idea and constructed a crude plan around it. Solomon told Mick that King would never willingly let any of them walk out of the old police station. His own men included. And even if King was able to kill only one of them, it would be one too many. So Solomon gave himself up so they could live. But that was only the beginning.

Mick was not about to let King walk away with Solomon. Not without a fight. After all, without Solomon there was no hope. But Solomon's idea did help Mick to gather the rest of King's men. King leaving the way he had helped to show his men that their allegiance was misplaced. And Mick knew King loved himself far too much to ever hurt Solomon at this point. By killing Solomon, King would in essence doom himself.

Mick instructed Robert and the rest of the men to stay behind at the police station. It took a little convincing, but Mick made him realize how such a large band of men would hurt their element of surprise. And they needed to beat the other three to The Facility. A small group was a fast group.

During the formulation of the plan, Alex told

Mick that he would take their group the long way to The Facility to buy him some time. Thankfully, King believed Sid's whole "they'll kill me" routine. Mick needed Sid with him.

"Are you sure they are going to let us in?" Mick asked Sid.

Sid turned. "No." He entered a set of digits in a hidden display on the side of a downed wall. "This might not go so well," he said. "You may want to be prepared."

Leaving his kids behind with that group left a sour taste in Mick's mouth. This was the same group that had held them all captive. The same group that had kept Ms. Stella and Solomon all those years. But Mick had little choice. He could not bring them with him. There was no telling what was about to happen. Chester, Deep, and Laurel were all there. Mick knew they would give their lives to save the kids. He just hoped it never came to that.

Five long minutes later the wall in front of them split down the middle. It then pushed toward the sides, revealing a thick door behind it.

"This is the back door?" Mick asked.

"Yes. This is it. Nobody noticed me the first time. But they are obviously paying attention now. I put in my code, but that was just to let them know we were here. Dr. Jones is the only person with the authority to open either set of doors now, according to Alex. Since those doors are opening, I can only assume it was done on Phillip's authority."

The door pushed open to reveal three heavily armed security guards dressed in dark-blue jumpsuits.

"Dr. Roth," the guard in front said. "Welcome back." His tone was less than welcoming. "Who is this?" he asked, nodding toward Mick.

"Jon," Sid said to the head of security, "this is Mick. Dr. Jones will want to speak with us. We found the immunity."

The guard soaked in the words and then reached for the communication device on his sleeve. He backed away. All Mick could hear was, "Dr. Roth has returned with the subject," as Jon walked away.

The two other guards watched both Mick and Sid. Their fingers resting lightly on the triggers of their automatic rifles.

"This way," Jon said. "Dr. Jones is waiting."

The guards parted only after patting both of them down and taking Mick's rifle.

"Not much to look at," Mick said as they walked down the pipe-lined hallway. Though it was strange to see the string of working lights that lined the hall. It had been ages since he'd seen electricity in action.

"The real stuff is upstairs," Sid said.

The small group went right at the end of the tunnel and stopped at the elevator. The guard pushed the button for the first floor. Mick felt as if he had gone back in time as soon as the elevator doors shut. He had not seen an elevator work since before Colossus. Now he was in a fully powered one, complete with working lights and even the digital display showing what floor they were on. To think this had existed the entire time made him both angry and sad.

"This way," the guard said, exiting the elevator.

He led them down a long white-walled hallway.

Many a scientist stopped dead in their tracks as they walked past. Mick heard one whisper, "He's the one." Another said, "I can't believe they let Sid back in after what he did."

Above all, Mick quickly realized how understated Sid was when he'd said the real stuff was upstairs. The Facility looked nothing short of something from another world. Pristine white walls. Clean glass. Electricity. Lights. People working. Everything he thought he would never see again in his lifetime was right there in front of him.

"Where are we going?" Mick asked.

"To see the man responsible for this mess."

The front guard stopped at Phillip's door. He opened it and held his arm out, signifying for them to enter.

Phillip stood from his clean desk. "Sid," he said. "Have you come crawling back?"

"This is Mick," Sid said, ignoring Phillip.

"Security told me as much. They also said that

he is the one we have been looking for?"

"That was a lie," Sid said. "But we have found the immunity strand."

Phillip quickly shook off his confusion. "Are you sure you've found it?" he asked.

"Positive."

"That is amazing news, Sid. Amazing. But where is that person?"

"They should be here soon. Alex is leading them to the front entrance."

"And why did you bring"—he looked at Mick—"him here if he is not the one we need?"

"Mick saved all our lives," Sid said. "He's been through hell. And he is the one that will lead us out of it."

Phillip chuckled. "Lead us out? Out of what? We are all that is left."

"That's not true," Mick said. "There are thousands of us out there struggling to survive."

Phillip smiled. "Let me rephrase that. We are all that is left of those worth saving." He then sneered at Mick. "No offense."

"There are children out there," Mick shouted.

"Please lower your voice. There are children in here, too," Phillip said. "However, these children have been raised in a manner more fitting the continuation of our species."

"More fitting?" Mick turned to Sid. "You were right about him."

The communication station on Phillip's desk began to beep. He reached down. "Yes?"

"Sir," came a voice from the device. "We have Dr. Cole outside the main doors. He has two with him. One is armed."

"I will be right there." He shook his head. "What a mess." He then waved Jon inside his office. "Escort these two to the front door. They will be leaving from it shortly."

CHAPTER 40

The same guards that had escorted Sid and Mick up from the sublevels also ushered them to the front doors. But when Mick arrived, he quickly realized these were anything but doors. They towered over his head, much taller than the secondary entrance they'd used only moments before. The doors rose twenty feet maybe and appeared to be made of solid steel. To Mick's right was a display panel with a collection of numbers and digital buttons. A closed-circuit television display was affixed to the wall above that. It showed what was outside the door. And what was outside was their salvation with their possible demise holding a gun to his back.

Dr. Jones walked over to the panel. He signaled to the head guard. "Keep these people back," he instructed, pointing over Mick's shoulder to the crowd of people that had begun to gather.

Mick looked back to see a group of maybe twenty or so people. All dressed in the same white jumpsuit with the same green circle with a helix atop it. These must all be people from The Initiative. They all varied in age, height, and ethnicity. It was a melting pot of survivors. All of them appeared clean and well-groomed. Exactly how Mick remembered people looking before the meteorites. Mick felt like the one grain of brown rice in a bowlful of white.

Dr. Jones pressed the intercom button. "Dr. Cole. I thought I had made it very clear that once you left, you would not be coming back?"

The display panel above their heads showed Alex listening to Phillip. He then walked over to the panel in the parking meter and pressed a button.

"This is Solomon," Alex said, pointing. "He is immune to the virus. Want to let me in now?"

The group behind Mick collectively gasped. They then began to whisper among themselves. When Mick turned, he noticed the group had doubled in size in only a matter of seconds. It was apparent that everyone there realized what was transpiring. To have this gathering of eyes and ears behind them was a part of the plan that Mick could never have envisioned, but it was one he was ecstatic to see happening. It would help to ensure Phillip could not sweep this away.

"Are you certain he is immune?" Phillip asked.

Alex said, "Very. We scanned him multiple times with a cellular scanner. He's clean. Even after being injected with your—"

Phillip let the button go, and the rest of Alex's comments were muted.

More whispers from behind them. A bit louder than before. Phillip's suppression of Alex had apparently not gone unnoticed.

"Aren't you going to let everyone know, Dr.

Jones?" Mick said. He turned toward the group of people that had just grown even larger. Maybe a hundred or so people. All of them listening intently to Mick. He figured now was as good a time as any.

Phillip nervously eyed the group. "There is nothing to see here," he said. "Please. We all have important work to get back to. This will all be over momentarily."

The group went nowhere.

"Why don't you tell them, Phillip?" Sid said. "Tell them how the test you sent out to your fellow man was no test at all?"

"Sid," Rebekah said, stepping out from behind the front of the group. "That's a pretty serious allegation."

"It's the truth, Rebekah. We've all been duped." Sid turned back to Phillip. "Go ahead, Phillip."

"Tell who, Sid? All of your fellow scientists? They know what needs to be done at times in order for science to progress. You and Alex are the only two who don't seem to understand that a few ants must be crushed on our walk to rebuild what we lost."

"Ants?" Mick said. "That's what we are to you?" He turned to the group. "That's what my children are to him. My children, who have suffered more than any father should see his child put through."

"No," Phillip said. "That's not what I meant."

"Then what did you mean?" Sid asked.

Mick saw the look in his eyes. It was fear. The same look they all had once they'd realized their world was about to change for the worse.

"Dr. Jones has been keeping secrets," Sid said, first to the security guard to his left, then turning to address the rest of the group behind him. "Those *tests* he sent out to the population outside our doors were not tests at all. The auto injectors contained a special concoction he made secretly in his private lab. It was an accelerant. Once injected, the subject had at most five days to live." The group gasped. Sid removed the note sent to Mick. He held it in the air. "This is what he sent out with the accelerant. A note. One that uses The Initiative's name to push his own agenda."

"All right," Phillip said. "I think we have all heard enough of your lies, Dr. Roth. Guards—"

"No," Rebekah said. "Let them continue."

"Sid's not lying," Mick said. "Our home, or, what we called home, anyway, was destroyed this past storm. It was nothing more than an old cluttered office building. But it was all we had after Impact. We didn't know any of this existed. I also lost someone very dear to me at the same time. We were left with no other option than to inject ourselves in the hope that the note was true. That someone from The Facility"—he looked around—"one of you, would come to rescue us. I injected my children with that stuff. I sentenced my own kids to five more days alive because of this man." He turned and pointed at Phillip. As he recounted,

Mick found himself getting angrier by the minute. He then doubled over and fell to his knees, coughing, hacking. A small bit of blood fell to the polished floors. Everyone watched in horror. The only sound was Mick's hacking at it bounced around the hall.

Sid put his hand on Mick's back. "This will happen to us all eventually. We are all going to die from this virus. You all know that. Only Phillip here chose to hurt these people further in secret."

"You're a naive man, Sid," Phillip said. "Do you really believe that without my intervention any of this would have happened?" He punched in his long string of digits. The red Close button turned into a green Open. "If I hadn't done what I had, would you have found your new sense of purpose and ventured outside these walls? If I hadn't been the one to come up with a solution to our problem—"

"A problem you created, Phillip." Sid turned to the group. "I wish the accelerant was the worst thing I had to tell you all." Sid turned to the head of security. "Jon, how long have we known each other?"

Jon shrugged. "Probably fifteen years. Around there."

"Have you ever known me to lie? To anyone about anything?"

"No. You've always been a stand-up guy."

Sid smiled at him for the reassurance. He then moved away from him and toward the middle area between the ever-growing group and Mick. "Then I need you all to listen carefully to what I am about to say."

"I think we have heard enough," Phillip said. "Guards. Take them to the holding cell until I have cleaned up this mess outside that Dr. Roth has brought to our doorstep."

The guards stood their ground.

"Go ahead, Sid," Jon said.

"The virus was not brought to this planet by the meteorites as we all have been told. No. The virus existed here this entire time. In Dr. Jones's head. That is, until he created it in his lab."

"That's insane," Phillip said. "The outside air must have screwed with your mind."

"It helped to clear my mind, actually. Being outside allowed me to see what I could never have in here. I saw the truth."

"Is this true, Dr. Jones?" asked someone from within the group.

"Of course it's not true. These people are suffering from some sort of neurological impairment. The virus must be more powerful outside of our walls."

"It's the same virus, Phillip. You should know that, considering it was you who infected all of us, as well."

Gasps.

Sid stared at Phillip.

Phillip stared back. He looked paler than he had a moment ago. His forehead began to perspire.

He gulped. "The virus was never meant for those of us inside The Facility. I assure you all. It was simply a terrible accident."

"So it's true," someone said.

"He infected us," someone else said.

Phillip held up his hands to calm the crowd. "It was an accident. A very unfortunate turn of events. One of the test vials that was used for the strand had a stress fracture. It broke. The virus was released that instant. I tried to contain it the instant it happened."

"By locking Dr. Shaker in the lab, you sentenced him to death," Sid said. "That's how he died."

"He was a clumsy fool."

"Don't you dare blame him for what you've done. He trusted you, Phillip. We all did."

"What I have done?" Phillip said. "I have kept you all alive for the past ten years. We have made great progress in so many fields. Once we rebuild, our civilization will be light-years ahead of where it was just ten short years earlier."

"All the progress we have made will mean nothing if the virus were to run its course," Sid said. "And the simple fact that you created the virus means you doomed us all with your own two hands. The deaths of all those that have already succumbed are on your head."

"Progress isn't always a clean process," Phillip said. "Do I need to remind all of you what we are up against? Or have you all become too accustomed to living at The Facility? Outside these walls is a war zone of unimaginable proportions. Outside these walls—"

"Are people," Mick said, getting back to his feet. "People you may have passed on the street ten years back. People with family's. People like me. That is what's outside the walls. And every minute of every day is a struggle."

Phillip turned to the group again. "The virus was never meant for any of you."

"And who exactly was it meant for then, Phillip?" Sid said.

"If we are to ever rebuild, we must start with a clean slate. We are the future of this world. We are the best and brightest. We give humanity the best chance of regaining a foothold. We must take this opportunity that has been given to us. We must use it to better ourselves. Weed out the weak and let the strong grow stronger."

"A new society built upon the bodies of the murdered is no society at all," Mick said. He began coughing again. "It's called genocide."

"You're a self-righteous fool," Phillip said.

"No, Phillip. You are the fool," Sid said. "What happened to you? You used to be such a brilliant mind. Now you are a delusional murderer."

"Enough!" Phillip shouted. "I've heard enough. I will not have my motives questioned."

"So have we," Jon said. The head guard nodded to the other two. They quickly went over and took Phillip by the arms.

"What do you think you are doing? Let go of me. We have work to do."

"I think you've done enough," Jon said. He then led Phillip away from the crowd that clawed at him as he passed down the long white hall.

CHAPTER 41

"What's taking them so long?" King asked.

"They are probably debating even letting us in," Alex said from a nearby piece of upturned pavement he had taken a seat on.

King looked up toward the camera. "Well, they better hurry."

"Or w-what? You'll sh-shoot us?" Solomon said. "Th-then you d-d-die, too."

King nudged Solomon with the barrel of his gun. "Maybe you're not as stupid as I thought, boy."

The large steel doors began to open. It became instantly clear to Solomon that their plan had worked. Mick stood next to Sid in the middle of a very large group of people dressed in white lab coats. Two guards each held their scoped rifles out. Both of them were aimed at King.

"It's over," Mick said, breathing more labored than ever. "Let him go."

King took stock of a situation he clearly did not expect. "Very clever, Mick." He nudged Solomon closer to the door. "But this little plan of yours must revolve around me doing what you ask. No? And, as it turns out, I have no desire to do that."

"This is the end," Mick shouted. "No more lives need to be lost because of your thirst for

341

power."

"Again, you act as if I care what you say. What you do. This," King said, looking around, "is all mine. All of it. You hear me!" He began to cough. "And nothing you can do will take that from me." He coughed again.

Another two guards came running up. One took the same position as the other two, his gun aimed at King's head. The other stopped next to Sid and Mick.

"Dr. Roth," the guard said. "The group you told us to expect has arrived. We put them in the infirmary."

"Thank you," Sid said. He patted Mick on the back. "Your kids are safe now."

A tingle ran the length of Mick's body. He smiled. It was a genuine smile. Something he had not done in what seemed like forever. Robert had kept his word. A surprising twist of trust that was never guaranteed. And it appeared that Sandeep was as proficient as Mick had figured he would be with the tracking device used to get them to The Facility. Mick's blue tracking dot thankfully still had a bit of light remaining in it.

"This is your final warning," King said. "Let us in or the boy dies."

Solomon spun to his left, catching King off guard. His right arm grasped a hold of King's gun as he turned. He tore it from his hand with his bearlike strength and tossed it aside. Solomon then clubbed King against the side of his head with his stiffened arm.

King dropped to the rubble he claimed as his own.

Solomon jumped on top of him and whaled on his face while pinning King's arms down with his knees. He then grabbed him by the throat. Solomon felt the anger of all the years of torment culminate in his hands. He choked King like he had Clyde. Only this time Ms. Stella was not there to stop him. But even though she wasn't there, he heard her voice. Her soft words pleading for him to stop. "No, Solomon," he heard. "A life as pure as yours does not need a death to soil it."

Solomon stared out past King. He ignored his bluish face and his gasps. He thought of only Ms. Stella. What she had taught him through the years. He remembered her love at that moment. He would not do anything to hurt her wishes. Her love for him was the only reason he let go of King's throat. He would not disappoint her, even in death.

King panted to regain his lost breath. He brought his own hands up to soothe his reddened throat.

"Good, boy," King said through gasps. "Now help me up."

Solomon smacked him across the face. "I'm n-nobody's b-boy." He then rose to his feet and started to walk toward The Facility's entrance.

"I wouldn't do that," Mick shouted, holding his rifle toward King.

King stopped inching toward his gun and

looked up. "I guess you win, Mick."

"You just don't get it. There are no winners here. The fact that you can't already see that is all the more reason to pity you."

"Pity me? I am King."

Mick nodded to Sid, who in turn entered a code and pushed the Close button. The doors slowly began to shut.

"Rule your kingdom," Mick called, not breaking eye contact with King. "Make the days the best of your life. Because they will be your last."

King wasted no time. He must have realized that he was watching his own death certificate being signed. He broke for the closing door, sprinting faster than he had ever probably run, trying to save a life that had already ended.

Mick watched. His face unflinching. His pity absolute. Even though he wanted King dead, he could not help but feel human sympathy for even the most inhumane of people.

"No!" King shouted.

The doors had only inches left to go when King reached his gun. He fired round after round. The first two Mick heard hit the outer doors. After that, it was silent.

CHAPTER 42

Two weeks passed.

King was never seen or heard from again. Mick assumed he eventually succumbed to the virus, alone in his kingdom of rubble. A just ending for an unjust man.

The remaining scientists formed a committee to decide Phillip's fate. Some wanted to throw him out of The Facility. Inject him with his own accelerant. Let him suffer the same fate as King. Sid convinced them otherwise. He told them that it was the wrong foundation to lay for humanity's new start. If they were going to rebuild, then it should be atop the lessons they had all learned, and not on more mistakes. They would need to build something that they could all proudly stand on. A foundation that would support the great new world they would start.

The security team's first effort was to restore the police station to a somewhat working station. Dr. Jones was banished to a lifetime within that station. The committee decided he should not be afforded the comforts of the jail within The Facility's walls. He would languish in the very cell that Solomon had spent most of his adult life, staring at the same water-stain mouse, dwelling in the same negative thoughts that the world outside brought.

Mick walked into one of the many rooms located within The Facility. The automatic doors slid open as he approached. They were going to take some getting used to.

"Hello," Mick said.

"Hey, Dad," Nate said.

"Hi, Daddy," Kathryn said.

He wondered how much longer she would call him that. He hoped forever. It made him feel younger.

"What did you learn today?"

Sandeep chimed in. "History. Nate insisted."

"Trying to be well-rounded," Nate said before Mick could ask. "You know, for when I go on job interviews." He smiled.

"That's my boy."

"I told you society always found a way to rise from its ashes," Kathryn added smugly.

"Yeah, yeah," Nate said. "You were right. There's a first time for everything, I guess."

It was nice to see them back to normal.

"Where are Chester and Laurel?" Sid asked.

Deep said, "Last I saw of Chester, he was finishing up the touches on his ministry. He seems happy to have an actual room now rather than a corner of the shelter. And Laurel is down in the medical ward. She can't soak in the information fast enough. She says they have really done some great things here."

"That's good," Mick said. "I'm happy to know

some good came out of this place. And how about you, Deep? How are you feeling?"

"Much improved. And I must say, sleeping in that bed for the past few nights has done wonders for my happiness. Much better than the cot used to."

"Almost too comfortable," Mick said. "All right. I'll let you get back to what you were doing. I was just checking in. I'm off to see Solomon's new digs. Sid said he gave him Phillip's old room."

Mick brushed Nate's head with his hand. He then kissed Kathryn on the crown of her head and left the room.

Solomon's room was at the end of the hall, past the bustling labs that at one time had produced the accelerant but now produced the cure. Solomon's genes worked beautifully to eradicate the virus. Typically within forty-eight hours of injection, the patient was virus-free. The team of scientists and engineers had worked on a method to introduce the cure in an airborne way. There were too many people to inject. Deep helped to create the air pushers that the security team were now scattering across the city. That would be step one in a long series of steps aimed at getting back what the meteorites had destroyed.

"C-come in," Solomon said after Mick pushed the Call button outside his door.

Mick entered to see Solomon behind a large desk. "What are you writing?"

Solomon smiled. "Ms. S-Stella t-t-told me t-to

write w-what happened so others w-w-won't m-make the s-same mistakes."

"She was a very smart lady, Solomon. I wish I could have gotten to know her better."

Solomon smiled warmly. He then went over to the bookcase to his right and removed a small wrapped box. He brought it over and handed it to Mick.

"What's this?" Mick asked.

"Open it."

Mick tore the thin wrapping paper off and smiled. "Who put you up to this?" he asked, thinking it must have been one of his kids. "Thank you, Solomon. It's just what I always wanted. My very own supply of canned meat."

Solomon reached out and pulled Mick close. He hugged him with all the love he had been robbed of for all those years. He hugged him for a future he'd never dreamed possible and a past he'd helped him escape. But most of all, Solomon hugged him because Mick was now family. And family stuck together.

THE END

www.ingramcontent.com/pod-product-compliance
Lightning Source LLC
Chambersburg PA
CBHW020328180626
46812CB00001B/104